The Mystical Spirit of the Ol' St. Joe

NORMAN PHILIP JEDDELOH

The Mystical Spirit of the Ol' St. Joe
Copyright © 2025 by Norman Phillip Jeddeloh
Cover design by Miblart

This is a work of fiction. Any characters, businesses, places, events or incidents are either the product of the author's imagination or are used fictitiously. Any resemblance to actual persons, living or dead, events or locales is entirely coincidental.

Printed in the United States of America

Hardcover ISBN: 978-1-965253-42-7
Paperback ISBN: 978-1-965253-43-4
Ebook ISBN: 978-1-965253-44-1

"Ol' man river that ol' man river
He must know somethin' but don't say nothin'
He just keeps rollin'
He keeps on rollin' along

Long ol' river forever keeps rollin' on.
He don't plant tater
He don't plant cotton
An' them that plants 'em is soon forgotten
But ol' man river he just keeps rollin' along
Ah, gits weary an' sick of tryin'
I'm tired of livin' an' scared of dyin'
But ol' man river he just keeps rollin' along."
—"Ol' Man River"
Show Boat
Jerome Kern and Oscar Hammerstein II

"I do not know much about gods; but I think that the river
Is a strong brown god—sullen, untamed and intractable."
—"The Dry Salvages"
Four Quartets
T.S. Eliot

Acknowledgements

Again, as with *A Boat Named Blind Faith*, I gratefully acknowledge the incredible assistance of my editor, Natalie Tighman, who once again guided me from rough dribble to respectable manuscript, and to my insightful beta editors Todd Scales, Killian Sweeney, Sue Lenski, Larry Hallock, and Fran Lope. It has been said that a saint is nothing more than an ordinary dead sinner revised and edited. Each of my editors has played a similar role in the creation of *The Mystical Spirit of the Ol' St. Joe,* although… "Saintly?"

Well, read for yourselves.

SHE OPENED HER EYES, moving them slowly, tentatively, as she absorbed her unfamiliar surroundings. Was she alive? Was she dead and in some sort of afterlife? Or was this only a dream? She raised her arm and let it drop back to the dirty canvas cot. Seemed like she was alive. She could move her aching muscles but felt like a stone— immobile, lifeless. If she had been asleep, it must have been long and deep.

The windowless room was dark, illuminated only by a bank of votive candles on a rack, like at some rundown shrine for a long- forgotten saint. It smelled musty and felt dank, reminding her of the cellar in her uncle's old farmhouse out in the woods. A heavy, dark-maroon curtain hung precariously from a tarnished brass rod. It covered a door; where it led, she didn't know. She sensed that she was alone but wasn't sure.

She groaned softly and stared intently at the candles, trying to stop the room from spinning. Suddenly, a gnarled hand pulled aside the curtain, causing a beam of light to hit her face. The brightness startled her, and she covered her eyes.

An old woman entered. She was dressed in a black robe with a hood that hung loosely on her gaunt frame. Her hair was gray, strag-gly, and looked as if it had been unkempt for some time. She had a hooked nose but piercing, probing eyes peering out above wrinkled cheeks. The appearance of this strange old woman spooked Semantha. She shivered.

"I've been wondering when you would wake up," the old woman said. Her voice was melodic, soft, unlike her appearance.

"Who are you?" Semantha asked as she lifted her head from the cot, rubbed her eyes, and looked around. She was confused and disoriented, not sure where she was or what had happened. Or even who she was. All she felt was a vague sense of panic—about what she could not tell—and the instinct to run—why, she did not know. She sensed she was in danger.

"I'm Erzulie, the one who brought you back from the dead," the old woman said.

"Dead?" A pulse ran down Semantha's spine. "Dead? How'd I...I... get here?"

"You're safe with me," the old woman said.

Semantha sat up and looked at her. She wondered why the woman had not answered her question. She wrapped a part of the old, yellowed blanket she had been lying on around her stomach and legs to cover her nakedness. What had happened to her clothes?

Vague images began flashing before her. She remembered a fight with a man in the river and everything going black. The name Marco sounded in her mind, like someone yelling in an echo chamber. A mixture of passion and terror burst through her body. She sensed she had been sent to capture this man, but why or by whom she could not recall. *Would she suffer because she hadn't gotten him?* It seemed so long ago, a nightmare in a past life. She coughed out some water. It tasted like fish and slime. When she tried to get up, she fell back on the cot, too weak to flee.

"I wasn't sure I could save ya, but you're back."

"Back from where?"

"From the ol' St. Joe. You were floating naked, face down. Not breathing. Probably that saved ya, maybe the river saved ya. Didn't want ya to die."

The old woman smiled, walked to the cot, and ran the back of her hand over Semantha's brow, almost like a nurse in a hospital.

"How'd ya end up in the river anyway?"

"I…I…I…don't…don't kn…remember." Semantha closed her eyes, put her palm over them, and began to cry. She felt like she was lost in a thick fog. Her lips trembled.

"There, there, my pet," the old woman said as she began gently stroking Semantha's hair. At first, Semantha braced when the old woman tried to touch her, but her touch—like her voice—was soothing, comforting. Her trepidation waned.

"You're gonna be fine."

As if her mother, she sat down next to Semantha and hugged her, holding her tight and rubbing her back. A straggly gray cat with a spotty coat and green eyes jumped up on the cot next to the old woman. Startled, Semantha jerked away.

"Oh, this is Macy," the old woman said, smiling while she scratched the cat's head. It purred and rubbed itself on the woman's arm. "Sometimes he helps me get in touch with the spirit world. Be nice to him."

Semantha smelled the woman's strong odors, those of someone who had not bathed for a long time. Nauseous from the stench, she turned her head away for a second.

"How'd I get here?"

"Pulled you out of the good old St. Joe River and threw you in the back of my pickup out there," the woman said, waving her hand toward the outside. "You're pretty heavy, but I'm strong. All that weightlifting I did in med school paid off." The woman smiled, displaying her crooked yellow teeth. It was a disarming smile.

"How long have I been sleeping?"

The woman smirked. "Long enough," she said as she got up to walk out of the room.

"Wait," Semantha said, wanting an explanation, but the woman did not respond. She left Semantha alone staring at the candles and wondering what was happening.

Semantha's head cleared a little more. Powerful images flashed in her mind, so vivid she felt transported in time and place. She saw herself on a boat in Lake Michigan scattering Pappie's ashes. *Cursed day*, she thought. *Pappie, oh my dear father, dead.*

She moaned. She felt her face begin to burn.

Then Saul's face appeared, a malevolent phantom.

Unholy animal, deceitful murderer! Hammering a stake in Pappie's heart, monster. No, no, no. She gritted her teeth, clenched her fists in anger and disgust.

But finally, an image completely different, sweet. A beautiful man on another boat. Their eyes met in a long-distance embrace. She was overtaken by passion and longing.

That beautiful man... God, oh my God.... She couldn't place him, but then she squeezed her eyes tightly. She flashed to Pappie's memorial black mass a couple of days after the encounter on the boat. Yes, he was there too. How or why he got there, she couldn't remember. From nowhere, the name Marco resonated in her mind. *Marco, my God Marco.* She felt dizzy. Her head began to spin again.

Him lying there drugged. Saul's plan to sacrifice him to the devil. *My God, no, oh no.* She gagged. Somehow, he jumped up and escaped. *How?* A splash as his body hit the river. She saw herself swimming after him. *Why?* Again, her mind went blank as she drifted off to sleep...but then dreamed a nightmare.

Finding him, the struggle, his arms around her holding her under water, frigid, gasping for air. Then her feeling of being sucked backwards and pulled through the water, back and forth, blackness fading in and out, then nothing. She again heard a voice shouting, "Marco," then again, this time stronger and more insistent than before: "Marco." Then practically a scream, "Marco!"

Semantha woke with a start, her eyes opening wide, her heart beating hard. Her shoulders shook and she screamed. The old woman rushed in, took her hand and gently stroked it.

"You'll be fine," she said. "I'm a doctor."

"Doctor? I don't believe that."

"Lost my license years ago. Michigan didn't like that I combined medicine with Santeria. It worked for my patients. Hell, it worked for you. That's all I can say. Potions with snake eyes and pig bile work about as well as penicillin, let me tell ya." She took a long drag on her corncob pipe, like she was thinking. Circles of smoke drifted to the rafters.

"Took some shots and incantations, lots of incense burning, getting in touch with the spirit world."

Macy's back arched. He let out a cat-like muted shriek.

"But my sweet, when you figure out how you ended up in the water, I'd like to know," the woman said.

Semantha looked at her with amazement and nodded. She was not sure what to make of this creaky old woman or her own Lazarus-like resurrection. She still felt the urge to run but knew she couldn't. She would need to build her strength before she could get away.

*　　*　　*

THE NEXT DAY as the sun was setting, the woman came into the room and smiled at her like a wet nurse about to suckle a new baby. She propped up Semantha's head on a pillow and held a chalice to her lips. She had filled it with a spice-laden concoction smelling like vinegar.

Semantha turned her head and balked.

"You want me to drink this? It smells terrible. What is it?" she asked.

"My own blend. Marrow from the bones of a suckling pig, turmeric, ground rat tail, some Maryjane, and a pinch of other beautiful herbs," the woman said. She winked. "Works every time. Some people say it's magic. When you're better, I'll tell you stories."

Semantha recoiled at the thought of drinking the potion, but she took hold of the chalice and let the liquid slide down her throat. It flowed easily. Instantly, she felt a slight rush and then smooth and detached. Dreamy and sort of spacey.

After Semantha finished the potion, the woman rubbed her back and legs with her wrinkled hands, she said to return circulation. Semantha grimaced and tried to push her away. She didn't like the idea of this old woman massaging her. But the woman insisted, and Semantha closed her eyes, let it happen. She didn't see she had a choice. So, she imagined that the woman's hand was a man's. *Marco, you*, she thought. She groaned slightly when it went close to her breast or crotch.

*   *   *

FOR WEEKS, Semantha laid on the cot in the overalls and sweatshirt the woman gave her, drinking the daily potion and sliding in and out of wakefulness. She and the woman hardly talked at all. Semantha forgot her name and the woman never asked for hers, called her "my little pet" or "sweet flower." As she lay there recovering slowly from her ordeal, she could hear the woman outside the room, cleaning and cooking, a tranquil rhapsody of domestic sounds played with comforting regularity.

In her foggy state, Semantha's resistance to the woman's advances waned. After a while, she surprised herself. She came to appreciate the woman's attention, motherly, warm and sort of innocent. She thought about the mother she never had. She felt better after these interludes and started to look forward to them. Then she responded by rubbing the old woman's frame, first only as a payback, but then more, letting her fantasies about a man's hands stock her sensations. *Oh Marco,* she again thought. Their physical contacts became more regular, almost sexual. As Semantha got used to the woman's distinct smell, revulsion changed to acceptance, and she let the woman lie with her for a while after the message.

One day, the woman's eyes leveled with Semantha's. A mournful, far-away look appeared on her furrowed face.

"I love you, sweet flower," she said. "Never—please never—leave me." She went silent for a second. "You're..." The woman took a deep breath and let it out slowly, sighing. "You're all I have."

Semantha smiled thinly and nodded her head. But the woman's strong declaration evoked a sense of disquietude in Semantha. She didn't know whether she could trust this old lady.

What was her name again?

*   *   *

"NO MORE of that drink," Semantha said one morning after a month lying on the cot. "I want to get up."

"I think you should rest some more, my pet. Let me get you some potion."

"No, I want to see the world outside again," Semantha said. She had grown tired of how she felt after she drank it, sort of numb. She wished the fog to lift, to be clear-headed and aware like before. No more of the oozy middle world halfway between dreams and reality. Maybe, soon, she would be strong enough to leave.

The old woman furled her forehead, looking disgusted and angry. She grabbed hold of Semantha's shoulder and yanked her to her feet, with her left arm wrapped tightly around Semantha's waist, so tightly that Semantha could not breathe.

"Not so hard," Semantha said. She tried to push the woman away but could not.

At first, when on her feet, Semantha felt dizzy and unsure. Then her balance came back. She could tell she had lost a lot of weight and felt the frailty which comes from a long convalescence. She wondered if the potion had something to do with her weakness. Probably, but it also seemed it had helped her recover.

The woman clasped Semantha's arm with a vise-like grip and yanked her toward the front door. "Careful, you're hurting me," Semantha said, wrinkling her brow, but the woman did not let go or let up.

She threw open the door and dragged Semantha outside. Most of the leaves were off the trees and the air was nippy. The bright sunshine of the late October day hit Semantha like a wall of fire. She raised her hand to cover her eyes. She looked back at the half-house, half-cave from which she had emerged. It blended well into the woods.

The woman walked Semantha down the pathway leading from the hovel to the road. Her steps were halting and unsure; she staggered and almost fell. Several times the woman caught her like a protective doe coddling a newly born fawn. Semantha wondered about this woman. She did seem pretty harmless. Maybe she had nothing to fear, despite the old woman's weird mannerisms and strange dress.

*　　*　　*

AFTER A FEW WEEKS of these walks, Semantha's physical condition and strength improved, her energy returned. But at the same time, her urge to flee faded. Semantha liked feeling safe and sheltered, all under this woman's watchful shield. It was the first time in her life she felt cared for by a woman, and there was consoling consistency to life in the hovel. She stopped having nightmares about Pappie, Saul's brutality, and the struggle with Marco. It seemed like she had crossed into a different world, a world of calmness and tranquility—so distant from her troubled past, filled as it had been with abuse and unrequited affection. She entertained the idea of staying with this woman indefinitely.

Semantha's reverie and contentment did not last. She became curious about her strange circumstances and antsy to find out more about them. When the old woman left the house, Semantha began looking around. Though the woman had told her to stay out of her bedroom, Semantha couldn't resist the temptation. She went in.

The space was a little bigger than the single bed pushed against the wall. Like Semantha's room, it was dark and windowless, lying inside the hill from which the hovel emerged. But here, on a plain nightstand next to the bed, sat a portrait of a man in a glossy silver frame, looking out of place in these barren surroundings. Clouded by the darkness, Semantha couldn't make out whose image was portrayed. It seemed that this old woman didn't have any contact with the outside world. Maybe this picture was the exception. She wanted to see.

Semantha lit the kerosene lamp sitting on the nightstand to get a better look. As the light from the lamp came up and illuminated the picture, an electric shock passed up Semantha's spine. Her jaw dropped and she gasped. She covered her mouth.

"No, no, this cannot be, cannot," she said out loud. She brought the picture close to her face to be sure she saw correctly. She had. It was a picture of a young Pappie, looking handsome and distinguished in a three-piece wool suit with a flower in the lapel, his jet-black hair combed back in a classic style. Mesmerized, she couldn't take her eyes off the picture. How she longed for him, how deeply she felt his loss.

Then she saw the inscription. It was signed, *To my sweet with love, Theo.* Jealousy and anger cursed through her body. In her mind, Pappie was hers and hers alone. Before he was killed, they had been inseparable, to Semantha, the best father any girl could have. The possibility that he had had some sort of intimate relationship with this old coot revolted her. Her blood began to boil. She stared at the picture. It was taken many years ago, back when Pappie was known as "Theo." Why was it still sitting there in this woman's chamber after all this time?

Later that same day, they went for their daily walk even though it had snowed, the first snow of the winter season. As they proceeded down the slippery path, Semantha built up her courage, then halted and put her hand on the woman to signal her to stop. She turned and looked directly at the woman. Furor streamed from her eyes.

"I went into your bedroom this morning looking for a comb," Semantha said with a slight tremor in her voice.

The woman glowered. "How many times have I told ya, never go in there."

"I saw a picture on your nightstand."

"You shouldn't have gone in there. Don't do that again. Never, ya hear?"

"How did that picture get there?"

The woman looked down, her head turned away, apparently pondering how to answer. After a moment, she looked back at Semantha. She scowled.

"What difference does it make?

Semantha's face reddened and her jaw tightened. "Tell me!" she yelled.

The woman's eyes widened, her mouth dropped open, as if she couldn't quite understand why Semantha was so insistent.

"What's gotten into ya? You go into my room even though I told ya not to, you see this picture, and ya go crazy. It makes no sense."

Semantha's face turned bright red, and she clenched her fists. "Tell me!" she screamed again.

The woman was silent for another minute. She began rubbing her hands together and shaking her head. Her body tensed.

"I can't imagine why this concerns ya so much, but I guess it doesn't really matter." She shrugged her shoulders then looked directly into Semantha's eyes. "If ya must know, we were lovers."

Semantha gasped. "No!" she screamed. Waves of raw emotion ran up and down her backbone. Her worst suspicions were confirmed. She gagged. "When?"

The woman did not answer. She looked forlorn. Semantha fell to the wet, cold ground, sobbing. She covered her face and eyes with her hands and wailed.

The woman sat down next to her and put her hand on Semantha's leg. "What's gotten into ya?" she asked.

"No!" Semantha again screamed and jerked herself away. She was shaking. She wanted to run but she was still too weak.

"How could you do such a thing?" Semantha asked between the tears.

"What ya talking about? This is none of your business, and after I saved ya, too."

Semantha groaned. The woman stared at Semantha for a moment as if she was in deep thought. Then her look of anger was replaced by one of concern. She took several deep breaths and then sighed.

"It was only an affair, for God's sake," she said in a half whisper. "But I have never forgotten him, the only person I ever loved…" She turned away for a second. "Until now, that is," the woman said, her lips downturned.

"An affair? God in all of heaven." Semantha's brain was still racing out of control. She could feel her heart beating. She felt betrayed. Pappie with another woman? No.

"Why does that upset ya so, my pet? I don't understand," the woman said.

Semantha decided she must explain herself. This person had given her life back after all. She thought for a minute.

"If you must know, that man, he's my…my…" Semantha shook her head. The words sputtered out. "…my FATHER. I loved him with all my heart. He always told me that I was the only one."

"No, no. You really must be mistaken. Theo couldn't be your father," the woman said. "He never married, at least that's what I heard." The woman's brow arched up. "But calm down, please calm down. This was so long ago. What I care about now is you and me."

Semantha stopped crying and dried her tears with her sleeve. Possibly she was wrong. "How did you meet him?" she asked to find out.

"At a science fiction fair at the Big Pavillion in Saugatuck on a hot summer night. He was dressed like a silly Star Wars character, but so handsome anyway with his long, flowing black hair and ruddy complexion. I was instantly attracted."

Semantha was now sure it was Pappie. The description, the time, the setting all lined up. Semantha pictured how Pappie must have looked back then. The woman's description of Pappie as a young man rekindled her anger and disgust.

"Get away from me, you whore!" she screamed. Semantha struggled to get up to flee. She fell on her face in a pile of leaves and hit the ground with her fist.

The woman bent down and touched her lightly on her shoulder.

Semantha recoiled. "I'm leaving," she said.

"Look, my flower, I don't know what has come over ya. But ya can't leave," she said as a tear dripped down her face. "Don't ya know I love ya, for Christ's sake?"

The woman was right. She didn't have the strength to go. She let the woman help her back to the hovel. What else could she do? No money, no clothes, no job. Alone in the world without Pappie. For now, she had no choice but to stay with this woman.

*   *   *

THEREAFTER, Semantha and this woman lived in icy silence. Semantha wanted to have as little to do with her as she could. She rebuffed every effort the woman made to be social or talk. And no more sensual massages and no warm touching. Semantha didn't care that the woman moped around the hovel looking depressed and rejected.

An early blizzard sent waves of lake-effect snow and buried the front of the hovel right up to the top of the window. Snowbound, the two survived mostly on nuts and dried berries the woman had accumulated in the crawlspace beneath the wooden floor. The woman melted snow for water, and they used a bucket to relieve themselves. Washing and personal hygiene was not possible. Their body odors blended together and became indistinguishable from the musty smells of their abode.

Each day trapped with this woman was torture. Semantha cringed at the thought of the warm touching she had shared with her, now exposed as her father's ex-lover. She kept track of the days with marks on the wall yearning for the moment she could get the means to escape.

Marco, oh Marco.

Free from the numbing effect of the drink, Semantha recounted with crystal clarity her otherworldly encounter with him in that ratty old kitchen moments before he had broken free and escaped from Saul's evil. It had been the most passionate rendezvous she had ever experienced with any of her many lovers, so powerful despite how brief it had been. She envisioned Marco sitting next to her, their first kiss, touching each other, him inside of her, the pinnacle of physical and emotional intimacy they had shared, the sweet conversation afterwards. In her loneliness and isolation, her reverie took flight and became an all-consuming obsession. He was all she thought about.

She conjured him as a great philosopher, maybe a scientist on the brink of an important discovery, something extraordinary. His perceived stature grew with each passing day. How glorious her life would have been had she met him years before! Respectable, calm, ordinary, normal, free from the weird perversions which had dominated her existence up to then.

Could he have been my eternal soul mate? Maybe in a past life. She wondered whether he had survived. Saul and Clem, his partner in evil, had likely given chase and found him. She shuddered when she thought about how they would have brutalized him, Clem's stock-in-trade. She was quite sure she would never see him again. *Marco,* just his name, *my oh my.* Every so often, she buried her head in her thin, stained pillow and wept with reckless abandon, thinking about his fate. Each time the old lady would pull away the curtain and appear in her doorway, standing motionless with a troubled look on her face.

"Can I help?" she would ask with a nod. While Semantha felt the woman's concern; she wanted no part of it. She would scowl and turn away. Each time, a tear would come to the woman's eye as she dropped the curtain and left.

*   *   *

EVENTUALLY, Semantha decided she wanted to find out exactly what this old woman and Pappie had done together. Her longing to know more about their affair trumped the disgust she felt. That day, a late winter storm made the wind howl and caused the front door to shake. According to her marks on the wall, it was the seventy-third day she had been isolated in this cold, damp, hovel-like cave.

Semantha came out of her chamber and sat down at the beat-up wooden table in the open area of the hovel. The woman was sitting there as well, drinking something she called "herbal tea." Three chairs were placed around the table. In one corner, there was a small galley consisting of a two-burner gas hotplate with a metal tea kettle and some cabinets with rag-like draperies covering the shelves. In another, a wood-burning heater flued to the exterior. Behind it, an almost depleted stack of wood the woman had chopped before the winter set in. To save fuel, they both wore winter coats all day.

Semantha sat there for a long minute staring at the woman and try-ing to muster the courage to break the silence. The woman spoke first.

"Do you remember my name?" she asked. Surprised and embar-rassed because she didn't, Semantha stuttered for a second, then sat there and fidgeted.

"It's Erzulie," the old lady said as she pulled on her ear lobe, took a long, deep drag on her pipe, and set it in the old saucer she used as an ashtray.

"Ok, I'm Semantha."

Erzulie smiled as she took another sip of the warm concoction. "I've been incanting to the spirit world every day, hoping you'd come back to your senses. Maybe they heard me." As the cat stared at her, Erzulie extended her finger to her forehead then moved it slowly to her crotch and completed an exaggerated, slightly lewd, sign of the cross.

"Oh, so you're into the spirit world?" Semantha asked.

"Yep. I'm… uh… a Santera in the local Santeria group," she said, shaking her head up and down. "My parents were in it, too, back in Trinidad. We're from Cuba."

"Santeria? Never heard of it," Semantha said.

"It's Cuban. My father, may God rest his soul, was also deeply com-mitted...my mom, well, in her own world."

Erzulie pulled up her scarf and moved closer to the stove. She had put in a new log on the fire and it was blazing hot. "It's time to tell ya about me," she said.

Erzulie recounted her affair with Pappie and her flirtation with satanism. She'd soured on the idea when the warlock head of the local coven they were attending told her that the devil wanted her to have sex with him. She didn't figure that should be part of it. Her relationship with Theo had never gotten past kissing and hugging, and that's the way they both wanted it, at least according to Erzulie's recollection.

"When Theo decided to form his own coven, this man Saul showed up," she continued. "I knew from the moment I met him he was pure trouble. I told Theo I was…" — Erzulie knifed the air with her hand — "…through." She knitted her brows. "By then, Theo was consumed by this idea of Satan and leading a coven. Nothing else mattered. He appeared sad as I walked out, but I've never heard from him again."

Semantha was relieved to hear that Erzulie and Pappie's relationship had been pretty innocent. It seemed less threatening. *Maybe she's not quite so depraved.*

"Saul killed Pappie. Theo that is," Semantha said, as she teared up and ran her hand through her disheveled hair. Her thoughts returned to the day on the lake, scattering the ashes of her beloved father. But then they compulsively shifted to the chance meeting with Marco's vessel. She still recalled how she had been so profoundly attracted to his sad smile, infused as it seemed, with pathos. *Oh, what would I do to see him again?*

"Pappie meant the world to me, Erzulie. When I was only six, he saved me from his brother's abuse and gave me a life. I owe my existence to him."

"Like to me, my little flower." A faint smile appeared on her mournful face. "I had a daughter once too," she continued. "Isabella. I loved her dearly."

Semantha cocked her head to the side. It was hard to connect this quirky old recluse with a daughter. To Semantha, the distance seemed too far.

"Tell me about her," she said.

Erzulie looked away, closed her eyes, and almost imperceptibly shook her head. She remained silent.

The way Erzulie acted—so sad, so sweet, the obviously painful mention of her own daughter, and the comparison to her beloved Pappie—it all struck Semantha deeply, bringing into crystal focus for the first time what this skinny old woman with a hooked nose had done for her. She saw now that she owed her a monumental debt, almost more than the debt a child owes her mother. A lump came to her throat. *If only I'd had a mother like this.*

Without another word, Semantha rose from the table and disappeared behind the drape into her sleeping space. Embarrassed and feeling guilty about how cruelly she had treated Erzulie up to now, she needed to reflect alone on how she had behaved. She spent the night tossing on her cot.

The next morning, when Semantha rose, she knew she had to make amends. She emerged and found Erzulie sitting on her chair at the head of the table, a cup of tea in front of her, as if she had not moved from the night before. The room was quiet and the howling wind from yesterday had abated. Semantha grabbed Erzulie, pulled her to her feet, and threw her arms around her. She whispered into the old woman's ear.

"Thank you, Erzulie."

Erzulie smiled. Her eyes became soft.

"All forgiven, then?"

"Yes. After all, we love the same man," Semantha said. She laughed, a laugh tinged with sarcasm and devoid of pleasure. Erzulie breathed a sigh of relief. Her eyes twinkled. She put her head on Semantha's shoulder.

Semantha moved away from Erzulie after a few moments in her arms. "How did you save me?" she asked, holding Erzulie shoulders at arms' length.

"You weren't quite dead when I saw you floating in the river face down. Maybe you've heard, but sometimes people's hearts and breathing slow almost to nothing, only to revive later. There was a case over in Berrien where I grew up when a body shrieked out as the undertaker made the first cut. I did my PhD thesis on the case. Fascinating physiology."

Semantha nodded. Her face broadened into a smile. It was a coaxed, thin smile.

"Maybe I'm one of the lucky ones."

Erzulie turned her head away and stared at the floor. "IF…if you call this world a lucky place, maybe you are," she said softly with a slight, almost apologetic smile.

"Why did Saul kill Theo? He would never hurt a flea. A dreamer, for sure, but not mean." Erzulie wiped a tear from her eye with her finger as Macy snuggled up to her leg and purred, her tail held high.

"Saul was the devil." Semantha shook her head and placed her hands on her temples. "He was jealous and wanted Pappie's Circle to do violent things. When Pappie refused, he hammered a stake into Pappie's heart. God." Semantha's eyes were braised with grief as she envisaged the weapon finding its mark.

"How'd you wind up in the river? Saul come after you, too?" Erzulie poured more tea into her cup, then offered some to Semantha. Semantha held up her hand as if saying "No thanks." She found tea made with dried oak leaves distasteful.

"No, this beautiful man showed up just before we were going to have a mass for Pappie. Saul got it in his head to offer him up to the devil as a human sacrifice, had him readied, drugged and stretched out on a chair before the altar. Macabre, but that was Saul. When the man somehow escaped, Saul sent me after him. I found him, we had a violent struggle, and the man tried to kill me." Semantha decided not to tell Erzulie about her ongoing fascination with Marco. That was too much to explain.

Erzulie scratched her head. "Kill you?"

Semantha closed her eyes and grimaced. She looked solemn, as if at a wake.

"I've never seen anybody so white hot as that man was that day. I was petrified by the power of his rage, out of control."

Erzulie let a minute pass.

"What happened to Saul?"

"I have no idea, but I suspect he and his side-kick Clem ran away. Knowing them, they'd want to find this man. Marco's his name. Get revenge." Semantha cringed.

"Clem?" Erzulie asked, raising her left eyebrow. She looked at the blazing fire. It seemed she had something more to say, maybe knew something else.

Semantha's eyebrows furrowed. "Erzulie, what..."

Erzulie placed two of her fingers on Semantha's mouth.

"Enough," she said.

*　　*　　*

Springtime came early that year in Berrien County, and soon Erzulie and Semantha were able to dig themselves out and get more firewood. Semantha was amazed by Erzulie's strength. She could split logs like she'd learned from Lincoln. While she helped Erzulie stack the wood, Semantha asked Erzulie if she would help her find someplace else to live now that spring had come. Erzulie's eyes dropped, filled with painful melancholy.

First, before she agreed to do anything, she said, she needed to get in touch with her oricha. It had been too long. She told Semantha she liked to go to a Toque de Santo[1] at a Casa near Paw Paw where the spirits were strongest. She invited Semantha to come with her.

"I don't think so. No more crazy black masses and devil worship." She shook at the thought. "I still can't imagine how Marco got out alive," she said.

"Maybe this Marco of yours was mystically possessed by an oricha,"

---

[1] A place where Santeria rituals are performed. Also called a "Casa."

Erzulie said. "They have supernatural powers, you know." Erzulie looked skyward, her face glowing. "I have my own oricha who lives with me and sometimes possesses me. We are one." She placed her hand on Semantha's shoulder and smiled. "It helped me cure ya. Come with me tonight and see her power."

Semantha's eyebrows shot up; her face muscles tensed.

"No more conjuring weird forces from dark places for me," Semantha said as she smirked. There was a tone of finality in her voice.

Macy jumped, then soundlessly ran after a mouse that had emerged from behind a cupboard.

"Santeria's nothing like that. It's based on Roman Catholicism, combined with an Afro-Cuban native religion. My oricha serves Olodumare, the ultimate source of Ache. That's the invisible force that permeates the universe."

Erzulie genuflected and again crossed herself. "I do want you to experience this for yourself."

Semantha shook her head emphatically no, repulsed by the idea.

Erzulie got up from her chair, walked right next to Semantha, and, her forehead furled, stared down at her intently. Erzulie's face tightened, and her eyes narrowed. Her gray frizzy hair seemed to stand on end.

"Look, you don't have a choice," she said, her voice raised. She shook her bony finger at Semantha. "You owe your life to Santeria, young lady."

"I thought you said you saved me," Semantha responded, yelling right back. The months of confinement had made her edgy and irritable.

"Through the power of my oricha, I did. Don't argue. We're going."

Semantha was taken back by Erzulie's near-maniacal insistence and was afraid to push the woman further. She needed Erzulie's help in finding her own place. She got in the truck, and they headed to the Casa.

The large living room in the old farmhouse in Paw Paw was filled with little dolls—some black, some tan, some white, some dressed like saints, some unclothed from the waist up. Bouquets of brightly colored plastic flowers were everywhere on shelves throughout the room. Along the wall, there was a table covered with a white cloth and religious icons, several of which were partially covered with bright red silk cloth. Three votive candles adorned with pictures of the Blessed Virgin of Guadalupe flickered next to a beat-up statue looking like a calypso dancer but with a halo over his head. A small incense burner spewed out a steady stream of light gray smoke, permeating the brightly lit room with a sweet and spicy- smelling haze.

Ten men and women, mostly Latin, dressed in white flowing gowns, stood around the sides of the room when Erzulie and Semantha walked in. They too were dressed in white robes, Semantha wearing one of Erzulie's extras. It was a little too short.

A man entered just after they arrived and sat down behind a set of steel drums in one corner. He looked out of place, a balding middle aged white man dressed in workout clothes, like he had just come from the gym. But when he began beating out a dramatic calypso cadence, shaking his head and shoulders to the rhythm, the room came alive as people gyrated to the beat. Several shook rattlers and one had a set of castanets. As if possessed, the dancers began to mutter incantations set to the music. A cacophony of sounds filled the room.

In another minute, a shirtless young male dancer wearing a turban jumped into the room and began spinning to the rhythm. His head moved violently, like he was enraptured, as he moved from person to person thrusting with his hips, sometimes grabbing a man or a woman and pulling them into his gyrations.

My God, Semantha thought, *I know him.* She hoped he didn't recognize her. They had been sex partners in high school, one of many for her. He was the best of the lot, but the last thing she wanted was to have any further contact with him. She turned to head to the door, but it was too late. He got to Semantha and grabbed her by the shoulders. As he led her around in his dance, he brought his face to her ear.

"Meet me outside after the sacrifice," he whispered as he winked and snickered impishly. In an instant, he smiled and moved on.

Semantha hardly noticed the rest of the ritual: the incantations, the attempts at divinations, the killing of the hapless rooster, and the offering of its blood to the spirits. All she could think about was Cisco and why he wanted to meet her. She could not imagine what he wanted. A hookup? To talk about old times? Tell her about his family and pregnant wife? Semantha shook her head with disdain. She didn't want any of that.

It had been so long since the two of them had connected. Pappie's housekeeper, a big local gossip, had told her once that he had gone to Lake Michigan College and gotten his associate's degree in community policing. Semantha could not have cared less about what he had done after high school. Once she went to college and then on to graduate school in physics, she had eagerly placed her unpleasant teenage years behind her. Now, how could she get away from him? He had seen her, so she couldn't just walk out unnoticed. Besides, they were miles away from the hovel, and it was dark.

After the ceremonies were over-close to midnight-Semantha looked for Erzulie, her ride home and her ticket away from Cisco. Semantha was sure that if they left together, Cisco would be put off and keep his distance. She found Erzulie sitting motionless on the floor in a corner, legs crossed, her back against the wall. She was staring blankly at the ceiling, her mouth agape.

Semantha tapped Erzulie on the shoulder. "Let's go," she said. There was tightness in her voice. Erzulie did not move. She remained stiff like a statue.

Another Casa member stood nearby. "Don't worry about her. She's been overtaken by Oshun, her orisha," the woman said. "She will come-to when she is released. It's ok."

"Oshun?" Semantha said with a question in her voice.

"The goddess of love and serenity and the patron saint of rivers. People say that sometimes they see Oshun in the St. Joe River looking for King Shango, her late husband." She smiled and winked, waving her hand toward the outside. "You should go to the river and have a look. Maybe you'll see her, too."

Semantha didn't want to hear about some crazy Santeria superstition. And she'd had enough of the St. Joe River for her lifetime.

"Who are you?" Semantha asked, looking at the short, plain-looking woman.

"Cecelia," the woman said as she extended her hand to shake. "Let's go outside and talk. Erzulie has told me so much about you."

Semantha furrowed her eyebrows. "Some other time," she said, not returning the offer of a handshake. "Right now, I only want to get out of here."

"You'll need to wait 'til she's ready," Cecelia said, nodding toward Erzulie. "Take it from me, I've known her forever. Disturb her at your own peril. She can get very upset."

That's for sure, Semantha thought. But having no interest in meeting anyone right then, especially a Casa regular, she turned away from Cecelia and went outside, hoping to slide into the darkness and avoid Cisco.

It was no use. As soon as she left the house, Cisco stepped out of a shadow, grabbed her by the wrist and tugged her behind the barn-like garage next to the house. She let out a little squeak and said, "No."

"Don't worry, girl," Cisco said. He pushed her against the wall of the barn and put his hands on her shoulders, holding her at arms' length. The only light was from the house, projecting large gargoyle-like shadows of them on the wall.

Is he going to try to rape me? Semantha wondered. But he only smiled, a big toothy smile.

"I thought you were dead," he said. Then he dropped his grip on Semantha's shoulders and ran the back of his hand lightly over her forehead, like he was happy she was alive. He did not move closer.

"Dead? How would you know?"

"I'm a deputy in the Berrien County Sheriff's office, you know, the local wetback-made-good thing. They gave me an arrest warrant to serve on you but then the next week they said, 'Don't bother, she's dead.'"

"Arrest? For what?"

"Sex with those two teenage boys at the science fair you judged." Cisco blinked and smiled. "I was jealous."

"Jealous?" Semantha thought about those boys and turned her face away. It was true that she had surrendered to her impulse, or maybe compulsion was a better word. But they were seventeen and she didn't understand why a few quickies was such a big deal. She was sure the boys had enjoyed it.

With two of his outstretched fingers, Cisco gently moved Semantha's face back so he could look her in the eye.

"Our rolls were great," he said with a small smile.

Semantha thought back to those days. She was embarrassed by how her omnipresent, powerful sexual urges had overwhelmed her then. She was relieved that her brush with death had quelled those compulsions, at least for now. She had felt asexual during her recuperation and had allowed Erzulie's approaches only because they were comforting and not threatening.

"Rolls?"

"You know, those times in the back seat of my car. I lived for them." He laughed and fluttered his eyes seductively. Semantha was a touch disappointed that Cisco didn't try to make a move. Not that she would have allowed anything to happen, but he was handsome and she would have appreciated the compliment if he had tried.

Semantha scowled. "What made the sheriff's office think I was dead?"

"My God, that whole thing about the house on the river and what happened there was the soap opera of the day all over town. Everybody in the office was talking about it after that doctor guy showed up and said he was almost killed by devil worshipers. Things like that don't happen in this town."

"Who?" Semantha raised her eyebrow high, surprised and curious.

"I'm not sure. Some Greek looking guy, a doc of some sort. I saw him walking into the courtroom once, tall, very good looking," Cisco said.

Could it be?

Semantha's heart began to flutter, her pulse quickened. She gasped.

"You remember his name?"

"I saw a file with his name on it. It's been a long time…Mark or something like that."

Semantha's shoulders tingled. *Could he be alive, my Lord in all of heaven?* The full moon came out from behind the clouds and illuminated Cisco's face.

"Yeah, and then he came back about a month later and met with the prosecutor, another knockout babe. Looked a lot like you. No dimples, though." Cisco shook his hand up and down as if to say, "Too hot to handle."

"What happened then?"

"Can't tell ya. I got reassigned to another station. All I know is that the prosecutor quit a couple of months after that."

Semantha was flabbergasted at this news, almost too much to take in all at once. She stared at Cisco, wondering what more he knew, but also worried about what more he had in mind.

Cisco raised his left brow, and his eyes went from bright and wide to narrow and focused, taking on an alluring form. His lips softened and parted slightly. He put his arms around her, pulled her tight, and kissed her on her lips. Preoccupied by what she had just heard, Semantha offered no resistance. But at that moment, Erzulie came out from the house and saw them embrace. She screwed up her face. Even from a distance and despite the dim light, Semantha could feel the cold blast from Erzulie's eyes.

"Cisco, you stay away from her," Erzulie yelled. Semantha pulled away and offered Cisco a Mona Lisa smile. She walked to Erzulie.

"Watch yourself, babe. Don't let 'em know you're alive. Hope to see you again," Cisco yelled out as Semantha climbed into Erzulie's truck.

On the ride back to the hovel, Erzulie was stony silent, repeatedly clenching and unclenching her jaw. She asked Semantha nothing about her reactions to the ceremony. In the grateful silence, Semantha's mind went into motion.

Alive, my god, he's alive. I've got to see him, I must. How, when… where could he be now? Maybe I could find him…we could…no that's too much to hope for…so much has happened since then…but still maybe good luck for once…

Good Luck? Semantha again thought back to the day she had last seen Marco. The splendor of meeting him, but that glorious moment overlaid by the evil plan hatched by Saul and his brutish sidekick Clem. Her fight with Saul in front of the others, the browbeating he gave her, her timid decision to give in to his abuse, and—horror of all horrors—her complicit acts in furtherance of his atrocity. She pushed the thoughts about the rest of that horrible night out of her mind.

Saul and Clem. What ever happened to them? Did they run away, are they still around?

"Gordon, meet cynthia, my new bride," Marco said with an ear-to-ear smile. This was how Marco introduced his wife to Gordon Fellsteon, his boss and head of research, at the Fermilab holiday party. It was held each year at The Drake, Oak Brook, one of the nicest venues in the western suburbs. The men wore tuxedos and the women floor-length evening gowns. Marco looked dashing dressed in black, his stiffly starched white shirt contrasting dramatically with his Ferrari-red cummerbund and his light olive complexion. A white carnation was pinned onto his lapel.

Cynthia wore a new gown, captivating red and low-cut. It fit her form perfectly. She liked the way the red accented her blond hair. Marco had bought her a miniature white orchid wrist bouquet, which beautifully complimented the dress.

Cynthia was ecstatic, eagerly anticipating the exciting social life that came along with Marco's new status as a scientific rockstar working on the leading edge of particle physics at Fermilab, one of the world centers for the study of subatomic specks.

This was something she had longed to experience all the way back to her days growing up in small-town Iowa. This event was the best, complete with a harpist playing traditional Christmas songs. The harpist's music blended harmoniously with tinkling cocktail glasses and the gentle hum of happy chatter.

"Very pleased to meet you, Cynthia," Gordon said. "Marco has told me so much about you." He tilted his head, then looked Cynthia up and down like he had something on his mind other than hosting a cocktail party. Cynthia cringed imperceptibly when he winked at her.

"Everything he said about you is definitely true." He breathed in with an exaggerated sound. "Ummm. I love your perfume. Is it French? Lilac?" Gordon's eyes fell on Cythia's cleavage. "And how you met, accidentally sitting next to each other on that plane ride. What great luck." Fellsteon slapped Marco on the back as if the two were at a campus frat party.

"But it didn't —" Cynthia said. Marco's face instantly went from happy to dark. He looked like he was about to jump out of his skin. He seized Cynthia by the elbow and pulled her away.

"Gotta get this lady some champagne," he said. "We'll catch up with you in a bit, Gordon."

"What was that about, Marco?" Cynthia asked once they were out of Gordon's hearing. She felt manhandled.

"What do you expect that I would tell everyone the sordid details about my time in Michigan? God, no." He spoke in an angry whisper, his mouth close to Cynthia's ear. "You think I want people to be poking around about what happened, who Saul was, all that? Heaven forbid they start asking about Saul electrocuted on the accelerator." He looked panicked and shook his head. "Absolutely can't go there."

Cynthia knotted her brow but took the flute Marco offered. She wondered why Marco was so concerned about the accelerator incident. She thought of Marco as a hero for fending off his attacker, hurling him onto the high voltage coils. But never mind. Her thoughts quickly returned to the reception, the beautifully dressed people and the elegant surroundings.

Marco spent the rest of the evening introducing Cynthia to his colleagues, all of whom responded like Gordon. A few of the men gave her a hug and let their hands drift to the wrong places. Cynthia felt everyone's eyes on her. She was charmed by the attention, but uncomfortable with it at the same time. She had made herself into a hotshot prosecutor. The role as a coquettish princess did not quite fit.

When they got home-it was after midnight- Marco ripped off her gown as if he was a boy opening his first Christmas present, threw her on the bed, and had her. For Cynthia, it was not great love making, only coupling, but it was late. Afterwards, Marco poured them a nightcap, which they drank lounging naked on the bed.

"You were great tonight, Cynthia. It almost made me hard to see how everyone loved you. I couldn't wait to get you here." He patted his hand on the mattress. "You're really going to help my career."

"Your career?" Cynthia felt like a dark cloud had passed briefly in front of the sun. The reference seemed so out of place, and it left questions in Cynthia's mind. What did Marco expect of her? Was she to settle into a role in the supporting cast for his rise in the scientific world? The Fermilab women's auxiliary? God no. That was not in her plan even if she knew what would be expected in such a role, which she did not. And what about her own career? She mused over how important her work had been for her.

"Yeah, just what I need to get my full professorship, and who knows from there? Exceptional conversationalist, beautiful blonde hair, and an accomplished lawyer, to boot. Tonight, all eyes were on you, my darling." He paused and looked away.

"Did you have a good time, too?" he asked, yawning, his eyes half closed.

"For sure. Gordon's a trifle...how should I say it? ...overly macho, though." She could have been more direct, but she didn't want to crush the mood.

"That's the way he gets after a couple of drinks. Usually, he's stiffer and more formal than a Marine general. You'll see."

Cynthia did not respond. All in all, it had been a great evening, despite Marco' s unsettling reference to his career. She could see she had moved up the social ladder a couple of rungs, to a place far more elegant than the rowdy beer parties at law school or when she was in the prosecutor's office. Maybe she really was entering the enveloping world of privilege and status. *Exactly what I've always wanted,* she thought, falling asleep with a smile.

*   *   *

ELECTRICITY HAD SPARKED between Cynthia and Marco right from the start, at their meeting in that buggy old courthouse in Berrien, Michigan. She had been assigned to prosecute him for the murder of that witch, whatever her name was. How lucky her boss took over the case shortly after it began.

Marco had dazzled her instantly, tall with curly black hair and chiseled features, almost like a Greek god. She was as much in awe as she was in love. It had been a sublime journey—their tender embrace on the top of the Empire State Building, she proposed and he said "yes," helping him work out the trauma from being held hostage by the coven, their marriage at the Morton Arboretum followed by a honeymoon in Tahiti. She felt she was living a dream, all that comes with being married to a nationally known physicist.

It had not been easy for her to give up her work as a prosecutor, but it would have been even harder for her to relinquish the chance of spending her life with this amazing man. Yes, Marco was somewhat chauvinistic, a touch arrogant and disdainfully proud. She didn't care much. He was also charismatic, the way he looked at her, cocked his head, smiled seductively, winked his eye. He filled the space around him with his ferocious intellect, physicality, and verve.

Before long, though, the humdrum of daily existence settled in. Two months into their marriage, Cynthia often found herself alone in Marco's upscale River Forest townhouse, filled with fancy appliances they seldom used and modern Italian leather furniture Cynthia didn't much like. It felt like his place, not hers, and Marco really didn't want to talk about changing it around. Already at age thirty-nine, he was set in his ways. When Cynthia suggested that they shop together to acquire some art to hang on the sterile off-white walls, Marco shook his head "no," insisting he liked the "minimalist feel" he got from the blank whiteness. Cynthia was disappointed, but what was she going to do? She was sure that, in time, the house would feel like hers as well.

To start with, Marco came home for dinner every night, which, as he pointed out repeatedly, was a change from his habit when he lived alone—and a real sacrifice considering how much work he had to do: experiments to design, articles to write—he had just been named associate editor of a journal on neutrinos which took a lot of time— grant applications to prepare, everything associated with being a scientist on the rise. Cynthia wondered if he was trying to make her feel guilty, but she decided to ignore it if that was his intent. *At least we're together,* she thought.

Along with dinner at home, the responsibility for meal preparation fell on Cynthia. At first that worked out pretty well. Cooking was not her strong suit, but Marco told her over and over how much he liked what she prepared and she tried hard to up her minimal culinary skills to please him. But soon she began to feel like the kitchen slave. Sometimes he didn't even bother to put his plate in the dishwasher after finishing.

At the dinner table, he could be an engaging conversationalist, but only if the mood struck. More typically, he gave monologues about Fermilab politics and the department of physics at the university. She listened intently but often she felt she didn't have anything to say. And Marco seemed uninterested in what was going on with her or what she was thinking. Usually, he asked her little more than how her day had gone.

Cynthia's answer was always the same. She got tired of telling Marco about the futility of her job search. It was the time of a big downturn in legal work and firms were downsizing. Most employers wanted someone experienced in Illinois, not Michigan, law. Her old job as First Assistant U.S. Attorney in Detroit didn't seem to get her very far in Illinois. One interviewer told her that he thought that practice in Michigan was rather arcane compared to Illinois, a comment which struck a blow at Cynthia's pride. She felt two steps down as a female lawyer in a man's profession and three steps down because her work had been out of state. The only offer she got was from a small divorce-law firm in a northwest suburban strip mall, but the prospect of dealing with whiny, entitled housewives all day was repugnant to her.

Unemployed and with not much to do, Cynthia hung around the house more and more. She read some and watched TV once in a while. She had no friends in Chicago and wasn't sure where to go to meet new people. Without Marco, she would not do well at social events for couples, and she definitely would feel strange going to places frequented by singles. She began to think that other people wouldn't want to meet her anyway, a feeling left over from her anxiety-ridden teenage years. Her hope for a happy new life dimmed.

Cynthia's days became centered on reading the Help Wanted ads, sending out resumes, going for an occasional interview, and waiting for a response. Then the rejection letters, each hitting her harder than the one before. Occasionally she would shed a tear after opening one. But then she would dry her eyes and go back to watching the TV game shows, feeling less self-assured, more inadequate, closer to empty. She feared she was losing the sharp edge of confidence that she had developed in Detroit from success after success dealing with the most heinous crimes. She didn't know what to do to keep her edge, except to hope that something would happen to rekindle her self-confidence. At that point, she didn't care what.

Marco began coming home late more and more often, many times after she was already asleep. The crush of work at the office, he said. She wanted to believe him, but she began to wonder about his frequent, ready excuses.

Is he already on the prowl? She didn't want to think he was, but… With his many absences she lost her interest in preparing a good dinner, relying instead on carryout when he did show. Her evenings became as empty as her days. Pleasuring herself, the haven for lonely housewives, was her only sexual outlet. Sometimes she would tear up without apparent reason.

*   *   *

"Let's start a family," Cynthia said as she carefully set her fork on her folded napkin after she was finished eating. She winked and offered a toothy but forced smile. They had been married four months and Cynthia thought it was time to discuss the issue. She knew she should have brought it up before, but she had been busy with wedding plans, much of which had fallen on her. Now she was worried about how he would react, particularly because he had seemed aloof and sullen of late.

To soften him up, she had prepared his favorite food, beef bourguignon with fingerling potatoes, and had set the table with some bone china they had gotten as a wedding gift, hoping that seeing the dishes would remind him of that wonderful day. At least he had committed to being home that night.

"Come on babe. Don't you think I've got enough on my plate? What's wrong with you?" Marco responded, shaking his head and furrowing his eyebrows. Cynthia had prepared herself for the possibility of a negative reaction, but he didn't need to sound quite so harsh. His words hurt.

"You're too damned busy, that's the problem." Cynthia squinted as the corners of her lips turned down. "Don't you want our relationship anymore?" Her eyes reddened and watered as if she was ready to cry.

"Don't be so clingy, Cynthia. A promotion will be good for you too. More money, lots of international conferences. You can come. See the world."

"I want a husband, not a trip to Paris business class."

Marco's face turned sour.

"You complain too much about every damned thing." He knifed the air with his open hand. "Pick up my clothes, take out the garbage, on and on. It doesn't end." He shook his head. "My life is out in the world, not in this godforsaken house."

"What do you think I'm supposed to do, rot?"

"Get a job, that's what. You're not trying hard enough. Getting fat and lazy. And cut down on the wine. I see the bottles in the garbage." He brusquely pushed his plate away and defiantly threw his wadded-up napkin on it. He jumped up and left the room. Cynthia heard the door to the bedroom slam shut.

Cynthia put her face in her hands and began to cry, feeling acutely the sting of Marco's rejection. How much of his attitude could she take? He could be so mean. But was she ready to throw in the towel? Maybe he was right. Get a job and everything gets better. After a few moments, she forced herself to stop crying and went to the bedroom, ready to say whatever she must to patch things up. She wanted to try to hold onto something which she feared was slipping away.

Marco was already asleep and snoring like a banshee.

*   *   *

ON THE SIX-MONTH anniversary of their marriage, Marco came home unexpectedly early, six p.m., carrying a bottle of Dom Perignon champagne and a box of Belgian chocolates. He was feeling guilty about how harshly he had treated Cynthia in recent weeks and thought it best to offer an olive branch. While he had his doubts, he was not quite ready to give up.

When he arrived, Cynthia was lying on the couch in the living room, the same couch where they had first embraced more than a year ago. Her pajama top was unbuttoned to the waist, revealing her breasts and the start of a paunch. She had not combed her hair, appearing like she had spent the day without getting dressed or even washing up. A half empty bottle of cheap California wine sat on the coffee table next to an empty glass.

As soon as he walked in and put down the champagne, Cynthia pulled herself to her feet and stumbled over to him. She hugged him tight, then gave him a juicy, wet kiss, slobbering as her lips touched his.

"Easy, babe," he said, stepping back and turning his head. "You need a shower."

"Oh Marco, don't be mean. It's so good to see you, darlin'," she said, slurring her words. She grabbed his crotch and put his hand on hers. "How's 'bout a littl' action, huh? It is our anniver…sarry." Apparently, she had not noticed the fine wine and chocolates. Marco forcefully removed her hand and pulled his away from her. He drew in his eyebrows and sneered.

Cynthia staggered as she lost her balance for a second. She grabbed Marco's arm to keep from falling. She began rubbing herself up and down against his body.

"Not now," he said and shoved her away hard. She again lost her balance, stumbled back, and hit the couch with a thud. Marco sat down next to her, but at arm's length.

"I brought some champagne," he said in a monotone, disappointment spread across his face. "I wanted to make it up to you for being mean in the last few weeks. But I see you don't need any more to drink." Eyeing the partially finished bottle, Marco gave her a look of icy rebuke.

"C'mon Marco, it's juss a glass of wine. What's wrong with that?" she said, still slurring her words but moving close. She threw her arms around him, opened her mouth wide, and tried to give him a kiss. "Our anniversary…" She tugged on his sleeve to get him to lie down next to her and again grabbed for his crotch.

Marco pulled away and stood up, looking down at her. Her arms were still reaching up to him from the couch as she started to tear up.

"What's wrong, Marco? Don't you love me any…any…more?" she asked, her voice a fractured plea. She reached for a tissue from the box on the cocktail table.

Marco's eyes narrowed and he snarled.

"You know, it's simple, my dear," he said. He looked down at her for a long moment. "I don't even recognize you anymore. Overnight, you've become a dull… whiny…." — he went silent as if searching for words — "clingy housewife, the sort I detest." He shook his head in revulsion. "Get yourself together."

Cynthia was outraged. *So unfair,* she thought. She stood up, moved almost nose to nose with Marco, and let out her venom. It was as if Marco had become the reason for what was wrong in her life.

"Get myself together?" she asked, spittle spewing forth. "What about you? Always gone, always working, nothin'…" she said, her eyes burning.

"I left my life work, moved all the way here, no friends, no job, no family, just to be with you…only to find you somewhere else. Wrong, you hear?" She stomped her foot. "So wrong. Even my self- respect…" She would have sputtered out more, but the words seemed to get lost in her troubled mind. She gasped for air, and, exhausted, fell back to the couch.

Marco left for the bedroom. Cynthia finished the bottle and moaned quietly. She fell asleep right there.

After that, Marco rarely appeared at the house before eleven p.m., and went directly to the guest room when he did show up. Sometimes he slept on the couch in his office. Cynthia seldom saw him.

*   *   *

"Don't even try to deny it," Cynthia said as she waved a scrap of paper. It looked like a love note, pink with a filigreed edge. Marco had just returned from work and had walked into the bedroom to take off his soiled, wrinkled clothes. He appeared surprised when he found the lights on and Cynthia still up.

Cynthia had waited all day to confront him. Even though it was close to midnight, she had not taken even a sip of wine. She wanted to have her wits when the moment came. She felt tricked, robbed, abandoned along the side of the highway like roadkill, a gentle doe battered by a reckless maniac truck driver. She decided to let Marco know this was the last straw.

"And after less than a year, holy God in Christ. What did I do to deserve this?" Cynthia said, her face red, her eyes throwing daggers his way. She wadded up the paper and pitched it toward him. It landed at his feet.

Not even peering down at the crumpled paper, Marco took a deep breath and swallowed. "What is this?"

Cynthia could read the blank look on his face well enough to know that he was hiding something. She was not taken in by his feigned look of innocence.

"I don't know what you are talking about. I've been spending my time engaged in res—"

"Lies," Cynthia said in hot frustration. "Get real. Why don't you read it if you haven't already? Some floozy talking about the wonderful evening you spent with her."

"Oh, come on, Cynthia, you're—"

"You never got over that witch seductress, did you? All that talk about the trauma you suffered. That was so much fuckin' shit. In the end, I never satisfied you like her, did I?" *I've been used,* she thought. She began breathing hard.

"Holy Christ, Cythia, that's so unfair. You of all people know the story. I killed her, for fuck's sake."

"Get out of my bedroom, you sleaze. Now!"

"Your bedroom? That's rare. In case you haven't noticed, it's my name on the deed."

Neither Cynthia nor Marco said anything more. Not moving, they stared at each other for a time. Then Marco gave a mechanical shrug, turned, and walked out, slamming the door hard as he left. A hanger on the hook behind the door fell off, making a tinny plastic sound as it hit the burled teak floor.

Dazed and heartbroken, Cynthia fell to the bed and buried her head in the pillow.

The next morning, she got up and looked at the clock. *Nine thirty. I'm sure he's long gone. Only thing that matters to him is his fuckin' career and sleeping around.* She put on her robe and headed to the kitchen to get some coffee. She began to plan how she would pull herself together. Maybe she'd go live with her parents for a while. Return to Detroit. Some people she knew still worked in the prosecutor's office there.

Definitely she needed to get back in shape. It had been a mistake to allow herself to be swept off her feet, to lose her edge and *savoir faire* for an illusion. Inside, he was still a self-centered bastard. His Michigan problem had not changed him, not in the least.

When she got to the kitchen, she stopped dead and froze. To her surprise, he was sitting there in front of an undrunk coffee staring into space, still wearing his dirty clothes from the night before. Overnight, they had taken on a distinctive odor.

"What you doing here?" she asked from the doorway, keeping her distance.

"I couldn't go back to work after last night."

"Hey, don't blame me if you miss a publication deadline or some such thing. I'm calling a lawyer today, so get ready to go to the cleaners. Best if you get back to the only thing you care about."

Marco stared up at her. "No, no. Please Cynthia, all I could think about last night was all the beautiful things we've done together, how wonderful you've been. I couldn't get it out of my mind how support-ive you were when I had problems performing in bed. How you helped me get my confidence back. I spent the night here in this chair with my face in my hands, sobbing dryly. It was the first time in my life I did anything like shedding a tear."

Cynthia shook her head, her lips turned down.

"I don't want this to end this way," Marco said as he stood and walked toward where Cynthia was standing.

"Keep your distance, unless you want to defend an assault charge along with the divorce. Is that what you want?"

"Oh my God, Cynthia. I've really hurt you, I'm so very…" He extended his arms as if inviting a hug.

"Waaay too easy. A quick and flip apology won't hack it this time. Don't even try. It's high time that you learned that you can't just treat a woman any way you want, so what if you're drop dead handsome."

Marco's jaw dropped and his eyes opened wide. He stared at Cynthia motionless for a long minute, holding his look of astonishment.

"Holy Lord, Cynthia, that's almost exactly what Semantha said to me before I drowned her." He didn't move a muscle.

Cynthia backed into the hallway. She was scared about what Marco had just said, but after she thought about it, it didn't seem like a threat. His words and the quiet, pensive way he said them made her feel sorry that she had spoken so roughly. She knew Marco had gone through a lot. Think of it—laying in front of those crazy people intent on killing him, the life and death struggle with Saul at Fermilab, deciding to voluntarily turn himself in for killing the witch, everything else. It was hard to imagine how he had even survived.

And it had not been easy for him to deal with her frustrations, not being able to find a job and having nothing to do all day long. She could see that part of the fault lay at her feet. She also knew that he was under constant pressure at work.

"You have a lot to learn, Loverboy," she said in almost a whisper, as she could no longer summon the gall for an attack. The slightest hint of a smile appeared on her face.

"Teach me then…" Marco closed his eyes and bowed, looking ashamed. She walked over to him and touched her lips to his forehead.

"Maybe we can figure this out," she said, this time speaking slowly in a deep, throaty whisper.

"Let's take some time off, then see where we are. I do love you…" Marco stopped. "And so do my colleagues."

Cynthia didn't know what to make of the reference to his co-workers, particularly at this moment. She wondered what was important to this man, but she still wasn't ready to give up the dream, which Marco's display of contrition had reignited.

*   *   *

Two months later, Marco took Cynthia to Charleston, South Carolina, hoping to put the seal on their reconciliation and rekindle a little passion. He reserved the top-floor suite in a romantic ante-bellum guest house in the oldest part of town. They had already gone for counseling and taken many long lake-front walks to try to talk through their difficulties. It had been arduous, tedious work, but they had managed to hang together.

At the end of their candlelight dinner the first night, right after they ordered their post-dessert cognac, Cynthia's face turned grave.

"Do you think counseling helped?" she asked, speaking in the quietest, calmest voice she could muster. She ran her hand over her perfectly combed hair. Her stomach fluttered, worried about how he might answer.

Marco hesitated longer than he should have. His eyes closed for an instant as he rubbed his chin.

"The sessions were okay, I guess. At least we were able to learn how to talk to each other without screaming."

The waiter brought the drinks and opened his lips as if he was about to speak. Marco frowned at him and motioned for him to put the glasses on the table.

"Don't you think that's rather callous?" Cynthia said in a rueful voice, twisting her forehead. She had wished he would have been more hopeful, more enthusiastic. She thought about her strained efforts to please Marco physically and how empty that had left her. Apparently, she had not been successful.

Marco looked past her.

"What'd you think would happen?" he asked.

Cynthia rubbed her forehead thinking about how to answer. She took a sip of her drink, hoping it would help, then centered her glass carefully in the middle of her napkin.

"For it to be like it was in the beginning." She smiled and winked, trying to be seductive.

Marco screwed up his face and looked somewhat lost, maybe feeling the effect of too many cocktails. His eyes drooped and his face became stoic, fixed.

"Cynthia, you've gotta' understand. I can't promise you I won't ever have an affair again. I just can't." He went silent for a time. "What I can promise is I will never leave you as long as you will have me." Marco's voice dripped with sadness and regret.

Cynthia didn't know how to respond. Why hadn't Marco been more forthright during counseling? Maybe if he had, they would have really gotten somewhere beyond only learning how to listen to each other. This even though the counselor had prodded them to more impactful interactions. What was he afraid of?

Marco's eyes narrowed and his face muscles tightened, like he was grappling with inner turmoil.

"Maybe I said too much." Marco nervously rubbed the back of his neck.

Cynthia reached out with her hand and touched Marco's arm. "No, no, no. Maybe it's…"

"I know what you are about to say, Cynthia. Don't." He moved his right hand as if to cut off her words. His face turned from hard to soft. "I'm gonna tell you something I've never told any person before."

Cynthia was drawn to Marco's beautiful green eyes. Her stomach twisted some more.

Marco fidgeted in his chair, picked up his glass and started furiously swirling the light golden drink in the snifter, like he was searching for courage. He looked uncharacteristically unsure of himself.

"I have a problem." He looked at Cynthia with expectant eyes and waited a second, probably to see how she would react. She said nothing but kept her eyes on him. "Intimacy scares me. It's safer to play around." He took a big gulp of the cognac and coughed a little as it went down. "Please don't judge me."

Cynthia's mind left the fancy restaurant, the posh surroundings, the charming town. There was nothing in her world except this man and what he was telling her.

"I don't understand, Marco. Why? You are so handsome and self-possessed." She pushed her glass away as if to say, "no more."

Marco seemed to disappear into the arid desert of his mind. He began playing with one of his curls. His knee bounced up and down, making the tablecloth on his side move slightly. A bead of sweat appeared on his forehead.

Cynthia sensed Marco was in uncharted territory. He looked like a scared child. She began softly rubbing his arm, wanting desperately to tell him it was okay, but not sure how. After what seemed like an eternity, he looked back up and stared into Cynthia's eyes.

"I can only guess. Maybe it has to do with when I was a boy. I didn't feel much loved or cared about." Marco took his napkin from his lap, touched it to his lips, then threw it on the table.

"That's so different from what you've always told me," Cynthia said. "Great home, wonderful, loving parents, lots of closeness, that's how you've described it."

"I don't like to talk about what it was really like, so I pretend it was great. Easier." Marco paused. "My parents thought of me as little more than a distraction. They were gone a lot and when they were in town, they spent their time on the phone or in meetings."

Marco rubbed his forehead like he was looking for an answer.

"They fought too, lots of yelling and screaming. Their idea of being parents was to hire a nanny, buy me something, and tell me to go play." Marco shook his head remorsefully. "I was a lonely, lonely child."

Marco pinched the bridge of his nose and then rubbed his eyes.

"And being handsome doesn't help. Playing around is too easy."

Marco sighed, sounding relieved. A slight smile appeared on his face. The waiter approached again. Marco waved him off with a frown and said, "Later."

Cythia thought that Marco had more to say and just needed the encouragement. "But tell me, my dear, why is this coming up now?" she asked, still in her very soft voice. She withdrew her hand from Marco's arm and began gently rubbing his cheek. He blushed and took her hand in his. Bringing it to his lips, he kissed it tenderly. For the first time, Cynthia felt deep pity for Marco. She had never before heard anything vaguely like these words come from him.

"Cynthia, I'm wondering whether I have it in me to settle into a relationship with anyone, let alone a great person like you." He put his hand in front of his mouth and cleared his throat. "Sometimes I think I'm like that witch I killed, on a never-ending quest to quench a thirst that doesn't go away."

Cynthia, puzzled, tilted her head. She waited for an explanation of this unexpected comparison. Finally, she spoke. "Marco, could you explain? I'm not sure I understand."

Marco stayed quiet for minutes like he was framing an answer or unsure how much to say.

"She was an up-and-up nymphomaniac. I think, for her, sex was a substitute for the real relationship she secretly craved but never had, no idea how to attain." He shook his head and batted his eyelashes, appearing about to cry. "That's me, too."

Marco acted unsure, embarrassed, like he had not intended to go that far. Then his eyes closed, and the corners of his mouth turned down.

"Well, ah…. Trust is…trust, is a real issue for me." Neither Marco nor Cynthia moved an inch. "It's very hard for me to trust anyone, let alone a woman I care about. So, I wander from woman to woman."

Cynthia was overtaken with compassion. She had no idea all this was brewing inside her husband. Compulsively she began rubbing the ivory pendant Marco had given her as a wedding gift. It felt comforting in her hand.

"Do you trust me?" Cynthia asked, petrified as to how Marco might answer.

Marco stared down for a very long time, like he was searching deep inside. Then he lifted his head, looked directly at Cynthia, and again ran his hand through his hair.

"I can't say…I mean…the words are there but how could you love who I really am? Maybe only what I appear to be." Marco stopped speaking and lowered his gaze. "I'm so scared."

Marco again ceased talking and rubbed his forehead, crossed then uncrossed his arms in front of his chest. He fidgeted in his chair and cleared his throat nervously.

"No, no, no…not true," Cynthia said. She felt more love for this man than she had ever felt before. She had come face to face with the human being he really was.

*   *   *

"Let's take a walk. I don't feel like going to sleep," Cynthia said as she stood up from the dinner table. It was a warm May evening, and through the restaurant's windows, they could see lots of people standing around the bars on River Street. They walked out, and after strolling around for a bit, found an out-of-the-way place in an alleyway for one more drink. It was called Mata Hari's. As they were about to go in, Marco pointed to a beat-up shop close by with a lit kerosene lamp in the window emitting a welcoming glow. The handmade sign next to the lamp read, *Fortunes Told, $25.00.*

"Let's go in," Marco said with his typical arrogant laugh. "Maybe we'll get some answers."

"Answers from the spirit world?" Cynthia asked in a mocking tone. "Aren't you Mr. Big Time scientist?" Cynthia coaxed a little cat grin. "That doesn't sound like you."

Marco chuckled. "Come on, it's just a little playing around. It'll be fun." Marco motioned in the direction of the shop. When Cynthia frowned and didn't move, he took her hand and pulled her toward the door. "Relax. Let yourself live," he said.

"Playing around is what we need, but not with a fortune teller," Cynthia said. She put her hand on Marco's chest and stopped him just before they were going to enter. She turned to him. "If you are in the mood to play, let's go back to the guest house." Even though they had tried, they had not been able to spark any passion between them. That worried Cynthia. Without passion, their relationship would be a sterile shell.

Marco was not deterred. When they entered the shop, they found an older, creole-looking man sitting behind a small, round table covered in dark green Naugahyde. Before him was a stack of tarot cards and a crystal ball. He wore a silk turban, and a flowing dark purple robe adorned with gilded stars. A deep scar extended from the corner of his left eye to his nose. His face was covered with age spots. The dimly lit room smelled of incense and cigar smoke. Posters containing occult symbols covered the walls and the skull of a goat was perched on a single wooden shelf behind the man.

"Good morrow, my name is Gramarye." He spoke with a thick Haitian accent. He motioned with his hand. "Sit down, please." He rolled his eyes up toward the ceiling. "The spirits are alive tonight."

Cynthia and Marco sat down across from the old man. Marco giggled as if amused by the game. He pulled out his wallet and handed the man two twenty-dollar bills.

"Join hands," Gramarye said as he took theirs in his. Cynthia found his hands smooth, almost feminine. The man closed his eyes and appeared contemplative. "Come, spirit world, and greet my fellow travelers," he said. After a moment of silence, he leaned down and breathed on the cards. He dropped their hands, then moved the cards close to Marco.

"Cut them," he said, peering at Marco with x-ray eyes. "As many times and into as many stacks as you feel. Then put them in a single stack and give them back to me."

Marco complied and the old man dealt five from the top of the stack, placed them face up on the table, and examined them.

"You are troubled," the old man said, pulling his brows together as he winced. He stared intently at the cards. "And you are in danger." He dealt two more cards. Speaking slowly, he appeared to weigh his words. "Be vigilant and you may survive."

Cynthia, who had been aimlessly looking around the room studying the posters, now focused her attention on the old man. She felt a wave of apprehension.

"I also see great passion and horror."

"How and when?" Marco asked as he smiled, then laughed aloud. "Soon?"

Cynthia could tell Marco was playing the old man for a fool. Why had he wanted to come in?

The old man picked up the cards and threw the two twenties back at Marco.

"Leave now," he said with a note of finality. He stood up and rushed out of the room through a dark curtain in the back.

After they got to the street, Cynthia looked at Marco.

"That was weird and a little scary."

"What's wrong with a little passion? I thought you said that's what we need."

"But horror and the way he walked out on us. I got goosebumps."

"Part of the show. Money says he does this to get people to return and pay him even more. Maybe he was mad I didn't take his babble seriously."

Cynthia gave Marco a blast with her eyes.

"Sometimes, Marco, you are a real prick. Are you ever going to change?"

IV

"I'VE GOT TO FIND HIM," Semantha said to Erzulie. They were finishing dinner and the hovel smelled of onions and garlic.

Erzulie shook her head. "Marco? Why? Stay here with me. Aren't you happy here?"

Semantha knew the answer to that question, but she decided not to burn her bridges yet, at least not until she had her life back together.

Erzulie raised her eyebrow slightly. "And for what?"

As Erzulie got up to clear the table, Semantha looked away but said nothing. She was sure Erzulie wouldn't understand that, in her mind, Marco had become her chance to escape from her twisted history and settle into a sweet future of conventionality.

Erzulie began washing the dishes, but then, after scrubbing a pot, turned and looked back at Semantha.

"Didn't you try to kill each other?" She scowled. Semantha remained silent.

What happened after Semantha and Marco had first shared those glorious hours together had become quite irrelevant in Semantha's mind. She knew Erzulie would not understand that, either.

Erzulie began stacking dishes on the drying rack.

"I'm starting my quest at the old house on the river," Semantha said, her jaw extended. She felt compelled to return to the place where

Marco and she had experienced each other for the first time. She braced for Erzulie to try to stop her.

"Remember what Cisco insisted," Erzulie said, still cleaning the dishes.

"All I want to do is go to the house…It's probably deserted by now."

"What if they are still there?"

"They won't be. Saul was deathly afraid of the cops. When he knew that Marco had escaped from me, I'm sure he cleared out and took Clem with him."

Erzulie came back to the table and stood over Semantha, a cold blast surging from her eyes.

"I want no part of this," Erzulie said, her voice tinged with anger. "I'm not getting close to that place, and neither should you." She paused. "I forbid it."

Semantha stood up and stared at Erzulie for a minute.

"Try and stop me," she said, shaking her head.

She left the hovel, went to the road, and walked the ten miles over to the old house. Her heart was burning inside the whole way, a mixture of passion and fear. Erzulie was right. She didn't really know what she would find. But she also knew she had to go.

The house was connected to the road by a long lane. She hated that lane. It was so dark and macabre. She couldn't help but think about what had happened on that pathway. She stopped and looked at the rock where she had sat when Pappie told her how he had been visited by Satan—a story that still befuddled and amazed her. Then she paused at the patch of thistle where she struggled with what to do after Saul had manhandled her. She thought about her resultant descent into the darkest pit of her being.

All the weird noises and sounds from the deep brush, trees, and hidden animals along the path still panicked her. *Best to try not to think about all that.* She quickened her pace.

She walked past the corral where the black goats once lived and then the beat-up barn where Pappie had presided over the black masses. She peered in. The table he used as an altar remained, as well as the chair where they had stretched Marco out in anticipation of the sacrifice. She went over to it, rubbed it like it was alive, then put her lips on it like a pilgrim kissing a relic. It felt sacred to her. The long black velvet drapes which had once descended from the rafters along the walls were lying on the floor, wet and molding. There were signs that a family of raccoons was using them as a nest.

She left the barn, her mind reeling, and walked to the house. It looked deserted, lonely. After another brutal winter, more paint was peeling and the vegetation looked more beat up. Even though it was early April and still nippy, the door to the kitchen was slightly ajar. The screen door banged in the wind. Everything seemed so familiar and, at once, so distant.

She pushed the door open and entered. The table and chair were still there beneath a single naked light bulb, no different than when she and Marco were there together. It felt like a shrine, a shrine to Marco and her passion.

Then she stopped dead. The red plastic cup she had given to Marco with the drug in it was still sitting on the counter, a reminder of her forced complicity in Saul's evil. She shook all over. She buried her face in her hands and yelled, "No!" The word echoed through the foul-smelling air. Guilt and remorse overwhelmed her. How could she do such a thing? And to a man for whom she felt such powerful attraction.

At that moment, Semantha heard someone walking down the hall-way toward the kitchen. She stopped cold as Clem appeared in the doorway, shirtless, suspenders holding up his stained pants, his face covered with stubble, but still with the beard of two cones, now over-grown and untrimmed.

"Wha' th' fuck!" he yelled and halted abruptly. "Who's ya?"

Semantha shrieked, turned, and ran for the door. Clem was strong and, without a car, she had no easy way to escape. She ran down the lane toward the road as fast as she could but tripped on a fallen branch and fell to the ground. When she tried to get up, searing pain ran through her right leg, and she fell back. Her leg didn't feel broken, but it would probably be some time before she could put full weight on it. She looked back at the house. Clem, wearing a long black winter coat, was slowly walking her way, appearing dazed like a zombie. Every so often he would yell, "Hey where'd ya go? Come 'ere."

In the hope Clem would not see her, Semantha crawled into a thick clump of brush, not the best hiding place since the leaves were still only budding. Yet Clem walked right by.

This guy is so dumb.

"Hey, where'd ya go?" Clem continued to yell as he walked down the lane. Semantha hoped he would get tired of looking and go back to the house. Then she could hobble back to Erzulie's. But at that moment, a snake fell from the branch of a tree and landed on her leg. Even though it was a harmless garter and quickly slithered away, she was startled and yelled out in spite of herself.

Clem stopped immediately, turned, and walked right to the spot where Semantha was hiding. Now he was only a few feet from her. She could hear his heavy breathing and smell his body odor, the stench of someone who had not washed for a long time.

"Hey, ya bitch, wha's ya doin' here? I knows ya's in there, so ya might as well come out. I kin wait." He sat down on a blown-over tree trunk and started humming to himself.

Semantha was trapped. She couldn't wait there forever. It was already late in the day, and she was not dressed for a long siege in this cold, uncomfortable hiding place. Nor was she prepared to fend off animals on the roam. Rumor had it that there was a large pack of wild dogs not far away and that every so often a farmer would find a cow or a lamb they had ripped apart. She had no interest in finding out if the rumors were true.

How could she handle Clem, maybe even get him to help her in her search for Marco? She hatched a plan. Though she could not outrun or outwait this creep, she was sure she could outsmart him. Saul had been able to twist him into knots. So could she. It was a cloudy blustery day, creating lots of cold gray shadows in the spooky lane. She waited until it got a little darker for maximum effect. Then she crawled out of the bushes and stood up straight, ignoring the pain in her leg.

"Helloooo, Clem," she said, trying to make her voice seem wobbly and mysterious. She remembered playing a ghost in a high school play once. Pappie's housekeeper had made her a costume out of an old bed sheet, and she had learned how to sort of howl.

Clem saw Semantha's face for the first time. "Holy fuc,' you's Semantha. Haint ya dead? I seen ya floatin' in the ol' St. Joe myself. Fuk, you's a fuckin' ghost. Shit," Clem said. The few hairs on Clem's head stood on end, his face drained of blood, and he began to shake all over. "Holy shit. Haint never seen no ghost before."

After a moment, he looked off and muttered almost under his breath. "Shit. Pappie were'nt blowin' no smoke bout them bein' ghosts and spirits. I shoulda listened."

He turned and ran toward the door to the kitchen.

"Nooo wait, Clem," Semantha yelled as he ran. "I have a message from Lucifer for you."

Clem halted mid step, took a few breaths, then slowly spun around. He was about thirty feet from the kitchen door.

"Don't hurt me please. I ain't ready to go." Clem held up his arms like he was about to try to fend off an attack.

"Please wait, my child. Come here," Semantha said, trying to sound mysterious but reassuring at the same time. Clem dropped his arms, hesitated, then slowly walked back to where Semantha stood. Semantha hoped she had him under her spell.

"Oh my poor Clem…" She let out an oversized sigh. "I've traveled so far from Lucifer's spirit world. He sent me to find out what happened to his high priest, Saul." She raised her arms and looked skyward as if evoking a spirit.

Still trembling, Clem dropped to his knees and clapped his hands together like he was about to pray.

"Is Saul here?" Semantha asked in an insistent voice, looking down at him.

"Please Semantha, please don't ya hurt me." Clem reached up with one arm as if begging for a favor. Semantha smiled. She had him.

"Well, we'll see. You've got to tell me where Saul is."

"Don't rightly know," Clem answered instantly. "A while ago, all the sudden he got a bur up his ass. He tol' me he heard where that man was—ya know the man you an' him were gonna send to Lucifer. Saul grabbed his dagger an tol' me he'd come back with the fucker's balls inna' bag. Never showed again."

"Saul's dead, then?" She hoped the answer was yes.

"Don't know that neither. I'da thunk he'd return by now. So maybe." Clem got back to his feet and brushed off his pants. He pulled his coat tighter and zipped it up.

"Why didn't you go with him?" Semantha asked. She tried not to let on that she, too, was freezing. She wanted to seem supernatural to this ignorant bugger.

"Said that where he was goin' he didn't want no fuckin' sidekick." Clem shivered some more.

"You know where he went?" she asked.

"Nah, Saul never tol' me nothin' ceptin' when he wanted me to do some bad shit. Tol' him I wanted to go, too. Ain't ya cold?"

Somewhere in the distance, some dogs barked.

"Cain't we go inside now? Them dogs is scary."

Semantha motioned for Clem to go back to the house. She followed him, slowly hobbling behind him. Her leg was feeling better though.

Inside the kitchen, Clem lit a big candle sitting on the old linoleum counter. Semantha presumed that the electricity had been turned off, probably for a while. How long had Clem lived like this? Most likely made him even more crazy and antisocial than he was before.

The shadowy flickering from the candle made the room seem haunted. In the dim light, Clem's high, pitched forehead gave him the profile of a Neanderthal and his protruding eyes the look of a frightened alley cat, scared but ready to attack.

"Lucifer is pleased with what you have done here on earth, Clem." Semantha tried to smile, but Clem's stench made her feel like gagging. She fought back the urge.

"Almighty fuckin' shit," Clem said. He bowed his head so low his chin touched his chest. The light from the candle reflected off his bald head.

Semantha took her hand and lifted up Clem's head by his chin. She did the best she could to look him in the eye.

"Lucifer knows Saul treated you pretty bad, Clem. I saw it myself when I was living here."

"Yeah, tha's true." Clem's eyes dropped and the sides of his mouth turned down. He touched the edge of his eye. *Was he wiping away a tear?*

"Took me for granted, he did. Always acted like I was kinna a fool, lik' I was his slave. Ya know, he stole all my ma's hard-earned money. Told' me it was for buildin' Lucifer's kingdom righ' here. What a liar."

Upon hearing Clem tell his story, Semantha felt a twinge of compassion for this degenerate excuse for humanity, but only a twinge. Clem was about as bad as Saul, only more stupid, easier to manipulate.

Semantha felt a sudden sharp pain surge in her leg. She sat down on the kitchen chair, the same chair where Marco had been tied up. It seemed to radiate warmth—in vivid contrast to the drafty old farmhouse. She rubbed her leg as she felt it almost magically get better.

Clem looked like a lightbulb had just flashed on above his head. He raised his eyebrows.

"Whoa, wait a minute there, Semantha. Wha' gives? Ghosts ain't supposta fall and git hurt."

Semantha thought for a bit. "Lucifer brought me back from the dead, so I'm human."

"Holy shit, and he sent you to me, littl' ol'me, holy shit."

"Clem, help me find Saul. Lucifer has a message for him," she said, unable to shake the urgency from her voice. She couldn't help it; her body itched with desire for Marco.

"How's I gonna do tha', Semantha?" Clem rubbed the side of his head.

"You find the man, and I will be able to find Saul," Semantha said, even though the last person she ever wanted to see again was Saul.

"Wha's in it for me?"

Semantha leaned over and kissed Clem on the lips. The smell of his rancid breath nauseated her, but she was prepared to do whatever it took to get what she wanted. She put her hand on Clem's shoulder.

"Find me this man and Lucifer and I will be grateful. You will like the way I show gratitude." Semantha winked at Clem and gave him a cartoonish smile. Even in the weak light, Semantha could see desire building in Clem's eyes, like a dog picking up a scent. He took in a short breath as if astonished by the idea.

"Where's ya staying these days? If you's human, yous needs a roof over your head."

Semantha hoped he didn't think she would stay there with him. *What a horrible thought.*

"This old woman with a hooked nose took me in. She's way out in the woods."

Clem's jaw dropped.

"Erzie?" he asked.

"You know her?"

Clem got up and walked toward the door.

"What'd I say, Clem? You know her?"

Clem stopped, turned back toward Semantha, glowered, then scurried out the house.

*   *   *

CLEM WENT to the public library the next day to see if he could find out anything about Fermilab and where that was. He still remembered from the man's ID that he worked there as some kinda doc. Then he got in touch with his old friend who worked as a janitor in the county public records department. He knew he was on his way to finding this man. For the first time, Clem found out his name: Marco Adamos.

Two days later, Clem took the train to Chicago and went to the house where Marco supposedly lived. He waited in the bushes to see if he could get a look at Marco again. He wanted to be sure it was the right man before he did anything more. He had always craved Semantha and if this was the way to get her…

V

M ARCO FELT A SHARP PAIN as something heavy smacked his head. He passed out and hit the pavement of the parking lot outside his lab with a wham. When he woke up, he was tied up—hands, arms, feet—, was blindfolded, and was gagged, lying in the dark trunk of a car traveling at what seemed to be very high speed.

The engine's throaty rumble out the fine-tuned muffler sounded familiar. As much as he could, Marco moved his hand around the dirty trunk, which smelled of grease and rubber. There were what felt like scientific journals laying around him. He was inside his own car.

What is happening to me?

He began to wiggle around to see if he could free himself, but he was tied up too tightly. He tried to holler out in anguish, but his screams came out only as muffled groans.

Again, he thought. *This can only mean one thing.* He knew where he was going and what he was facing. Another fight for his life. *Lord, please, Lord, not again.*

Eventually, the car came to a stop and the front door opened. Marco made out heavy, noisy steps on the gravel surface, like those made by a very large man. *Oh no, not Clem,* Marco thought as the driver lumbered back to the trunk and opened it.

"Hello, doc,'" Clem said in a voice steeped in sarcasm. He sneered. "Git the fuc' out." When Marco didn't move, Clem grabbed the ropes around Marco's chest and pulled. "Out," he said as he yanked Marco from the trunk. A tire jack scraped Marco's face. He could feel the blood seeping out.

Clem cut some of the ropes with his dagger and stood Marco up. He was stiff from being stuffed in the trunk with his knees in his chest for hours. He stumbled.

Clem laughed meanly. "Rough ride, doc?" he said.

Clem took off the blindfold, turned Marco around, and pressed the point of the dagger against his back. He pushed Marco toward a heavy woods, right by the ratty old house where he had been held tied up and then by the barn from which he had fled. A shot of anxiety ran down Marco's back. *No, please Lord, no.*

Clem pushed him along for maybe fifty feet, pulled aside a curtain of vines, and threw him against a tree in a clearing just big enough for the two of them. The tangled web of vines shut out most of the light, and the wind whistling through the brush gave the space a sinister feel. With only a light leather jacket, Marco felt exposed. Clem took some more rope and bound Marco up tightly to the tree, hands and feet. He sealed Marco's mouth with duct tape. Marco gagged, nauseated by Clem's smell. He was weak from hunger.

Twisting Marco's ears, Clem spoke in a fierce whisper.

"Welcome back to good ol' Michigan, doc. We's been hopin' you all come back and see us. An' now you're here." Clem slapped Marco, then laughed, sounding like the Joker in a horror movie. "I hopes yer trip weren't too bumpy. Those ol' cars lik' you got don't ride so smooth, but yous probably know that. And in all that fancy Italian leather shit." Clem grabbed Marco's shirt at the collar and pulled. "See, you weren't exactly dressed fer the trip"

Marco tried to speak but couldn't. He was paralyzed with fear but yearned to cry out for mercy.

Clem cleared his throat like he was about to give a speech. He grabbed Marco's chin and lifted his head. He put his face right next to Marco's.

"Jes in case ya don't know, you's back at the ol' house wit al us real folks. But don't ya worry, nobody gonna hurt ya. Yous' gonna be a trophy fer my brand-new wife. I'm gonna give ya to her when she's broke in." He sneered. "So yous got a little wait, I hope ya don't mind. Meantime, yous gotta be real quiet, no noise." He grabbed Marco's throat and squeezed hard. "'Cause I don't want to have to do nothin' bad, you know what I mean? But that's up to ya. Got it?"

Marco was silent.

"I said got it, didn't ya hear?" Clem squeezed harder. Marco gagged and mumbled.

"That's better. I'll be close by and if I hear from ya, I'll be right here. Don't ya forget, now." Clem punched Marco in the gut, causing him to double over as much as he could considering the ropes. "Gotta go and pick up my new wife. I'll be right back." Clem turned to leave but then stopped and looked back.

"But one last thing ya faggot. Saul's dead, right?"

Marco didn't know how to answer. Would Saul's death be good or bad news to Clem? He didn't want to give this animal any excuse to abuse him more, maybe kill him. Marco nodded affirmatively, tentatively, fearing the consequence of his admission. He got ready for a punch.

"Good riddance," Clem said.

Phew, Marco thought.

Clem replaced the blindfold and left.

Alone and blinded, Marco felt isolated and desolate, sensations potentiated by the blackness. He heard the put-put sound of the motor on some pleasure boat close by on the river. So close, but yet a universe away. He thought about the river, all the secrets it held, some his own.

He began to cry. Again, caught by these subhuman animals, again tied up, again in grave danger. And now being told he would be some woman's "trophy." What could that mean? Who could that even be, married to a disgusting creature like Clem? He couldn't imagine. Chained up and used to serve a woman's sexual pleasure? He shook his head in disbelief.

Only two days ago, Cynthia and I were in Charleston, a good healing trip, he thought. *But now this. When will this private hell end? What did I ever do to deserve this?* He recalled the fortune teller's face after he cut the cards. He jerked.

And how long would he be here in the woods? Were there animals? What would happen when it got pitch dark? Tied up, he would be incredibly vulnerable to attack, especially after nightfall. Despite Clem's warning, he tried to shriek, but nothing got past the tape.

Moments later, he felt something nibbling on his shoe. He kicked it away as much as the ropes around his legs would let him. But whatever it was came right back and continued to nibble. He jerked again and the nibbling stopped, only to commence once again after Marco stopped moving. How long would he need to keep doing this? His shoes were a very thin leather easily eaten through. Then the creature bit into his flesh, sending a jolt up his leg. Then again and again as he ran out of energy to continue to kick it away.

What am I going to do? Where is Cynthia when I need her? What must she be thinking now?

*   *   *

THREE DAYS AFTER Semantha's brush with Clem at the house on the river, Erzulie went into town for food and to take care of some business. Semantha stayed, scared by Cisco's warning. She sat and listened as the sound from Erzulie's noisy muffler gradually faded. She was happy to be alone, happier to have some peace away from Erzulie. She thought of ways she could put some money together to get away from this godforsaken town.

She also thought about seeing Clem. Why had he reacted so strongly when he found out that she was living with Erzulie? There must be some history there. Semantha couldn't imagine what. Was Clem her son? She remembered Erzulie telling her she had a daughter. Nothing would surprise Semantha anymore. At least she was proud of herself for wrapping Clem around her little finger and sending him off to look for Marco. She didn't think there was any chance Clem would find him, but it didn't hurt for him to try.

Maybe he would get in trouble and never return, not a bad thing. Then she would have the house on the river all to herself and she could go there any time to sit on the river's edge and feel closer to Marco.

About twenty minutes after Erzulie left, she was surprised to hear a car coming down the lane, definitely not Erzulie's truck. It sounded sporty and powerful. She pulled the yellowed lace curtain aside and looked out as the car pulled up to the door. She couldn't believe what she saw. Clem was getting out of a classic BMW 2002, not like one she would expect him to drive, if he ever drove at all. She wondered how and why he had gotten this car.

Clem had cleaned himself up and trimmed his beard. He walked up to the front step, pushed open the door without knocking, and charged in like he owned the place. He seemed taller than when Semantha saw him at the house.

"Jes saw that ol' jezzie leave," Clem said. Semantha detected the scent of alcohol on his breath. "Good, I don't want no trouble this morning, 'cause I's got some good news." Clem stared at Semantha for a second, then displayed a mean smile, like a boar about to go in for a kill.

"I's got yer man."

"Oh my God, you found him. How?" Semantha's heart fluttered. Dizzy with expectation, she had not heard such good news since she had been pulled out of the river. She almost couldn't contain herself in her own body. Then she thought again.

Got him? What could that mean? She felt a twinge in her back. She instantly worried that he had brutalized Marco rather than merely locating him and letting her do the rest. This is not what she had wanted or expected. Maybe she had employed a blunt instrument to do a task requiring surgical precision.

"Found 'im over in Chicagae, drove 'im here an' got 'im tied up in the bushes near the house on the river. Lots of places to hide things around there. No one could ever find 'im."

The prospect of this poor man in Clem's clutches made her nauseous. Her mind jumped into overdrive. She had to find Marco and soon. The woods around the house were full of nasty creatures. What if a crow or river rat decided to make a meal of Marco? She trembled.

Semantha groaned. *What have I done?*

"Clem, what…" Clem placed his hand over her mouth, stopping her from speaking.

"Shut up. I's gonna take ya to 'im." Saying no more, he grabbed Semantha's arm and pulled her outside to the car, opened the door, and threw her in. She noted a River Forest, Illinois village sticker on the window. Is that where Marco lives? It sounds fancy.

Together, they drove to the house on the river and Clem motioned her to get out. He then clutched her by the elbow and dragged her into the kitchen. It was a sunny day and much warmer than a few days ago when she had sent Clem on his mission. It had rained heavily the night before, but now spring was in the air.

Clem spun Semantha around and put his hands on her shoulders. "Now I's ready for my reeward," Clem said with a smirk. He made a jerking motion in front of his crotch. His lips broadened into a smile, showing his stained, rotting teeth. He looked like an alley cat in heat.

Semantha stiffened. She had forgotten what she had said to get him to go looking for Marco. Surely, he couldn't be serious, but she felt her heart pounding.

"Where is he?" she asked.

"What's they say on TV? Yer wish is my command or sumpum lik' that." Clem unzipped his pants.

"I asked you, where is he?" Semantha stomped her foot, feeling a mixture of frustration, anticipation and fear. She was not in the mood for playing around.

"Al' in good time, Sama. You's knows what's next." He stuck his hand in his pants and began rubbing. He appeared deadly serious. Why was he no longer afraid of her like when she told him she was the devil's messenger?

"Don't be silly, Clem. I've got to see him first." She had no intention of submitting to Clem's demand, but she had to placate him somehow. She turned and walked toward the door, as if Marco was just outside.

"Not so fast, ya cunt." A nasty look came to Clem's face. He clenched his fists. "We's got a deal, an' now it's yer turn to pay up. An wha' they say at the laundry, 'no tickee, no shirtee.'" Clem giggled and began to move toward Semantha. Semantha backed away.

"No, Clem." She held up her hand as if to resist but he slapped her on her cheek. She reeled from the blow and felt where he had hit her.

"Clem, what are you doing?" Semantha tried to look stern. "Remember Lucifer sent me. Hurt me and you will answer to him."

"Tha's so muc' fuckin' shit, Semantha, you's jes a big fat liar." He grabbed for her blouse as Semantha pulled away. A button pulled off, revealing her bra. Fear raced up Semantha's spine. The situation was spinning out of control.

"Clem what's gotten into you?" She shook her head. "When I saw you before, you believed me." Clem let out a mean snicker.

"Tha' ol' boyfrien' of yours gotta biiiig mouth. It's all over town that you jes passed out, didn't die, an' yer bac'." Clem again grabbed Semantha by the shoulders and put his mouth close to her ears. He spoke slow and rough.

"An now if ya ever wanna see yer ol' loverboy you's gonna do what I say, maybe spend time with me." He winked in a menacing way and spit in her face. "I's got it in my mind I'm gonna finish up what Saul wanted but was too greedy to get. Cum 'ere." Clem threw his arms around Semantha's chest, pulled her tight, and began pumping his crotch on her hips as he ripped at her clothes.

"No, no, no," Semantha pounded him with her fists. She was no match for Clem.

*　　*　　*

"Ooh-wee ooh-wee, ooh-wee" screamed Erzulie from the door to the kitchen, sounding like a cross between a growling bear and a shrieking buzzard. Her hair stood on end and her eyes were as big, white, and round as golf balls. Clem pivoted around, looked at Erzulie, and turned to stone. His massive size seemed to shrink. Semantha was never happier to see anyone in her life, even Erzulie.

"Get out or you die," Erzulie said, squinting her eyes and furling her brow. She pointed her bony twisted finger at Clem and shook it. "The curse of Olodumare fall on you. Now get out."

Clem stood motionless, looking slow-witted. Erzulie pulled out a knife and lurched at him. He deflected the knife and swatted it to the floor, hitting with a bang. He smirked and cleared his throat like he was about to spit.

"What's ya doin' granny? We's all know that your black belt has done gone an' expired. An' no more of that there magic like inna old days. That's expired too. You'se lucky I haint got no gun, elsewise you'd be full of holes right' now."

"Don't screw with me, Clem," Erzulie said. "And don't test the magic of Santeria again." There was a wild look on her face, and black anger in her voice. Her intensity seemed to fill the room like electricity shot from a laser gun. She extended her arms, causing the folds of her robe to open like a crow and she looked toward the ceiling. "Mechialik, come," she intoned. She joined her hands together inside the sleeves of her robe, forming an enclosure. Then she raised her arms higher as a large puff of smoke emerged and bathed her in an eerie haze.

"Git…if you want to keep those low-life balls of yours, you slime!" Erzulie screamed, sending a white-hot look his way. Erzulie's eyes had grown even larger and her cheeks were bright red. Spit accompanied every word.

Semantha had never seen Erzulie put on such a powerful display. Semantha was stunned by Erzulie's might.

Clem shook as if he had just seen a ghost. Surrendering, he raised his arms above his head as he ran for the door. He zipped up his pants as he ran, accidentally kicking the leg of the chair on his hurried way out. Erzulie went to the door and peered out.

"That'll take care of him, at least for now."

Semantha emitted a large sigh of relief. "Oh, my God," she said. She could only imagine what Clem would have done to her. She sat down, closed her eyes, and put her head in her hands. She began breathing intentionally in a long, slow, even tempo, trying to calm down and moderate the pounding of her heart. After a moment, she raised her head and looked at Erzulie, her mouth agape.

"How? Why?"

"Something told me to come back from town early, maybe Michalik. When you were not at the house and I saw the tracks of a car in the mud, I got the idea you had come here." There was a stiff, unemotional tone in Erzulie's voice and a hard look on her face. "You disobeyed me."

"Marco's outside," Semantha said as she adjusted her disheveled clothes.

"When are you going to listen?" Erzulie looked like a stern schoolmarm who had caught one of her female students kissing behind the outhouse.

"I've got to find him."

Erzulie grabbed her by the ear and twisted. "No, you're going home with me," she said as she began pulling Semantha toward the door.

"Please, no. You must help me find Marco." Semantha pulled away. Erzulie's eyes narrowed and she pursed her lips. Her nostrils flared.

"Can't you see, I saved you…again. Show a little gratitude. Come home with me and forget this man. After all, he tried to kill you."

That comment struck Semantha hard, but this still was not the time to explain what the idea of Marco had come to symbolize in her mind. And him outside at that very minute. She shook all over. *Maybe someday Erzulie will understand what it's like for the idea of a man to take over so thoroughly.*

"The ploy with the smoke was incredible. How'd you do it?" Semantha asked in a matter-of-fact tone, hoping to get Erzulie to think about something besides forcing Semantha back to the hovel.

"It wasn't, how did you say, a ploy, young lady." She winced. "Be respectful of my power."

Despite her flip question, Semantha was flabbergasted by Erzulie's resourcefulness. Was it magic? Could she get Erzulie to use her power to help find Marco? Appeal to her humanity? *She did have a daughter after all.* Semantha had frequently wondered what ever happened to Isabella.

It was already midafternoon. Darkness was coming, and with it all the dangers of the night. There was no time to lose. Without thinking, Semantha fell to her knees in front of Erzulie and wrapped her arms around Erzulie's skinny legs. She squeezed hard.

"Oh please, Erzulie, if you love me, you must help me find this man. My life…" She stopped for a second. "I love him."

Erzulie looked down at Semantha. There was melancholy in her eyes.

"I love you too. What about that?"

Semantha was cornered. She needed Erzulie so much right now. It wasn't just finding Marco, but her presence was also a check on Clem, no doubt lurking somewhere outside. She could imagine only one way to get Erzulie to help her, as distasteful as it might be. And so she stood up, threw her arms around Erzulie's shoulders and kissed her passionately, tasting Erzulie's sour breath with her tongue.

"Oh Erzulie, you are at the core of my being. We have gone through so much together, you nursing me back to life, our isolation during the blizzard, our two separate existences blending into one, even our smells… Don't you see that?" Semantha's eyes stared intently into Erzulie's She hoped she was penetrating Erzulie's stubborn resistance.

Erzulie stood in iced silence not moving, not returning Semantha's gaze. She looked suspicious, incredulous. Her lips turned down slightly.

"You want this man. Where do I fit in?" Erzulie's eyes were flat and gray. Semantha could see a yearning in Erzulie's eyes, the unrequited longing of an ancient to whom life had given only disappointments.

"Ok, let me say it plainly." Semantha swallowed hard. She was not sure she could bring herself to say what she needed to, but anything to save Marco. She went silent for a long moment, garnering her resolve, then looked down at the floor.

"I, I, I …. pledge myself to you," she said slowly, returning her gaze to Erzulie. She worried Erzulie would sense a dupe. "But please, please, we must rescue Marco. Once Clem realizes he is no longer bait to snare me, I am sure he'll dispose of him or let him die."

"Why should I trust you?" Erzulie said. A tear came to her eye. She wiped it off with her finger. Semantha waved her hand hoping Erzulie would look at things differently.

"I am Pappie's daughter, and you loved him."

"Theo left me too," Erzulie said, with a small shake of her head.

"You said you left him, not the other way around." Semantha tilted her head slightly.

"He left me to chase after his fantasies. Even more impossible to fight than the allure of another woman. His mind had left me, so I walked out." Erzulie's face took on an edge of weather-beaten sorrow.

Semantha's heart went out to this forgotten old woman, painfully alone. She felt guilty for how her father had treated her and didn't want to hurt her again like he had. But could she really spend the rest of her life with this smelly recluse? She wasn't sure, but she did know she had to fend off Clem and save Marco.

Erzulie took her long bony arms and grasped Semantha by the shoulders. The sleeves of her robe extended between them and bathed them together in darkness. Not moving a muscle, she stared intently at Semantha for what seemed like an eternity. Her breathing was heavy but even, like the beating of a bass drum.

Semantha could think of no more to say. She saw that this decision was so like the choice that Erzulie had to make about Pappie when his fantasies overtook his reality.

"No more pain, child," Erzulie finally said, dropping her arms and turning her head. "You are on your own. Go after the man you love. I hope it turns out better for you."

"No, no, no," Semantha moaned. "Don't leave me, please, no,

please. You saved me. I love you, really, I love you. I'll do anything, anything." She again dropped to her knees, letting her breast slide slowly against Erzulie's body, then she thrust her face hard into Erzulie's crotch.

"No," Erzulie said coldly. "The moment has passed," Erzulie said, pushing Semantha's head away, then lifting Semantha to her feet. She turned to head for the door.

"No wait, Erzulie, at least tell me why Clem is so afraid of you?"

Erzulie stopped and turned.

"Thirty years ago, I summoned Mechialik in this very room to beg him to cure his mother's cancer. It was a wild night." A faraway look appeared on Erzulie's face, and she smiled, a closed-mouth, sorrowful grin.

"The house shook from the wind and lightning hit on the river and all around, bringing trees crashing down and sending round after round of thunder. It was one of the worst electrical storms I've ever seen. Even the river was angry, throwing waves up in the backyard, joining in nature's attack. Clem was only four. He thought all this was caused by Mechialik, who he believed was here and present. You know the mind of a four-year-old. He thought I was some sort of powerful witch, had nightmares for years. Ever since, when I summon a Santeria spirit and he's present, his mind goes back to that terrible night." Erzulie stopped for a second and her face softened.

"But his mother survived and lived to old age."

Erzulie spotted the dagger she had dropped when going after Clem. She picked it up and gave it to Semantha.

"May Mechialik be with you." She shook her head and walked out, letting the screen door slam shut as she left. Semantha knew she had lost something important and realized that her battle had only just begun.

*   *   *

SEMANTHA slipped the dagger beneath her pants. It felt cold and threatening against her stomach, but also remarkably reassuring. She buttoned up her blouse and tiptoed outside so as not to telegraph her movements to Clem, wherever he was. She mulled over her options. How could she find Marco and get him out of there?

It was late afternoon on a sunny day in early May, unusually hot for the time of year, and the tall oak trees growing behind the house made the backyard between the kitchen and the barn almost dark. At the edge of the yard, there was a large clump of brush, thick and about shoulder high. She could hide there to see if Clem returned. She had played enough chess to realize that sometimes the best strategy is just to avoid being captured and mark time until the other player makes the mistakes.

After Semantha had waited about thirty minutes, Clem came back, sneaked up to the door to the kitchen and peeked inside, clearly on the lookout for Erzulie. Finding no one, he unzipped his pants and relieved himself. Then he yawned, gave out an "ahhh" and sat down on an old rusty lawn chair on the porch next to the house. He put his head back against the wall and appeared to fall asleep.

After a short nap, Clem woke. He scratched his head as if he had forgotten something. He went inside, came back out with a bottle of water, and walked off into the brush whistling "Dixie" as he went. He returned in about ten minutes, the bottle empty. Clem sat back down and began snoring like a walrus basking in the arctic sun. The sounds reverberated through the woods.

Semantha was relieved. The water had to be for Marco, so he must be very close, and more important, alive. Maybe she could find Marco and get out while Clem dozed. It did sound like he was out cold. Although the forest around the house was like a jungle, thick with overgrowth, she knew all its clearings, pathways and hiding places from the time when Pappie brought her here as a child. She vaguely recalled at least a dozen places where Marco could be.

Semantha couldn't go snooping around like she did in the old days when she was a girl. That would make noise and possibly alert Clem, especially in the super quiet woods. To get Marco out would require a precision hit, going directly to where he was on the first try and taking him out before Clem knew what had happened. Probably at most she had five minutes from the moment she made any noise.

She recalled a rock formation close to two stories high about a quarter of a mile from the house. If she could get to the top of it, she could look around and refresh her recollection, perhaps see some unusual movements or a route marked by disturbed brush.

She left her hiding place quietly, slowly, heading to the formation, being careful as best she could not to make any noise. It was impossible not to break a twig once in a while, sending a cracking sound toward the house. She hoped that didn't awaken Clem. She had to climb over and under the brush at every step, getting scratched and poked in the eye by stray branches. Thistles stung her legs. Flies bit her arms.

Every so often, she would stop and listen. The monster had stopped snoring, but the forest was unsettlingly quiet and still. Pappie would have said that the creatures were hushed because they sensed something evil in the air. Semantha felt like she was being watched.

When she got to the rock formation, she remembered that, along the side, partly hidden by weeds, there were a series of irregular, ledge-like protrusions, like steps, making the climb to the top easy. She went up. She had not been up there since she was about ten, but it seemed so familiar, right down to the stones and pebbles that littered the top. She and her friends had used the smaller ones to play soldier. She had once been quite good at pelting her buddies from her perch on top. It was a nasty game, but nobody got seriously hurt.

Before she even had caught her breath and looked around, she heard the forest stir. It sounded like someone was coming. A shiver went up her spine. It must be Clem. Within seconds, he appeared at the foot of the rock.

"Semantha, is that ya up there? You'se easy to follow through them bushes. What's ya doin'? Haint trying to figure out where I's got yer lover boy stashed, are ya?" There was a note of uncertainty in his voice.

"Just a little walk down memory lane, Clem." She tried to sound nonchalant. "Getting myself ready to pay up," she yelled down. "And I hope you know what I mean, lover boy."

Clem groaned. It was a groan of carnal anticipation, not agony.

"Com' on up, babe. I'm ready." Semantha hated to sound like she was playing cat and mouse with Clem, particularly as scared as she was. What if he figured out how to climb up the face of the rock or found the steps?

"How'd ya git up there, huh?"

Semantha peered over the edge down at Clem. He was rubbing his forehead like he was trying to figure out what to do.

"Right there, right up the side. I did it, so can you. Show me what a man you are," she yelled, wanting to sound seductive and hoping he would take the bait.

"I'm a comin'. Git yerself ready." He giggled. Semantha could tell Clem didn't have a clue. She looked down again. Clem had big, clumsy feet and even bigger leather-bottomed boots. He would get up a little, then slide back, sometimes dislodging pieces of rock. He grabbed twigs growing out of the side to lift himself up, but they broke from the weight. "Fuck!" he yelled. "Fuck!" He stomped his feet. "How'd ya do this?" he screamed, sounding frustrated and angry.

"Come on, Clem. Come on up and claim what's yours," Semantha yelled. He looked up. Semantha rubbed her crotch and groaned. She was happy to see this beast struggling and, now that it was pretty clear he would not be able to climb up easily, she pleasured in taunting him.

But there was no time for hesitation or second guessing. She gathered up some rocks, the largest she could lift, and waited for the right moment. She couldn't miss.

Finally, Clem reached a small ledge about seven feet below her. Semantha took the largest of the rocks and hurled it at him as hard as she could. It hit Clem squarely on the forehead.

"Ahhh," he groaned as he lost his grip and fell backward. He rolled down, hit the ground below with a thump, and didn't move.

Semantha smiled. *Easier than I thought.* She knew he would

come to and continue after her, but for the moment, she could rest and regroup, and zero in on where Marco was. But she could also see the sun was low in the sky. She shuddered, knowing she was running out of time.

From her vista, she surveyed the woods. She saw some vegetation that had been recently disturbed near a small clearing close to the house. She knew it well from when she used to play castles and dragons there as a child. It was just large enough for a person or two and was surrounded by heavy brush. A well-trod pathway led to an access point covered by thick vines. If Clem also knew about this spot, it would be a logical place to put Marco, close enough to keep his eye on him but far enough away so that he would not be visible from the house. That must be the place.

Semantha climbed down and headed for the clearing, carefully stepping over Clem's bulbous body. He was breathing heavily but wasn't snoring. She gave him a hard kick in the head to make sure he was out.

She propelled herself through the foliage on her way to the clearing in delicious anticipation of seeing Marco again. As she ran, she recalled the months of sadness she had felt without him and how she had pined for him after she found out he was still alive. *Maybe…finally now. My waiting is over.* As she got to the clearing, she heard a muffled groan. It was him, had to be.

She pushed aside the vine curtain and came to an abrupt stop. A river rat as big as an alley cat scurried away. But she stood there thrilled, mesmerized. There he was, Marco, it was him, really him. *My God, I've found him! Safe!* A quiver ran through her body.

Semantha looked him up and down. He was exactly as she remembered, but with a few gray hairs replacing his jet-black curls, maybe some slight wrinkles under his eyes. He began mumbling through the tape. It sounded like, "Help, help…"

"Marco," she said as she took off the blindfold and pulled the tape from his mouth. He winced, then blinked. He looked at Semantha and turned ashen white. His jaw dropped and his eyes opened wide.

"Semantha…Good Lord! I killed you. What are you doing here? What's going on? Am I dead?"

"No, and neither am I. You may be a great physicist but you're not so good at drowning people." She giggled and kissed him on the lips.

"Please, please untie me."

Semantha took the dagger from under her belt and cut the ropes. Marco stood up and shook out his limbs. Then he rubbed his arms. He bent over and felt his foot. There was a small hole in his shoe and a bright red spot right next to his little toe.

"Nasty critter. That smarts," he said. "Just getting through to my bone when you came."

"Oh Marco, I'm so happy to see you safe." She threw her arms around him and tried to give him a passionate kiss. He turned away and made a mean face.

"Whoa, whoa. Whoa. What's goin' on here?" He tried to give her a push, but didn't seem to have the strength. She held on. His face turned from ashen to a boiling bright red.

"Holy fuck!" he screamed in Semantha's ear, close enough to bite it off. "I get clubbed in the head, brought here, tied up to this tree by that freak." He shook his head.

"Then f-ing magically, you show up alive and throw yourself at me like we're two drunk sophomores at a spring frat party. No way." He struggled to free himself from her embrace, but Semantha continued to hold tight. He pushed harder and finally broke her hold. The sides of his mouth turned down in a fierce frown.

"One thing at a time, babe. Last, I recall, you and Saul were trying to sacrifice me to the devil."

Semantha dropped to her knees, put her head in her hands, and sobbed. After a moment, she looked up at Marco. He was standing there like a statue, stiff and not moving.

"Oh Marco, my love, my sweet." She raised her arms as if offering Marco a petition. "That was so wrong. How can I explain?" She stopped for a second.

"But wait, I hear someone coming," she said. Marco listened too. "Your buddy Clem?"

VI

Cynthia decided to spend the weekend with her parents after the hopeful but unsettling time in Charleston. Going back home was a trip she did not relish, never enjoyed, returning to her parents' neat and tidy brick ranch on the outskirts of tiny Elk Horn, Iowa. It was surrounded by other houses with their well-manicured lawns almost all the same, maybe the light posts in the front yards were different. It brought back memories Cynthia had tried to forget but couldn't, her bland, unexciting childhood, standard in every way, including her time as captain of the cheerleading squad. She was sure that she was selected more because of her cleavage than her talent, something she knew she didn't have much of.

Cynthia had spent a lifetime trying to escape from this stultifying world and to overcome her persistent feeling that she didn't quite measure up. That's the main reason she went to law school. It had been a fortunate choice because the mantle of her legal career empowered her, serving as a potent antidote to her tendency toward depression. The truculent demeanor and bellicose style she adopted as a lawyer masked a shaky self-image. And her gift for words overpowered her natural squeamishness in confrontations.

She felt obligated to visit every so often, but even more than the return to her white bread roots, she dreaded the annoying so-called "heart-to-heart" conversations with her mother. They always felt like unwanted prying, and they were always the same.

"How's married life, dear?" Millie would ask, seated on the clear plastic-coated couch in the "front" room. Cynthia bristled. Before Cynthia married Marco, it was about who she was dating. It was part of the inevitable ritual.

Her father Manfred, wearing his standard suspenders and tan work shirt, sat next to Millie, mute in "his" brown upholstered recliner. He nodded his head at appropriate moments but was otherwise lost in space. In recent years, a folding aluminum nightstand for his medicines had been placed next to his chair.

Cynthia hated the condescension in Millie's voice, as if Cynthia was failing at the one and only task for her life: meeting a good man and creating children. Cynthia wondered what her mother would think if she really told her everything, right down to helping Marco overcome a bout of sexual dysfunction after he was almost made a human sacrifice. Millie would be more than scandalized.

"Everything's fine, mom," Cynthia replied, sounding noncommittal and mildly irritated.

"You know, your father and I pray for you every day. We worry about you."

"Yes Mother, I know." Cynthia had to work not to tell her to mind her own business.

Manfred stirred. "All we want is for you to be happy." He drifted off, then opened his eyes. again "And some grandchildren." Cynthia visibly flinched.

Millie laughed as if embarrassed and told Manfred to hush up. He closed his eyes and began to snore quietly.

"You don't take care of yourself, Cynthia dear," Millie continued.

"Okay Mom, I know." It was easier for Cynthia to be agreeable. Fighting with her mother was useless.

"It's important to clean your gut out every day, mind me," Millie said.

Cynthia didn't reply. It was statements like this that made Cynthia worry about her parents' well-being. How much longer could they live independently? She looked at her father and noted his expressionless face as she settled in for Millie's monologue about what was going on around town, blatantly uninteresting gossip as far as Cythia was concerned.

"Now my dear, you remember Martha Williams, that old spinster who lived over on Elm?" Millie sniffed in a haughty way. "Well, she…."

Cynthia tried not to listen but the more she tried, the more aggravated she got. She could not appreciate her parents' narrow world and even narrower views about life. There was no having a decent conversation with them about anything: religion, their minds were already made up; politics, typical right-wing nonsense; international travel, not for them.

But while she sat there pretending to listen, she was struck with a revelation. *Am I really the same as these folks? Oh my God.* Maybe that was part of the problem with Marco. It was not enough for her to leave Iowa or become a more powerful version of her parents. How could she make herself enticing to a worldly man like him? Maybe learn physics? Take up belly dancing? She had to figure that out.

The next morning, Cynthia got up late. She didn't want to see Millie, who would surely chide her for sleeping in. Thankfully, Millie was not in the kitchen when she went for a glass of water. Cynthia looked out the window above the sink and saw her on her hands and knees, weeding the strawberries. Through the open back door, she heard her mother singing, "Amazing grace, how sweet the sound…" She sang with a flat, off-key voice. It looked like Millie was going to be a while, so Cynthia thought it safe to have a drink, free from Millie's remonstrations. She took out a bottle of wine hidden in her suitcase and poured some into a water glass.

It was a beautiful Sunday afternoon. Light from the sun streaked into the kitchen, past the old-fashioned lace drapes and onto the scratchy blue linoleum countertop The wine put Cynthia in a relaxed, contemplative frame of mind. She closed her eyes and felt the warmth of the sun hitting the side of her face. So much to think about. Sure, about how she needed to find a job and get herself back on a regular workout regime. Yes, finding a way of making herself more intriguing, like she'd thought about last night. Definitely all that, but mostly she thought about Marco and how much she craved to be with him.

She was happy they had more or less reconciled. Sex was still a problem, but that had never been that important to her.

She couldn't imagine life without him. Coming back to Iowa was a poignant reminder of how isolated she had been when she was growing up, how she thirsted for but didn't have any real close friends, how she had never found anyone to love until Marco came along. He had been her escape from the tedious Elk Horn sort of life. There was no going back to that. She would fight to the death to keep him and save herself.

She smiled. She thought back to their conversation in Charleston, when he admitted he had problems with trust and intimacy, how for the first time he had dropped his haughty veneer and told her about his sterile, lonely upbringing. Cynthia was gratified that Marco had decided to trust her enough to let her see this part of him.

Maybe underneath was a sweet child, wanting to be loved and cared for...

She imagined Marco as a small boy and her as a young girl skipping through a field, picking wild daisies together and playing "She loves me." How they laughed when the last petal landed on "She loves me." In her reverie, the sky was blue, the air warm. They hugged and kissed each other innocently. No confusion, distraction, complexity. This pleasant dream beguiled her. She put her head down on the Formica-topped kitchen table.

Cynthia's mind drifted from her sweet dreams to her unsatisfying conversation with Marco in the airport the day after their wonderful dinner. They were waiting to board their flight back to Chicago.

"Marco, I thought we made progress last night. I was so happy," she had said. Marco made a face as if he had sucked a lemon.

"We better go to the gate. Boarding soon." Marco waved his hand.

"But what about last night?" Cynthia felt a sinking feeling in her gut. Was he going to answer?

"Yeah, our first time getting our fortunes read together. Great." He emitted a shallow, cold laugh.

"No, I was talking about the restaurant." Cynthia grabbed his hand, but he pulled away.

"I thought the steak was overcooked. Let's go. We don't want to miss the plane." He jumped up and grabbed the bags, leaving Cynthia sitting alone.

Cynthia's thoughts returned to her mother's kitchen. She shook her head. She and Marco were still some distance from lasting intimacy and real communication. She worried that a wall she had no idea how to penetrate still separated her from Marco, even though a crack had appeared in Charleston.

Let down your wall, Marco. Cynthia feared that her dream of a beautiful life with him would sputter and evaporate.

*　　*　　*

Cynthia pulled into the driveway in River Forest at about eleven p.m. Marco had promised to be home early to greet her when she arrived, but no lights were on and when she opened the garage door, she was quite surprised—his car was gone. She unlocked the door to the mudroom and discovered no shoes. She walked through the house, turning on every light, only to find that there was no evidence that he had been there all day—or maybe for the last couple of days. No dirty dishes—he never put them in the dishwasher; no loose piles of clothes—he never hung them up after he took them off; no wet towels in the bathroom—he never folded them and put them on the towel rack like she wanted. It was like he had not been there since she left on Friday afternoon. The empty house felt stark and cold.

Cynthia's first reaction was rage. She kicked his favorite kitchen chair. *How could he do this to me? We worked so hard and the first chance he has, he goes off and has an affair who knows with what sort of slut.* Then she began to calm down. *Wait a minute, Cynthia. Marco is right.* She did tend to overreact and turn everything into World War III. "Don't cry until you are really hurt," Marco would say.

She started to worry that maybe something bad had happened. What if he was in an accident? What if he had had a health emergency? Surely she would have heard.

Perhaps he merely got consumed at work. Once in a while he slept on the couch in his new big office at the lab. But again, if that had happened, he certainly would have let her know.

And why hadn't he called her all weekend? Could be he didn't want to bother her when she was with her parents. Who knows?

Cynthia began to shake as she ran from room to room looking for any clue as to what may have happened to him. She called his brand-new flip phone. It rang and rang like it was turned off. She called the land line at his lab. No answer. She called the police. They had no information about any missing person or accidents.

Then, she had a disturbing thought. That slime bucket Saul was dead, but what about some of the other animals who were a part of that evil enterprise? Maybe they had come looking for revenge. Cynthia dismissed the thought as too remote. How would they ever find him all the way over here in River Forest? Marco had been careful to secure his address and other contact data. Besides, why was the car not in the garage? That told her he had gone somewhere. The thought of Marco in the arms of a beautiful twenty-one-year-old returned and infuriated her. "Damn him!" she yelled.

Cynthia spent a sleepless night, alternating between anger and worry, as she played out the possibilities over and over. Regardless of what had happened, she was petrified. He may be gone for good.

When the morning came, Cynthia went outside for some fresh air. She walked down the driveway toward the street and spotted a piece of thick stiff paper lying next to the bush at the side of the garage door. It was soggy from a couple of weekend rain showers. She picked it up and read it. Her eyes widened and her body shook, jolted by a wave of anxiety. It was a one-way Amtrak train ticket from Benton Harbor to Chicago for the previous Friday night. She screamed, dropped to her knees, and wailed, "Oh no, oh no, oh no."

"You okay, Cynthia?" their next-door neighbor Phil asked as he ran over from his backyard patio where he was having his morning coffee.

"Too awful for words," Cynthia said between tears, shaking her head. "I think Marco's been kidnapped."

Phil lifted her up and gestured for her to come over and sit down. Cynthia shook her head. "No time for coffee. I think those lunatics from that coven over in Benton Harbor have grabbed him again."

"What are you going to do? You better call the police."

"Police? Benton Harbor? No. I know those rent-a-cops over there all too well. They're idiots. They'll start to poke around, and he'll get killed. Besides, they are so corrupt. You never know whose side they are on." She creased her eyebrows. "I'm going myself. My husband's in trouble and that's where I belong."

"I wouldn't do that," Phil said. "What do you know about kidnappings and murder? You'll only make matters worse."

"I've got to go, do what I can. If they are going to sacrifice someone, maybe they'll take me instead."

"Marco must mean a lot to you."

Cynthia smiled at Phil through the fear in her eyes. She did not answer.

"I still wouldn't go. What good are you to him dead?"

Cynthia grimaced, then went back to her house, her mind racing as she planned what she was going to do. Marco could be anywhere, but most likely the lowlifes would take him back to their home territory. Even still, Benton Harbor was a pretty big place, and they could have taken him to a slew of different locations, even that old farmhouse on the river. She had visited that ramshackle place when she thought she would be prosecuting Marco for murder. She hated going there. It seemed to emit a cold, unnatural chill. She dismissed the possibility that he was there, too obvious after all that had come down. Or was it? These folks didn't seem too bright.

She also thought of calling Martin Dunland, her old boss in the county prosecutor's office. But she wasn't sure she could trust him and that would be a great way of ensuring that the police would become involved. Besides, from her years as a prosecutor, she was confident she understood the criminal mind and how bad people operate. She herself had investigated scores of crimes, each with its own malevolent twist. Of course, she had not anticipated that one day she would need to get to the bottom of a crime against the man she loved.

She turned on her computer to see if she could get any recent news about what was going on around the town. She saw a news article in Benton Harbor's *Herald Palladium* from about two weeks previous. The headline read: "Israelite House of David files suit to Quiet Title."

Interesting.

She remembered the Israelite House from her days in the prosecutor's office. Supposedly, it was a religious sect, but there were plenty of allegations about all sorts of improprieties: brainwashing, sexual exploitation, financial irregularities. Still, nothing had been proven. The newspaper story told about a house at 1356 West Wigmore Street in Benton Harbor that had been inherited by the two children of Sebastianus Papadiamantopoulos, a leader of the sect, but only for their lives. Now that they were both dead, the deed went to the church, and it was claiming title.

Something about that information seemed familiar to Cynthia. She thought for a moment. Then she recalled. That was the last name of the woman whom Marco had killed. How many people with that last name could there be in Benton Harbor? There had to be a connection of some sort. That's where she should begin her search. Maybe someone living at the house on Wigmore Street, or a neighbor, could point her in the right direction.

Either way, she was wild with anxiety, consumed with fear, but steeled with resolve. Her fight had begun.

VII

Semantha tucked the dagger back in her pants, grabbed Marco's hand to guide him through the vine curtain. "Come on, quick," she said, pulling hard. "Time for talk later."

Marco resisted. "I don't think I can trust you," he said.

"You've got no choice, if you want to live."

Marco shook his head and followed Semantha as she led him to the road. As they reached it, an earth-shattering "Fuck!" echoed through the woods.

"I guess he figured out you escaped," Semantha said. "Now we really have no time to lose."

It was an overcast night and pitch black, but the flat terrain made for easy walking. Still, Marco limped, favoring the foot the rat had nibbled. Every so often, he would wince from pain and had to stop to let it subside.

After they were a little way down the road, off in the distance, a car engine started with a throaty *varoom.*

"It's Tristan," Marco said.

"Tristan?"

"My Beemer. That's how he got me here."

"Get down," Semantha said. They dropped to their knees and fell flat in the gooey bottom of a shallow roadside drainage ditch.

In a moment, the car came roaring down the road, with no lights on except the spotlight right up next to the steering wheel. Clem was using it to scan the fields on both sides of the car every few feet.

"Powerful lamp," Semantha whispered.

"Yep. I don't do things half ass."

The light flashed directly on them and the car stopped.

"He's seen us," Semantha whispered. "Run for it." She pulled Marco to his feet and ran away from the road as fast as she could, holding on to Marco tightly. His running was getting increasingly labored. They were at the edge of a large, freshly mowed winter wheat field surrounded by an electrified metal wire fence.

"Remember how to do a low crawl?" she asked. "Don't touch it," she said as she pushed Marco toward the fence. They fell to the ground and went under. The ground was dry and hot.

"Come on Marco," Semantha said, pushing him along. A fleeting picture flashed in her mind of what Clem could do if he caught them. Surely, she would be raped and Marco brutalized, maybe killed.

"We've got to put some distance between us and Clem," she said, emphasizing the words "got to."

"I'm doing the best I can. It's pretty painful."

As they started to run across the field, Clem threw the car into reverse and backed about one hundred feet down the road. There he revved the engine, floored the accelerator, and sent the car flying over the ditch into the field where Semantha and Marco were running. As the car broke through the fence, the wires went flying and sparks lit up the night.

"Good pyrotechnics," Marco said with an ironic smile.

Clem, not injured by the impact, turned on the car's headlights, and aimed directly toward Marco and Semantha.

"Look out," Marco yelled. He pushed Semantha away and jumped to the side just as the passenger-side rear view mirror skimmed his shoulder. "Split up!"

Marco ran in one direction and Semantha the other. Clem drove to the edge of the field, turned around, and got Marco directly in his sight. He put on the bright headlights, which sent an eerie beam down the field, temporarily blinding Marco. But he heard the *varoom* of the engine as it headed for him. Marco tried to run away from the sound, but Clem steered the car exactly where Marco was running. At the moment of impact, Marco darted to the left, again narrowly avoiding being hit. His shoe ripped open. He screamed when his foot landed on the stubble left over from the harvest.

As Marco struggled to get up, Clem slammed on the brakes and threw the car in reverse. Instead of going for Marco, now pretty much a sitting duck, he drove around wildly, scanning the field for Semantha. The lights fell on her as she was running for the side of the field. This time, Clem had a good, long track to build up speed. He again revved the engine and headed directly for Semantha. She turned, saw the lights, and stopped dead. As Clem got close, Semantha raised her arms exactly like Erzulie had and yelled at the top of her voice, "Meechiiialikkkk!" The car veered to the right and slammed into a fencepost, knocking it over.

Semantha took out her dagger and ran toward the stopped car. Clem was inside, unconscious, but he did not appear to have been seriously hurt. *Gotta get Marco out of here. I'll deal with him later,* she thought. She assumed she had time since the car's engine seemed to have been knocked out. She ran to the part of the field where she saw Marco jump and found him lying in the dirt, rubbing his bloody foot.

"I'm not sure I can move," he said.

"Guy, you've got no choice." Semantha pulled him to his feet, put his arm around her shoulder, and began dragging him toward the side of the field. She was not sure where her strength was coming from. Ahead, she saw a stone fence the car could not scale. Maybe on the other side they could get help. They heard the car engine restart.

"He's coming for his next pass," Semantha said. "Move." With her adrenaline pumping overtime, she ran at top speed, dragging Marco along. As they got close to the wall, the now-single headlight from the car zeroed in on them like a laser beam from a gun sight. Clem gassed the engine, and the car came careening across the field right for them.

"Faster," Semantha yelled. Marco could only groan. It was just a few feet to a small opening in the fence, but the car was closing in fast.

"I said, 'faster!'" She now had Marco on her back, almost carrying him. He was so tall his feet dragged on the ground. He yelled out in pain, but Semantha thought of nothing but getting them to safety.

"Almost there," she said. "Hold on."

They got to the fence at about the same moment as the car. Semantha jumped through the small opening, carrying Marco with her, then dove down behind the stones.

The car smashed against the fence, making a horrific crashing sound as metal twisted and glass broke. Then there was an explosion and they both felt the heat from the burning wreckage. The light from the fire reflected on the branches of the trees above.

"I guess we made it," Marco said.

"Time to spare," Semantha said with a blank smile. "But I'm afraid your car is a goner." Marco hobbled to his feet and watched his lovely Tristan go up in flames. Neither noticed whether Clem was still behind the wheel.

"What now?" Marco asked. "I really can't walk."

"Let's see if we can find the river. It's very peaceful this time of year. Maybe there's a gazebo or shore house somewhere where we can rest and wait for the morning."

"Okay. But how about some answers," Marco said insistently.

Semantha didn't answer. She again put Marco's arm around her shoulder and began to walk. Before long, they made it to the river and discovered a small boathouse that was unlocked. Inside it was cool, but at least they were away from the coyotes, racoons and river rats. Marco took off his tattered shoe and began rubbing his foot. Semantha found a kerosene lamp and a match. The lamp filled the space with a warm glimmer but also illuminated the blood oozing from Marco's toe.

"Got to get you some help," Semantha said.

"How about an explanation? I'm abducted, manhandled, and brought to this god-awful hell hole—again! What's going on?"

Semantha shook her head and touched Marco lightly on the cheek. She looked down, then smiled for a second, but her lips quickly turned into a frown.

"No, but…"

"And what about me becoming a sex slave?" Marco's face was bright red, and his eyes were flaming.

"Oh my God, Clem is a monster."

Marco grabbed Semantha by the arm and squeezed hard.

"That hurts."

"Somehow, I think you had something to do with this. Way too convenient that you magically show up here at exactly the same time as I do."

Marco let go of Semantha's arm and glowered. He shook his head, then wrinkled his brow. His lips pressed together. He looked directly into Semantha's eyes.

"How do I get out of this insanity?"

Semantha teared up.

"No, no, no. I love you and can't live without you. You can't leave."

Marco looked incredulous. "So, you have me kidnapped? Pretty sick."

Semantha began to cry.

"All I wanted was for Clem to find you, nothing more. Please believe me. He got carried away. I craved the chance to meet you, explain everything and see if I could make amends. That's all. I've thought about little else besides you for the last year."

Just then the door burst open.

"You's firgittin one littl' thing, Miss Semantha," Clem yelled as he walked in. He was breathing heavily, and his nostrils were flared like a bull in the ring. Big beads of sweat appeared on his forehead and blood dripped from a gash by his eye. He pranced around the boathouse knocking things off shelves and breaking whatever wasn't nailed down. His arms swung violently from side to side. He grabbed a wooden plank and hit it hard against a rowboat turned upside down on sawhorses. The noise echoed through the shack.

"You made me jes' a little promise, an' I'm here to collect from ya. An' as long as he's here, he kin watch." He took the plank and threw it over his shoulder like a baseball bat. "Maybe git some pointers 'bout how real men fuck their womenfolk. Maybe he'd like a little up his ass, too. I seen he can't really walk so not much he could do about it." Clem laughed. "Maybe yous'e good fer sumpin, ya faggot."

Clem kicked Marco hard in the head. Some blood oozed out of his ear, and he passed out.

"That'll take care of him fer right now so's we can have some privacy," Clem said, staring intently at Semantha.

Semantha had seen Clem's violent side before, but never this extreme. She was beside herself with fear and revulsion, but she knew she had to keep her wits about her if she was to save herself and Marco. She probably had only one chance. Clem didn't appear to have a weapon and that would help, but she had also seen him easily deflect the knife when Erzulie attacked him. It would take more than just a frontal assault to bring him down.

She fell to the cold concrete floor. Her hand moved to her pants and then to behind a box next to her. In the dim light, she was pretty sure Clem hadn't noticed.

"Oh Clem, how could you doubt me? I want you so bad," Semantha said, squeezing soft words from her mouth. She forced her lips to fake a smile.

Clem stopped pacing and looked down on Semantha sitting there. "Why'd ya run away then?"

Semantha saw how she could play with him. As disgusting as it would be, she thought she could have him.

"Oh Clem, you're so strong and brave." Semantha batted her eyelashes like a schoolgirl. "But I was worried about Marco." She couldn't believe she was saying these things. In all her years of knowing Clem, she could never have imagined this. She swallowed nervously.

"Besides, you've never heard of playing hard to get?" She extended her arm to him as if making him an offer. "I can't wait," Semantha said.

"Well…'" Clem's breathing slowed, and he stopped grimacing. He looked like he was thinking.

He's so gullible, she thought, but she was steeling for the affront she was about to endure.

Clem began to shift back and forth on his feet like an anxious fifteen-year-old. "Gosh," he said.

"But ya gotta be nice, not mean like Saul. He treated you bad. Me too. That's over. Time for you to be treated real good. And treat me good, too." Semantha laid down on the floor near the box with her arms spread out like angel wings. She unbuttoned her pants and slid her hand underneath. "Come and get me."

Clem instantly threw himself on top of Semantha, still fully clothed. He began pumping with his pelvis. He moaned. Semantha pushed him away. She wanted to get him in a more compromised position.

"No, no, no, Clem," Semantha said, cooing. "Make love to me. Take your clothes off and then come and lie down." Semantha couldn't believe she was saying this, inviting her own rape. The thought of his penis inside of her was revolting. *This better work.*

Clem readily complied, now with a rapacious, lustful smile on his face. Stripping off his pants, old tee shirt, his shoes and his socks, he stood there in his yellowed boxer shorts. His body odor, no longer contained by his clothes, filled the small boathouse.

Clem dropped to his knees and started ripping at Semantha's clothes. His breathing became heavy, and his pelvis thrust violently in Semantha's crotch. Semantha gritted her teeth, her stomach tied in knots. She tried to pretend that Clem was one of her ex-lovers, but that did not ease the revulsion. She could not escape the sense of violation and indignity.

Clem entered her and began pumping. She felt a sharp pain. It was time to act; she couldn't take any more. She reached behind the box, pulled out the dagger, quickly raised it over Clem, and thrust it into Clem's back as close to his heart as she could get it.

"Aggg!" he screamed. His eyes became anguished slits, and his eyebrows knitted together. A stream of blood trickled from his ear. "You fuckin' cunt." A big wad of spit dripped from his open mouth.

Not out, Clem could do anything. Semantha got ready for a painful death. *At least make it quick,* she thought. Clem slapped her, then put his hands around her throat. He squeezed hard. Semantha thought about Pappie. She was on the way to join him.

But Marco had just come to and, seeing Clem chocking Semantha, he sprang into action. He picked up the plank, tiptoed over to Clem, and hit him hard on the side of his head. "Brute!" he yelled.

Clem passed out and fell on Semantha. She rolled him off her and he lay there next to her, still breathing but with heavy, labored gasps. Semantha took a second to look at Clem. How silly he looked naked, with his big beer gut, the smallest tuft of body hair growing on his chest, and the tiniest member she had ever seen. She pulled out the dagger and adjusted her clothes.

"We gotta get out of here right now, Marco."

"Why? You got another act like him waiting in the wings?"

"No, there are warrants out for my arrest and if the police come, I'll be thrown in jail. I want to get away and spend time with you."

Marco furrowed his forehead and glowered. "What do we do about him?" he asked, pointing at the swollen body lying in a lake of its own blood.

"No choices," Semantha said as she took the dagger and slit his throat. A bubbling sound emitted from Clem's neck and more blood oozed out. "Done." She sounded like a country doc who had just removed a wart. She helped Marco up, opened the door, and ran with him on her shoulder out of the boathouse. A light in an adjacent yard turned on and the back door to a house opened.

"What's going on out here?" a middle-aged man yelled into the night.

Semantha ran as hard and fast as she could carrying Marco on her shoulders. She hoped against hope she and Marco had not been seen.

*   *   *

THE EMERGENCY KEY was still hidden inside an old rusty watering can behind the garage attached to Semantha's childhood home, the stately Georgian mansion at 1356 Wigmore Street. For Marco, it had been a long, difficult slog from the gazebo on the river, but Semantha had assured him he could recuperate there and that as soon as he felt better, she would help him catch the train. That sounded reasonable to Marco. Anyway, where could he go at three 3 a.m., no phone, no wallet and his clothes in tatters?

Semantha unlocked the back door and ushered Marco into the kitchen. The house looked like it had not been lived in for years. Dust was everywhere and it smelled musty, with a hint of mothballs.

Marco's toe was now so inflamed he could no longer walk. Semantha flicked on the old-style fluorescent kitchen light and deposited him on the long, wooden bench in the cozy-looking break-fast nook. It was still stocked with slightly yellowed paper napkins in a chrome holder embossed with an inverted cross. He slumped down, holding his head in his hands.

"Uhhh, it hurts," he said.

"Let me see what I can find to get you some relief," Semantha said. She left the kitchen, walking down the walnut-paneled hallway toward the stairs. Marco watched her as she walked. Even though his foot pained him a lot, his eyes were drawn to her alluring swagger. She got as far as the entry to the dining room. Stopping abruptly, she fell to her knees and pressed her cheek against the dark, thick Oriental carpet. She began to whimper with gasps of sorrow.

"What's wrong?" Marco asked. He was puzzled by the intensity of her reaction, forgetting for a minute about his foot. He wasn't sure why, but something inside of him wanted to comfort her in her distress despite everything that had happened. He momentarily thought back to their encounter on the lake and their otherworldly rendezvous in that old farm kitchen. It was hard to forget passion that powerful, especially for him. Rarely had any woman excited him so much. He never could get enough.

After a moment of furious weeping, Semantha rolled over and sat up. "This is the exact spot where Saul killed Pappie," she said tearfully. She got up and walked back to the kitchen table, sat down next to Marco, and put her head on his shoulder, letting her long blonde hair fall on his arm. Marco sat there without moving but fighting the barest shadow of a smile. She began to weep afresh.

"I loved him so much. He was everything to me. And he loved me too. I couldn't have asked for a better dad."

A tear came from Marco's eye and ran down his cheek, thinking about his own indifferent father and the emptiness of their relationship. Without a thought, he threw his arms around Semantha and pulled her closer. She still smelled sweet, even after all she had gone through.

"I'm lost without him. So lonely, so isolated. Sometimes I want to die." She placed her head on his chest. Marco didn't resist. Instead, he stroked her hair, soft and smooth, and brushed a few more tears from her eyes.

"Don't talk like that," Marco said, almost pleading. He was touched to the soul by her melancholy. A part of him wanted to help relieve her pain if he could. "Someone will come along and sweep you off your feet."

Semantha stopped crying; the sadness on her face disappeared. She tugged herself away from Marco's arms and looked him in the eye. Her blue eyes blinked seductively.

"That's already happened." She waited a second, then offered a coquettish smile, highlighting her dimples.

"That's you," she said and moved closer as if wanting to kiss Marco on the lips. Almost automatically, Marco touched her right dimple with two of his fingers, but then the corners of his mouth abruptly turned down. Dropping his hand from her face, he pushed her away brusquely and hard.

"Wait a minute, my friend," he said, squinting his forehead. "What's going on? Let's get back to reality," he said with a penetrating, serious look.

Semantha's mouth opened a little as if she was about to ask a question.

"I don't get it," he said. "The last time we saw each other was when we were standing in the river right after I escaped. We had an argument, and you said some choice words. Then I tried to drown you. I was mad-dog enraged. I still remember it like yesterday. No question, I wanted to kill you."

"So…"

"So… So? Holy shit. After all that, all the sudden you show up yesterday as if nothing happened and make a herculean effort to save me from that so called 'friend' of yours. And you try to tug at my heart strings with all this about the murder of your stepdad. Doesn't add up." He stopped. His eyes narrowed.

"That, all of this." He made a sweeping motion with his hand. "Inexplicable. If it was me, I'd be looking for revenge, not trying to rekindle passion, or whatever is on your mind." He winced and looked at his foot. It was still bleeding, and he could feel it throb, though taking the weight off had eased the pain.

"I really don't get it," Marco said with a quixotic scowl.

"Wait, wait, Marco. Try to understand." She took Marco's hand in hers. "From the moment I saw you out there on the lake, remember? I was passionately drawn to you. Even from across the water, I felt your sadness, like inside you were suffering from some great tragedy, some terrible loss, something." She shook her head and tried to brush her hand through his hair. He held up his arm to stop her and shook his head.

"I instantly felt an uncanny kinship with you, almost like we were fellow travelers on the road to perdition. Maybe it was because of my own loss and all the pain I had to endure when I was a child." She went silent, wanting to give Marco a chance to think about what she had said.

"Was I wrong to feel that?" Semantha eventually said. Marco softened, again drawn in by the intensity of her emotion.

"I've…well, I've had some bad times too… not as bad as yours," he said.

"Tell me," Semantha asked, wishing to seem interested and as solicitous as possible.

"Some other time," Marco said. He was not ready to get into his past traumas. But a fleeting recollection of his high school sweetheart flashed in his head. Melissa—he had loved her so much—and how depressed he had been, almost suicidal, when she turned him over to pursue a career out of the country. He thought about her dimples, how compelling he had found them. Marco turned red. He desired to touch Semantha's dimpled cheek.

"But really… I tried to kill you."

"Yes, but I also said some terrible things that were not true. I didn't believe them then, but I said them anyway. I was furious, too, totally confused and disoriented. Saul had sent me to kill you. I had a dagger in my underwear. So, you were right to be wary."

"But…" Marco began.

"I am sure your mind was in disarray," Semantha continued. "I can see how you acted impulsively against your own nature. I don't blame you. Long ago, I forgave you."

Marco said nothing, astonished by Semantha's declaration and overwhelmed by everything that had happened since Clem had grabbed him. His thoughts veered in one direction then the other, like jumping beans in a bottle.

The house was intensely quiet, only the slow *drip, drip, drip* from the ancient faucet over the sink. It seemed like a metronome counting the seconds. Neither Marco nor Semantha looked at each other. The single bulb in the ceiling light flickered. After five minutes or so, Marco broke the silence.

"Surely, there are others…" he said.

"But none like you. I dream of being the woman at your side as you climb to the heights. Can I say it, Marco? I need you so very much. Please, oh please, believe me."

Marco's jaw tightened and he scratched his head. *Am I insane? Is this really happening?* His body convulsed as his anger spiked.

"All this is unbelievably hard to take in," he said gruffly, shaking his head. "Don't forget, I saw you at the black mass, standing up there behind the altar with Saul like you were gleefully anticipating the dagger plunging into my heart. And beforehand, you giving me the poison to drink. As far as I could see, you were part of the plan all along. But now you are saying wonderful things, like a distressed lover craving reconciliation.

"No way," Marco said as he knifed the air with his hand and frowned.

Semantha waited a moment, then placed her hand on Marco's knee and peered into his eyes.

"Saul had terrorized me. He had that power over people. He knew exactly how to whip up a crowd and turn people over to him. He had emotionally bludgeoned me, almost to the point of death."

"Okay, but…"

"By the time I was standing there, like you say, at the altar, mentally I had shut down. Everything seemed so unreal, like your worst nightmare. Regardless of what you say about how I looked, you are mistaken. I was catatonic. Saul had taken over my mind."

Semantha looked down at the mosaic tiled floor. A distant appearance came to her eyes, maybe recalling a scene from her childhood.

"He gave me orders to bring back your private parts in a plastic bag, but I think he knew I couldn't do it. Probably, I was to be a decoy for him to hunt you down, do the job himself. But I was quite sure that if I didn't do what he said, I would suffer an agonizing death. That was Saul."

"Lord in heaven," Marco said.

"It's all true." The corners of Semantha's lips turned up slightly. Marco began to understand, at least some.

"I guess I was lucky to get out alive," Marco said.

"We all thought you were drugged and out cold," Semantha said.

"I didn't drink the poison. I figured out there must be something going on."

"Smart. Your powerful intellect working overtime," Semantha said as she reached over to hug him. She offered her open mouth as if asking for a passionate kiss.

Marco visibly jerked, taken back by Semantha's aggressiveness but intrigued anyway. *She is hot. Maybe...* But then startled by his urge to touch her, he slid down the bench away from her and looked down at the floor. *Get a hold of yourself. Think with your mind and not your penis. And what about Cynthia?*

"What did I do?" Semantha asked. Her words sounded like a plea.

Marco shook his head a bit, folded his arms, and closed his eyes as he disappeared into the black forest of his thoughts. He remembered his pledge to Cynthia, but here was this beautiful woman...

So much like Melissa.

Maybe this was God sending him his heart's desire on the rebound. He felt his lust and emotion tugging at him against his reason.

Look at all that this woman has done. Could Cynthia pull that off? Right now, she was probably sitting at home absorbed by *Judge Judy* and eating some Chinese carry out. Cynthia is a bright, decent woman, but prone to depression and given over to weakness. She doesn't turn me on like this woman does. Not only is she beautiful—those titillating dimples—but she is exotic, mysterious, with one foot in the spirit world. And here she is, offering herself to me without condition or limitation.

No, Marco. Stop it. If he gave into Semantha's charms, it would almost surely ruin his marriage, maybe his career. And what about the arrest warrants?

"Marco? You, ok?" Semantha asked. Marco opened his eyes and looked at Semantha with steely indifference.

"Let's get all of our cards on the table," he said, his voice cold and unemotional.

"I'm married."

"Oh," Semantha said with an indifferent sounding tone in her voice as she raised her right eyebrow. "That's a surprise. How did that happen?"

"After I thought I killed you, I turned myself in. She was the prosecutor, until she was removed from the case."

"Turned yourself in? Why? No one could have known what you tried to do. There wasn't any evidence linking you to the crime. No witnesses and definitely no body." Semantha ran her hand through her hair.

"It was a question of my integrity, taking responsibility for what I believed I had done," Marco said, peering at the floor.

Semantha smiled. Love was written all over her face.

"What happened? Apparently, you didn't go to jail. My old boyfriend would have told me if you had."

"There was a plea deal. The chief prosecutor wanted to keep things quiet, didn't want to blow up the community with a public trial. You know, a witches' coven, human sacrifice, all that…"

Semantha went silent, perhaps considering what Marco had said. Then her lips formed a carved jack-o-lantern smile. "Well, we can still be friends, can't we?" She reached over to give Marco a hug but accidentally kicked his wound with her foot. A wave of pain went up his leg. He recalled he was injured and let out a groan.

"Now we really do need to get you something for that," Semantha said. "It's looking bad."

Marco put his hand on his forehead. "I'm beginning to feel pretty dizzy, too."

Semantha's face twinkled. She brushed Marco's cheek softly with the back of her hand. "Pappie's mother was a kleptomaniac. Let me see what I can find."

Before long, Semantha returned with some pills, ointments, and a bucket filled with soaking salts. She carefully cut off what remained of Marco's blood-soaked shoe and sock and cleaned the wound. Marco winced when she plunged his foot into the boiling water but felt relief when she took it out and bandaged it. She kissed his infected toe like a mother would.

Marco was drawn in by Semantha's apparent caring and compassion.

"Tomorrow I've really got to go. I'm sure my wife is concerned," he said, but he felt the emptiness of his own words. Part of him wanted to stay with this woman and make love to her.

"Sure," Semantha said. "But for now, let's get you upstairs and into bed. You need some rest." She again put her arm around him and cobbled him up two flights of stairs to the master bedroom, helping him avoid putting any pressure on his foot. She laid him on Pappie's mahogany four-poster bed, still covered with his grandmother's embroidered golden bedspread, and carefully helped him undress.

Marco noticed her hair brushing against his chest as he pulled off his pants. He tried to ignore how delectable her hair felt. He wanted to reach out and pass his hand through it, kiss her dimple. *Don't! You beggar,* he thought.

Then she took off her own tattered clothes and threw them on the heap with Marco's. She started to climb into bed. Marco noticed a bit of blood ooze out from her crotch.

"Careful now, Semantha," Marco said, holding out his hand, signaling her to stop and keep her distance. But his face betrayed his passion. She looked disappointed but resolved.

"Gotta get us a change of clothes," Semantha said. "Let me see if I can find anything."

After a few minutes, she came back into the bedroom dressed in a skintight pants suit from the 1950's with a robe thrown over her arm.

"I'll have to go into town tomorrow morning to get you something, but here's Pappie's robe. Put it on for now." She gasped when she saw him lying there in the robe. "I love the way it looks on you," she said. "And look at my aunt's outfit. It fits me perfectly."

It sure does, Marco thought, feeling a tug in his crotch. *Whoa, watch it.*

*   *   *

THE NEXT MORNING, Marco slept until close to noon and when he awoke, he looked at his foot. Twice the normal size, it was bright red and throbbing more than before. Then he looked around the room. It took him a moment to realize where he was and to recount what had happened the day before, but when he did, he whimpered. Immediately Semantha walked in, still dressed in her aunt's skintight pants.

"I was waiting outside for you to get up, sleepy head." She smiled from ear to ear. "Better get you to a doctor with that foot."

"I've got to call my wife," Marco responded.

"Call from his office."

Semantha found the key to Pappie's 1965 Buick Electra still parked in the garage and stuffed Marco in in the back seat, wearing only Pappie's robe. She took him to a physician her father had known well. He treated Marco with a couple shots of IV antibiotics and gave him a prescription for more, plus some pain medication, no questions asked. He told them that Marco had been infected with an antibiotic-resistant bacteria, which could have killed him.

"No laughing matter," he had said. "Soak your foot as much as possible. And no travel or vigorous activity… including sex," he said, eying Semantha with his own calculating, lustful eyes.

"And here's something more for the pain," he said as he gave Marco another jab. Immediately Marco felt smooth and detached. Calling Cynthia slipped out of his mind.

After returning from the doctor, Semantha spent the next couple of days nursing Marco like he was a newborn baby, soaking his foot, putting on fresh dressings, and reminding him to take his pills. She got some food and Marco some clothes.

Marco loved the attention, although he felt guilty. He needed to find a phone and call Cynthia. But wasn't she still visiting her parents? Marco had forgotten how long she would be gone, but it was a while. There was no rush. She was always preoccupied when she went there. He could complete his healing under Semantha's watchful care before figuring out how to get back to Chicago.

In the meantime, he spent his time distracted by Semantha's every move as she worked around the bed, cleaned up, and brought him food. She was an extraordinary nurse. And they talked, Semantha, about the glory of her old teaching days, Marco a little about the importance of his physics experiments, but mostly complaining about Cynthia, complaining a lot. She was getting fat and lazy, bitching about almost everything he did, and demanding more and more of his time, time he didn't have, he said.

As he got better, he also felt his animal passion rising. Semantha wanted him. He wondered whether he should oblige. But he needed to try to control himself.

Don't be a fool. She's not Melissa.

VIII

THE DAY AFTER finding the one-way ticket, Cynthia dressed in a jungle fatigue uniform she had bought for a costume party and headed for Benton Harbor. Saving Marco from his evil captors would be a daunting task. She felt like she was descending into a deep cave without a lantern.

On the way, she stopped by a shabby-looking gun store in Indiana. A salesperson stood behind a showcase filled with mean-looking weapons.

"Going to war?" he asked, smirking like he was amused.

Cynthia ignored the dig and coaxed a narrow, artificial smile. The man reminded her of her father, bald with suspenders stretched over a beer gut. She didn't want to get contentious.

"I…I've got to be ready," Cynthia replied.

"Ready? For what? No war games nearby today," he said.

Cynthia frowned and sent him a "none of your business" look.

"Well, you're dressed for it," he said, laughing out loud. He got out several weapons from the showcase and put them on the glass countertop.

Cynthia eyed them, appearing confused. She picked up one by the barrel, inadvertently pointing it directly at herself.

"Not that way," the dealer yelled and pulled the gun from her. "Here, try this one."

She took the gun the dealer offered but couldn't get her finger on the trigger. Her hand was too small. Cynthia thought about how her grandfather had looked when she had first tried to ride a bicycle. The dealer's pained expression was exactly like that.

"C-C-C-Can I get a license to carry one of these?" Cynthia asked sheepishly.

"License no problem," the dealer said. "You know how to use um? They're not toys, ya know."

"Well, uh…" Cynthia said.

"You seem like a nice young lady. Take my advice. Don't buy one of these unless you know how to use it."

"But I think I may need to defend myself."

"Not so simple. More people are killed with their own guns than anything else. Get a dagger. Less potent, but it has its advantages. That's what I recommend." He pulled one from a drawer behind the counter and gave it to Cynthia. It came with a belt and holster.

Cynthia looked it over, then took out her card to pay.

"Remember, be careful." The dealer knotted his eyebrows. "Even this thing can be turned on you." The dealer's words were disquieting, but Cynthia was undeterred. She knew she would feel better with some kind of weapon and the dealer was right; she hadn't the slightest idea how to use a gun. She clicked on the holster and left.

Now armed, she drove on to Benton Harbor and then to the house on Wigmore Street. After thinking some more about her quest, Cynthia had already decided that it was pretty unlikely that Marco's captors would have taken him to a location in the middle of town. But yet, as with any criminal investigation she had ever conducted, she wanted to be thorough.

When she got there, Cynthia took a good look, hoping to spot some clues. The house, a bit in disrepair, appeared deserted. The green shutters had been closed, except for one on the second floor, which was half open, revealing only darkness within. A few tiles were missing from the green slate roof, and the front yard was overgrown with weeds. An unpruned Japanese lilac at the corner of the house was shedding its blooms, and a bright orange sign plastered on the front door said *Legal Notice* in bold letters.

She parked, walked up to the door, and knocked. No one answered. She knocked louder. Silence. She banged insistently. Still nothing.

Her suspicions were confirmed: a dead end. She kicked herself for wasting time coming here. But now she could scratch this house off the list. She walked back to the street down the brick front walkway, marveling at its intricate inlaid design.

As she reached her car, a shriveled-up, hunched-over old lady with a cane hobbled up. She wore a tattered blue cloth coat and a pink babushka tightly wrapped around her head. A few strands of white hair peeked out from underneath.

"You's in the special forces thing?" she asked. Cynthia made a face.

"No," she said, sounding mean. "I'm looking for someone."

"Uh, Pappie?"

"Who?"

"Oh, you know, that old guy—somebody told me he was a warlock, ya know, a male witch. Got himself killed right over in that house a ways back." The lady nodded her head in the direction of 1356, but then she went silent as her head dropped and she leaned hard on her cane. After a bit, she lifted her head and seemed to come to. "Lots of people come looking for him."

Cynthia recognized the name "Pappie." So, this was where he was living when he was stabbed. A tingle coursed up Cynthia's spine. A lot had happened there.

"Anybody living here now?" Cynthia asked.

"Livin' here? Uh…" Her voice trailed off, and her head dropped again. "Living…erh." After a little, she continued. "I don't think so. Well sometimes, ur uh…not as best I can tell." Shen began to wobble on her cane. Cynthia worried she was about to topple over.

"I live right there," she said, waving her arm at the house across the street from 1356 while keeping her eyes on the ground. When she again lifted her head, she straightened up and her eyes opened wide.

"Come to think of it, I did see a young girl goin' in there a couple of times the other day. Looks like they're getting ready to sell it. I think she was going to clean. She was carrying some grocery bags, maybe supplies."

"Did you see what she looked like?"

"Sort of familiar, but…uh. But I don't…. I really couldn't place her." The lady's eyes clouded over.

Cynthia wasn't sure whether the information from this old lady was reliable. But she didn't see that there was more to do at this place. It didn't sound like Marco had been there.

As she drove away, she did not notice the face peering out from a dormer window.

IX

SEMANTHA WALKED INTO the bedroom wearing a tan tank top showing off her cleavage and tight form-fitting pants, almost exactly the same outfit as she had on, now several years ago, when she had come into the kitchen of the house on the river and untied Marco. She had cleaned up, fixed her hair, and smothered herself in perfume smelling of lilacs. How did she know that was Marco's favorite scent?

His foot well on the mend, Marco was resting on the bed half asleep. She tapped him lightly and said "Hi" in a soft, sweet voice.

He opened his eyes, looked at her, and quivered. He was transported back to the excitement of their first encounter and the passion he had experienced then. He felt his resistance waning.

"Babe, you're beautiful, I confess," he blurted out without thinking. Semantha dipped her head slightly and winked.

"You know what you can do about it, don't you?" She gave a flat-lipped smile, making her dimples stand out.

"No, I can't do that…you know." Marco's voice lacked conviction.

"But just once, what could that hurt? I'm not going to tell your wife. What was her name again?"

Marco only smiled.

Without another word, Semantha moved to the bottom of the bed and pulled the sock off Marco's healthy foot. She dropped to her knees and began to kiss it passionately and rub it seductively.

A quake surged up from Marco's toe through his legs and spine to his brain, like a grand wave building momentum to break.

She's right. What would it matter, only once?

What would it matter? He knew. Closing his eyes, recollections of Cynthia's compassion and caring flashed in his head, her help in overcoming the trauma from his first capture, how understanding she had been when he could not perform sexually, so much more. She's a gentle soul, kind, decent, caring. He imagined her sitting next to him. Marco shook his head.

She doesn't deserve this. A flash of guilt swept over him.

But then he opened his eyes to Semantha licking his feet. So unlike Cynthia, she was all he ever wanted in a woman. *Licking my feet. Licking my feet!*

No more use denying it. *Give into it, you know you're going to.* Her smells intoxicated him and her body—God, her body.

I want her with everything I have. I must have her. Cynthia be damned. Marco felt his member fill and throb. He sat up and reached down to her, put his hand under her blouse and began rubbing her breast, so firm and petite.

"Oh my God," Semantha said and moved up to lie down next to him. She melted into him, and they caressed intimately. He licked her dimples on one side, then the other. He had resisted too long.

Marco's hand wandered, sliding under her brassiere, moving not with intention but as if possessed. Her breasts, the small of her back, the wonderment of her cleavage, her intimate parts covered with delectable curly blond hair, the powerful feminine smell filling the room intertwining with the extravagant fragrance of the perfume. He wanted to touch her, kiss her, consume her if he could. At that moment, nothing else mattered to him.

Melissa, my God, Marco thought, as the recollection of his first love became the reality of his immediate passion. No longer was she gone away; he had mystically reunited with her in the form of the woman next to him.

Marco let his tongue explore Semantha's erogeny freely, without inhibition, as it probed deeply inside her in blind, fevered thrusts. She softly quivered and her hips undulated back and forth. Marco undid her bra and lightly touched her nipples, rubbing them in a circle with the small of his hand.

Oh Semantha, my life, the power of you. He lusted to be inside her but he cried out to become a part of her. With her, he would escape from the humdrum and explore the extraordinary, the otherworldly. *Just the sex alone...* A lifetime of passion was captured in this moment. Poetry, harmony, rhythm, exciting agitation. This was to be his.

She lifted his legs and offered him her tongue in the most intimate of intimate places, soft, warm, sweet. He was launched toward the stars. Never before had he experienced such a feeling, no other woman.... Cynthia, she would never. He was ready to abandon his past banal existence and live in the world of the unknown, the undiscovered.

"Now take me," Semantha said as she rolled onto her stomach and offered him her trim, supple bottom. Marco's member throbbed in anticipation. *I've always wanted...* Marco thought as he obliged Semantha's urging, like a schoolboy, enthusiastically readying himself to submit to her desires. He thrust himself inside her with a heavy push. Semantha jerked.

"Not too hard," Semantha said. She pulled away, rolled over and put her hand on his chest.

"Again, but easier. I'm small..."

This time taking it slow, Marco gradually entered her. Then both of them groaned as if singing an aria.

*   *   *

Afterwards, they rested on separate parts of the enormous bed, looking away from each other, recovering from the powerful but passing oneness they had shared After a while, Semantha rolled over, looked at Marco, and let her arm fall on Marco's still partially erect member as if by accident. She rubbed it lightly with the back of her arm. He dozed off and she closed her eyes too.

Marco awakened when he heard a knock on the door, then another. He looked at Semantha. She opened her eyes when someone knocked a third time, louder and seemingly more insistent than before. Semantha got up, went to the dormer window, pulled back the drape, and looked out.

"That's strange. Some woman, dressed up like a jungle soldier, complete with a dagger on her waist," she said.

Marco recalled Cynthia's costume for the Mardi Gras party last spring. It couldn't be, he was sure.

"Maybe she's someone come looking for Saul," Marco said. He was not about to tell Semantha about Cynthia's costume. Semantha's face became troubled as if Marco had hit a sore spot.

"Whatever did happen with Saul?" she asked, turning away from the window.

"Let's say he got too involved in a physics experiment…it killed him. I'll tell you the details some other time. But I've been wondering about something myself. What about these arrest warrants?"

"Yeah, before I met you, I had sex with a couple of seventeen-year-old high school boys in a science project I was judging. I hate myself for doing that. It sort of ruined my career as a physics teacher."

Marco's mouth dropped open.

"Is that your kink?" he asked. He wondered, who is this person with whom he had just been so intimate?

"Sex with teenagers was the exception, but my overpowering urge is gone now. It feels good to be liberated. I haven't had sex with any man since you and I had that passionate night together in the kitchen. Haven't wanted it, haven't craved it. You cured me."

"At least I'm good for something," Marco said with an uncomfortable laugh. "No sex with anyone then?"

Semantha looked away and growled.

"What did I say?"

*   *   *

LATER the same afternoon, still lying on the bed with Semantha, Marco became antsy. He figured Cynthia would be getting back from Iowa, and he needed to get to work. He had some experiments underway which had to be tended to. Besides, his breathtaking liaison with Semantha had, at least for the present, depleted his passion, permitting him a return to full-throated reality with his thoughts relatively unclouded by his urges.

Sex with her had been an amazing interlude, but, as he lay there, he didn't see how it could develop into more than that. Semantha would not fit well into his life. How could he explain her to his colleagues at the department holiday party? How embarrassing it would be. "Here, Dr. Fellsteon, meet the witch who tried to sacrifice me to the devil. I tried to kill her, but now we're lovers." And what about the arrest warrants? They couldn't be wished away, and probably, before long, she would be spending a good deal of time in jail. A relationship with Semantha offered the potential for so much more pain than their passion ever could confer pleasure.

And Cynthia? He couldn't just walk away from her, especially after they had both worked so hard to keep their relationship alive. And a long, bitter, expensive divorce would be very damaging to his career, which had taken off with the data generated when Saul hit the accelerator coil. With Cynthia by his side, he could go even further.

"I've gotta go home," Marco said. "Can I borrow the car?" Marco got up from the bed and began dressing.

"No, no, no," Semantha said. "You can't go." She jumped out of bed and prostrated herself in front of him. She reached for him, but he didn't move closer. He stared at her blankly, marveling at the intensity of her feelings but also troubled by them.

"Stay with me. Please, please," Semantha said, her voice trembling. "We can run away and find a place, maybe somewhere in the North Woods, far away from the world and all its problems. Live our lives alone with nature." She kissed his feet.

Marco looked down at her. He recalled how beautiful her dimples were when she smiled, her petite breasts he had just rubbed, her delectable ass he had just…. He couldn't deny his passion for her even though now muted after the intensity of their recent encounter.

"I'll come back," Marco said, but his tone was noncommittal. At that moment, he wanted to return to his work and normalcy. He wasn't sure about forever.

"No, it'll never be like this again. I can't live without you." She looked up at him, her eyes contorted and her mouth wide open, riveted in a silent scream.

Marco quickly turned and headed for the door.

X

Cynthia drove to the house on the river right after leaving Wigmore Street. Her anxiety almost overwhelmed her. What would she find? Would Marco be there? Was he being held prisoner, maybe about to be sacrificed?

As she slowed down to turn onto the narrow, one-lane gravel road leading to the pathway to the house, she almost ran into a huge tow truck that pulled out directly in front of her. Trailered behind it was the beat-up, burned-out, mangled mess of a car sitting on a wheeled dolly. She slammed on the brakes, scarcely missing getting hit. The tow truck driver was apparently in a hurry.

Cynthia was jolted by what she saw. While quite disfigured, there was no mistaking it, a BMW 2002 of the same make, color and model as Marco's car, complete with a scorched but recognizable Illinois license plate. While the numbers were badly burned, the first two letters were "MA." The car had to be his.

She took a good look at the vehicle as it passed by. There were no signs of blood or serious injury. *Could he walk away from that mess?* she wondered. He had led a charmed existence up until now, even fending off Saul's brutality. Had his luck run out this time? She felt a knot in her stomach thinking about what might have happened to him. She pined for answers.

She immediately turned around and chased after the tow truck, flashing her lights and honking her horn. The truck pulled over, Cynthia right behind him. She jumped out of her car and ran to the driver, her hair blowing in the wind.

"Whaddya want, lady?" the driver said.

"That's my husband's car."

"Was, is more like it."

"Do you know what happened?"

"All I know is I got me a call from this nice young lady to come and, you know, tow the car. She gave me the credit card number for some man. As I recall, she said she was his girlfriend or something like that. Don't really recall what she said. All I know is the card went through, and I got paid."

"What was the name she said was on the card?"

"Don't righly remember. Marc or sumpum like that."

Cynthia felt her face warm and her blood pressure rise. Girlfriend with Marco's credit card number? Feeling betrayed, she envisioned thrusting her dagger into Marco's balls and twisting hard. He had a lot of explaining to do. Now, if for no other reason, she had to find him and make him pay. *Fucker.*

She tried to remind herself, though, she needed to remain calm and logical until she knew all the facts, but it didn't look good.

She left the tow truck, turned back around, and drove to the pathway and parked. She walked down through the dark, over-grown cathedral of trees and bushes. Last time she had had two sworn officers with her. Now that she was alone, it felt different, eerie, chilling, almost haunted. The air was oppressively stuffy, an unholy scent lingered in the air. The bushes shook when she walked by as small animals scurried away and starlings high in the trees cackled. She was unnerved.

Cynthia felt a dark sense of evil as she reached the barn. She was startled by a possum running away as she peered in. Upon entering, she imagined what it had been like for Marco sitting in that old wooden chair anticipating his own death, fearful he could not pull off the escape. She envisioned the terror he must have felt.

Her thoughts turned to that woman Semantha, dressed all in black, standing with Saul behind the altar, which was still there. She pictured the scene that night—a bunch of witches dressed in black robes, the four large kerosene torches, all that chanting and incense, and Marco lying there naked, exposed, vulnerable.

A shiver flashed through Cynthia's body as she thought about him like that. She found him intensely attractive, body and intellect. She so much wanted him not to be the double-dealing bastard she feared he was.

Cynthia left the barn and walked to the house. She entered the kitchen. She had been there before when she came with the cops, but it felt different being alone in this disquieting setting. The table and chair were still there, the site of Marco's tryst with Semantha. A cold wind seemed to blow into the room from nowhere. She shivered and pulled her coat tightly around her neck.

"What's ya doing here?" a voice screamed. Startled, she turned and saw a middle-aged bald man wearing overalls standing in the doorway. He aimed a shotgun at her and cocked the trigger with an audible snap. Her shoulders shook.

"Don't shoot, please," Cynthia said, her wobbly voice giving away her fear. "I don't mean any harm. I'm looking for my husband."

"Pretty fucked up place to look for a husband." The man walked over to Cynthia and stuck the rifle in her gut. She noticed he walked very slowly and with a limp in his left leg.

"No, please no." Cynthia instinctively raised her hands. She tried to sound as defenseless as possible. The edges of her lips turned down as if about to cry. "I…I…I think he's been kidnapped. I thought maybe they brought him here. I saw them towing his car."

"Look, you, git off my property. I live next door. Bought this place because my wife an' I are sick and tired of the craziness goin' on here fer years. We live alone and want some peace and quiet. Chantin', goats, cars parked for miles on the road all night long, that noisy sailboat of theirs. Too much shit and evil. Yesterday, we found this weird lookin' guy with two beards lyin' naked in our boat house, throat slashed. Enough."

Cynthia gagged. She thought of Marco's description of Clem.

"All we want is solitude," the man said apologetically as he lowered the rifle.

"Do you know what happened?"

"Haint got no idea. I heard a commotion in the boat house an' by the time I got up and threw on some clothes, all I saw was a pretty youngish woman sort-a dragging a very tall man with curly Greek lookin'hair. It was like he was drugged. Found a trail of blood when it got light."

Cynthia gasped in surprise. She began to put the pieces together.

The Amtrak ticket, Marco's burned-out car, Clem's murder. Clem had taken the train to River Forest and abducted Marco to bring him here. But why, and why was he then murdered? By whom?

It sounded like Marco was injured. In the car wreck? When he was trying to run away? But who was the woman? Where does she fit in?

Was she trying to save Macro from Clem? Did she murder him to get away? Was she the same woman bringing cleaning supplies to the house on Wigmore Street? A piece of the puzzle was missing. Maybe Cynthia should go back to Wigmore Street.

"Can I at least look around?" Cynthia said with a wide, sweet smile. She winked.

"Make it quick," the man said.

Cynthia went outside where she noticed a piece of pink cloth hanging from one of the bushes near the black door, like it had been ripped off when someone in a hurry had passed by. She walked over and felt it. It was soft and a little dainty, like a woman's blouse. She saw that the bushes nearby had been disturbed. Branches had been broken, and the leaves had just withered. Whatever had happened, it was very recent.

A woman chased through the bushes? By Clem? Cynthia felt she was on the right path. She needed to look around some more.

The neighbor came to the kitchen door and peered at Cynthia poking around the bushes.

"Time to git," he yelled.

"Please sir. Only a few minutes more."

"I said git." He again raised his rifle as if he was about to shoot.

Cynthia looked at him, looked at his rifle. Would he really use it? She made a quick assessment. This old eccentric should be easy to ditch especially with his bum leg. And she hoped that somewhere near the house she could find more clues.

Cynthia turned around and ran as fast as she could, heading toward the back of the barn. She heard a shotgun fire and some loud cursing, but the old man did not follow. She stopped and looked around. She listened. Nothing.

That was easy. She smiled. This had been the first time she had ever faced down physical danger without so much as a blink. She felt proud. Maybe her swagger as a prosecutor was coming back.

She continued to look around. She saw a pathway to some vines which had been recently disturbed. She walked over and lifted them up, exposing a small clearing. At one side of the clearing, a pile of ropes lay on the ground. She examined one. It had been cut cleanly by a knife. She picked up the others. The same. She looked at the ground and saw a pool of freshly coagulated blood atop some dried leaves. Was it Marco's blood? Maybe Marco had been tied up in this clearing.

Seeing this, Cynthia felt relieved. Clem had brought Marco here, tied him up, and some woman had freed him, killing Clem to get away. Now she was fairly sure that Marco was alive and somewhere nearby. With the woman? Find the woman and she would probably find Marco. She decided to go back to the house on Wigmore Street.

First, she needed a cup of coffee.

*   *   *

MARCO grabbed the keys to the antiquated Buick and drove into St. Joe to get something to fortify himself for his long drive back to River Forest. There was only one restaurant open, an old-fashioned diner with Formica tabletops and red Naugahyde chairs and booths. He took a booth next to a window and ordered a cup of coffee.

It had only been a few minutes since he left her, but Marco was already beginning to feel Semantha's visceral pull. It was not going to be easy to walk away from her. He was not settled that he could live his life never seeing her again. He had to think about what to tell Cynthia when he saw her back in River Forest. With a long drive ahead, he had time to figure things out, think through an explanation.

As he finished his coffee and was about to get up and leave, Cynthia walked in. *No. My God, couldn't be,* he thought. *Her? Here? Now?* He was not prepared to face up to his wife yet. He became overcome with guilt for what he had done and ashamed of what he was thinking maybe he might do again.

Cynthia spotted Marco and stopped cold. Her eyes wide in shock, her mouth open, she hung motionless for a time. Then she smiled extravagantly, spread her arms open wide and rushed to him like a young girl running to greet her boyfriend returning from war.

"Marco! Oh my God, you're here and safe. Thank God! Oh my God," she said, her eyes filled with tears of joy as she kissed his cheek and wrapped him in a tight hug. Marco gave her only a loose embrace without standing up. Seeing his reaction, Cynthia dropped her arms; and her smile evaporated. She stepped back as her face took on the appearance of stunned dismay.

"What's wrong?" Cynthia asked.

"What are you doing here?" Marco scowled, masking his grave embarrassment and remorse. He wanted to escape, not so much from Cynthia as from his own dalliance. What would he say to her right then?

"Coming to find you, my dear." Her lips were twisted as if from pain.

"What's with the outlandish garb? Going off to war? And a dagger?" It had been her knocking on the door at 1356. He fought the urge to run to the car that instant and drive as far away as he could.

Cynthia's face reddened. "Wanted to be ready for anything. Aren't you going to invite me to sit down?" she asked, her voice filled with hurt.

Truth was, he didn't want her to sit down. He needed time alone. His impulse to flee overtook him.

"Look, Cynthia, I have no idea how you got here, but I'm late for a doctor's appointment and I really can't talk right now." He slid over on the bench of the booth and stood up. He gave Cynthia a peck on the cheek and headed for the door.

"Wait, what happened? What about your car? I saw it."

A sour urge overtook Marco.

"I'll call you," he said as he pushed the door open, not looking back.

Cynthia stood there, her mouth agape, frozen like a stone. She raised her hands to her eyes and sobbed dryly.

*   *   *

ABSOLUTELY THE WRONG MOMENT *for her to show,* Marco thought as he opened the car door, but he was amazed that she had figured out how to find him. He wouldn't have expected that from docile, meek Cynthia, couch potato Cynthia. *Maybe I underestimated her.* And he blanched when he thought how brusque he had been toward her. *I hope she understands. She does know how moody I can be.*

Marco's plan to go back to Chicago immediately changed. No use returning to the lab. He would be too distracted to get anything done.

Marco felt like he was in a whirlpool and had to swim hard against the current to get out. He was afraid he could never live without Semantha's intoxicating power. It set his soul on fire. But he worried that he needed dependable, resourceful Cynthia by his side to navigate his future. And he feared that he may have pushed her too far. He was quite sure that there was a limit to the abuse she would take. He needed to level with her and beg her forgiveness. As for Semantha, he couldn't leave her hanging. Whatever he did next, he knew it would change his life forever.

He started up the old Buick and began to drive. Without purpose or intent, he found himself drawn to the house on the river. He thought of the river, the tranquil flowing river, like a spirit, imbued with a sense of all humanity. He was sure the house was deserted now that Clem was dead. He hoped that he could sit on the bank and collect his thoughts, think about everything that had happened in the last two years, and make some decisions about his future—a future that now seemed more unsettled than ever. He didn't know what to do.

What he did know is that whenever he was with one of these women, he longed for what the other offered. He was in an impossible dilemma.

*   *   *

SEMANTHA WAS DEVASTATED when Marco left. Since Erzulie pulled her from the river, her hope of seeing him again had dominated her existence, given her a reason to carry on. Her past life, living with Pappie and teaching physics at the Berrien high school, good as it had been, was long since dissolved into history. She had nothing left but her fantasies about Marco. She could not let him go, not at least without a fight.

She went to Erzulie and begged her to use her truck—to go for a doctor's appointment, she said—and then drove to the house on the river, that house which had been the scene of so much of her life, that house where she had made real, passionate love to a man of substance for the first time, that house where she had gone from being a child to a woman, that house with all of its fond memories of Pappie, everything.

Maybe if she spent time alone at the house sitting on the shore and watching the water flow by, the river would help her compose herself, give her the strength to carry on...without Marco, if she had to.

*   *   *

Cʏɴᴛʜɪᴀ sᴛᴏᴏᴅ ᴀʟᴏɴᴇ in the diner after Marco walked out, crying and shaking. An old woman dressed like a gypsy and wearing a turban walked over. She put her arm around Cynthia and hugged her.

"There, there my sweet. I saw what happened. Men are all alike. Ur ah, don't you mind him, he'll be back, yes indeedy."

"Who are you?" Semantha asked.

"A friend in need is a friend indeed. I guarantee he'll be back."

"I don't think so." Cynthia leaned on the old woman's shoulder and cried some more. "I hate him."

But then she looked at the empty booth where he had been sitting. The coffee cup he had drunk from was still there, along with a spoon and a napkin next to a pile of sugar bags. She thought about how he would always say, "I like my sugar with a little coffee in it," wink, and chuckle as if he had told the greatest story in the world.

Coffee? Goodness. She thought back to their morning coffee on their honeymoon in Tahiti, every day for a week, watching the sun rise and drinking the best coffee she had ever tasted, followed by a champagne brunch and then a glorious swim in the south Pacific. She also recalled that wonderful night on the observation deck of the Empire State Building where Marco and she had professed love and became engaged, a highlight of her adult life.

There had been so many great times like this. Sure, he could be moody and dissolute, but then he would recover his charm once again, playful, sweet, and engaging. She still had profound questions, but, for her, he alone had offered her a route to escape her trite Iowa upbringing.

A life without him? Possibly, but she would lose so much.

She shan't be so hard on him.

Cynthia's white-hot anger dissipated. She realized that she was tethered to Marco by the violent force of stormy adoration. She played with a curl of her hair.

"But I need him…. I guess love him, too," she said quietly. "My God, my God, so much."

"Er, why'd he leave? A lovers' quarrel?" the old woman asked.

"I don't know. Sometimes it seems like he's in his own world."

"Men are all like that. That's why I never tied the knot. But my dear, by God's footstool, I've got some advice for you. Go someplace quiet and think this through. You've gotta clear your mind a little."

The old woman then told her about a quiet place along the river, now completely deserted, where she had spent many happy hours. Cynthia said she knew the place—all too well she knew it. She decided this old woman was right. Go back, avoid the old neighbor with a limp. She'd be quiet so as not to disturb him. A few hours watching the river go by might help her put the issue with Marco in perspective.

"What's your name, my dear," Cynthia asked.

"Memmie. I'm a friend of Erzulie."

"Who?"

"If you don't know her, find her. She will help you sort out what's happened. But for now, here's my advice: Fight for him with all you've got. Sometimes, that's what a woman gotta' do."

*   *   *

CYNTHIA WAS FIRST to arrive. She walked around the beat-up old house, then to the river, sitting down along the bank on dried leaves the wind had blown into a pile between the gnarled roots of an oak tree. It was like a little sanctuary abutting the river, hidden from the house and the rest of the shore by the tree. It felt like her own little world, a perfect place to calm her soul. She looked out on the water, seeking its guidance.

By now the sun was low in the sky, casting its rays on the gentle waves formed by a light breeze. She looked across the river and saw the autumn colors as the trees prepared for winter. Cynthia knew from Marco that this was the spot where he had jumped in the water to escape. It seemed too bucolic to have been the scene of such a horrific event.

As she took in the scene, she imagined the river water washing away her cares, her anxieties, even her passion for Marco. She buried her head in her hands and begged the river for peace.

*   *   *

SEMANTHA WALKED slowly down the lane and then to the house. And as she walked, she thought. *So much, so, much, so much.* Tears flowed and a couple of times, she sat down on the cold ground, overcome with emotion. The pain, my God the pain. *What did I ever do to deserve this? Finally, a man I could trust, but taken from me by a self-important, arrogant bitch.*

Samantha could feel her anger grow as she continued to walk toward the river. *The injustice of it all, the injustices I have suffered, now this.* A wind had kicked up, making the screen door on the kitchen bang against its frame. She stopped and thought about that kitchen, her time with Marco there. For her it was a temple.

She braced herself with desperate resolve. She was prepared to do what she had to do to hold onto this man and make him her own. Maybe Pappie would appear in the mist along the shore and guide her. But for sure seeing the river and tapping into its power would help her prepare for the task ahead.

Semantha had not seen or been in the river since the time Marco had attempted to kill her. She was not sure she could dive back in, but she decided to try, sort of a crude baptism to stiffen her resolve in her fight for her man. She walked up to the edge and slid easily out of the jumpsuit she was wearing. She dove in, her body bristling from the cold, but she felt empowered by the plunge. She shrieked.

*   *   *

UPON HEARING the splash and a shout downstream, a tingle passed up Cynthia's spine and the hair on the back of her neck stood on end.

Cynthia thought that she had been completely alone, but she was not. Who could be in this deserted place?

As she got up to find out, she grabbed the handle on her dagger for comfort. It hung loosely from the belt around her waist. Facing down the old neighbor with the shotgun had been easy. She had correctly judged him more scared than she was. Now she was no longer so sure of her capacity to confront real danger. Powerful dread threatened her tepid bravery.

The wind began to blow harder, making the river's waves beat furiously against the shore. A tied-up rowboat banged the dock like a hammer on an anvil. Cynthia moved out from her hiding place slowly, one step at a time, horrified by what she may find, a feeling potentiated by the troubled water.

When she reached the open, Cynthia was startled by a person outlined against the setting sun, drying herself. Her anxiety went up a notch.

"Who in God's name are you?" she asked, her voice trembling.

Semantha, also obviously taken by surprise, stopped and looked at Cynthia. For a minute, neither moved.

"What do you mean, who are you? I'm the owner's daughter. You have no right...."

Cynthia had seen the owner. Was this really his daughter? The man had told her he and his wife lived alone.

"The old guy who lives next door?" Cynthia asked.

A sad look came to Semantha's eyes.

"My father was killed, but before he died, we came here all the time. This is MY place. Now you go." Semantha gestured with her hand.

"No, you're not the own..." Cynthia said, but then hesitated as she thought, *the old warlock who was killed?* She stared at the naked woman in front of her, water still dripping from her hair.

"Semantha?" Cynthia asked after a second. Cynthia's stomach churned like it was filled with slithering snakes. Her body shivered.

Semantha nodded, threw on her clothes, then walked close to Cynthia so they were almost nose to nose. She hurled Cynthia a mean look.

"You know my name. How?" she asked, her voice a twisted demand.

Cynthia opened her mouth, but words did not come out.

"Come on, tell me," Semantha said as she gave Cynthia a push on her shoulder.

Cynthia stepped back. *So, she's not dead after all, the Jezebel Marco secretly craves?* And they're still in contact. This must be the person who called the tow truck and saved Marco from Clem. What betrayal, what evil. She clenched her teeth, hot with anger.

Her rival for Marco's affection stood defenseless before her, and she with a weapon. She thought about plunging it into Semantha's heart. Her hand moved toward the dagger but then she stopped herself. Despite this person's incarnate evil, she could not imagine taking someone else's life, even for Marco. Then what else could she do to respond to this affront? She felt weak, impotent. Inadequate.

"I..I..I…"She turned to run.

"Oh no, you wait one hot minute." Semantha grabbed Cynthia by the arm and twisted her around. She held tight.

"I've seen you before. Your clothes. You came to my house this morning. Why?"

Cynthia began to cry. She nodded her head back and forth. Her skill with words was of no use in fending off Semantha's physicality. She had no way out.

"My…my… h-h-husband," she blurted out meekly without thinking. Somewhere a tree branch broke off and crashed to the ground.

Semantha's eyes narrowed and she wailed as if leading a cadre of mourners. A thin, sinister smile parted her lips. She stood there, staring down Cynthia.

"So, you're the cunt who stole my man from me?" she declared. A blast from the wind blew Semantha's hair in 17 different directions at once, giving her a Medusa-like appearance.

The woman's crudeness offended Cynthia, neutralizing some of her galloping fear. She felt a call to action.

"You're supposed to be dead," she said. She sensed her heart pounding hard.

Semantha frowned and pointed her finger at Cynthia. "You wish, but I'm not so easy to kill. He's my man and I'm going to have him," she said.

"Marco? Your man? He's not…" Cynthia put her hands over her ears. "I will not listen to this dribble." Semantha's audacity revolted her. But was she ready for a fight?

"No, you listen. He loves me passionately. And you…."

Cynthia was pushed into a corner, no more escape.

"No, no, no. He married me. He loves me." Cynthia shook her head back and forth, tears streamed down her face. Unsure of Marco's love, her words lacked certainty.

"You bore him, don't you know that?" Semantha pranced and kicked her feet like a stallion in the starting gate, getting ready for a big race. "Look at you. You even look stupid dressed like some camouflaged tin soldier."

"I…I…" In her years as a criminal lawyer and prosecutor, Cynthia had never experienced invective like this. She was unsure how to counter it.

"You offer him nothing." Semantha's voice trembled. "You drain his energy and leave him starved. Starved for love, hear me? And you…"

"No, not…"

"Now I suppose you say, 'I'm his wife and go away,'" Semantha continued. "It doesn't work that way. Not in my world…"

"In your world?" Cynthia's fear evaporated. Her mind cleared for the struggle, but she saw it as so much more than a fight with this woman over a man. No, this was a clash of their upbringing, their passions, their unresolved agonies.

Outraged finally by Semantha's attacks, Cynthia's old prosecutorial swagger and self-confidence, long dormant in her luxurious River

Forest prison, surfaced in full force. She was impassioned like for a closing argument in a capital case. She shook her fist in Semantha's face.

"And what's that, the world of pain, misery, evil?" She looked away then glowered. "I'm sorry he didn't finish you off!" she yelled.

Semantha did not flinch.

"You don't own him," she exclaimed. "Why did you marry him anyway? Love? Or just trying to prove something to yourself?"

Cynthia's face turned bright red, and her eyes took on a menacing glint. Samantha's statement had hit too close to home. Her furor expunged the last vestige of her timidness. She, too, began to prowl back and forth, like a wolf eyeing its prey.

"You know nothing of love, getting all hot and bothered with every teenage boy in town," she said.

"Enough!" Semantha yelled, her eyes flaring with fiery intensity. She went for Cynthia's dagger and got her hands on it. But Cynthia knocked it to the dusty ground before Semantha had a good hold. Without the dagger, Cynthia felt laid bare. She had to get it back.

Semantha grabbed Cynthia around the wrist and squeezed tight, forcing the breath out of Cynthia's chest with a loud wheeze. They began to struggle, yelling and groaning, kicking and biting, pulling at each other's hair. Cynthia felt her clothes wetting with sweat. Semantha's strong lilac perfume turned her stomach.

Powered by passion and feeling under mortal attack, Cynthia fought as if to the death. The two fell to the ground, both trying to grab the knife. Their fight kicked up a cloud of dust that enveloped them.

*   *   *

MARCO SCREAMED as he walked around the side of the house and saw Semantha kneeling over Cynthia with a dagger held high.

"My wife!" He threw himself at Semantha to get her to stop but the momentum from his body drove the dagger deep into Cynthia's neck. She groaned as a river of her blood spurted out, spraying both Semantha and Marco. Her eyes glassed over.

"No, no, no!" he yelled. He ripped off his shirt and held it against her neck trying to stop the bleeding. It was of no use.

Cynthia looked at Marco for the last time. She reached up to him with her finger. He touched hers in return. Then her hand fell back. By the sweet look on her face, Marco sensed that she forgave him. Her breathing became shallow and her complexion bone white. As she closed her eyes, she whispered, "Marco, I love you and always will." Then she moved no more. The wind became still, as if holding its breath, and the river went flat, as if overwhelmed by the tragedy.

Marco's guttural cry echoed through the air. He fell to the ground next to Cynthia and hugged her with all his might. "No, Cynthia, don't leave me! I love you, too!"

Semantha stood motionless, dagger still in her hands, watching Marco hold Cynthia's body. When Marco finally looked up, his pale and blotchy face was bruised with grief. His puffy, red eyes sent a hateful blast toward Semantha. Semantha, her brow furrowed, smiled and chuckled quietly.

"Now you are free, Marco," she said, dropping the blood-covered knife to the ground.

"Free? Free? No, you have just killed the only person…." — he howled, his body hot and trembling — "…I ever loved. How could you do this…"

"Oh no."

"… to me?"

"But what about all those terrible things you told me about her back at Pappie's house? I did this for you, for us!"

Marco was disgusted by her impudence. His eyes took on a savage deadness. As he looked at this beast before him, he filled with undistilled hatred.

"No, my sweet babe, you did this for yourself. Don't you ever think about anything but your own desire?

"No, no, God, don't say that. No. I—I—I love you." Tears streamed down her cheeks as she threw herself at Marco, arms outstretched. "I've given up everything for you, even my relationship with Erzulie."

Marco's mouth opened wide. "Who?"

"The woman who brought me back to life. She loved me and wanted to take care of me for as long as she lived."

"You mean...." Marco glowered. "Lovers?" Marco winced and turned his head away. *The final outrage*, he thought.

Semantha tentatively shook her head. "No," but she looked confused. He hesitated again, still waiting for her reply.

"Not exactly. Well..."

"Get away from me. You're a whore. You know nothing about love!" Marco screamed. His face had turned bright red, his eyes became enormous and protruded. He reached down and grabbed the dagger. He lunged at her, dagger held high. "This time, it's going to stick," he said. He fixated on the pleasure he would get by destroying her.

Semantha jumped to the side. The knife missed her body, but it ripped her blouse and made a surface cut on her chest. While Marco readied for another try, she ran toward the house and picked up a large branch.

"Don't come any closer," she said, as she waved the branch in the air. Marco stopped but still held the dagger high.

"Please, listen to me," Semantha said. "Didn't I show you my love when I carried you out of that field? When I killed Clem to protect you, when I nursed you back to health? You live today because of me."

"Pretty twisted. You low life," Marco said. "I'm here because you had me kidnapped and brought here for who knows what." He spit on the ground.

"No, dear Marco, you are here because you always have been driven by your own narcissistic lust. Nothing more, nothing less. Only difference between you and me is your mind fuck at that lab. I'll bet the truth be known, you probably even cooked the books to get the data you needed. Look at yourself, Mr. Marco."

Marco's body twitched. She had guessed the awful truth.

*   *   *

FOR A WHILE, Marco and Semantha stood like statues glowering at each other. The smell of Cynthia's death hung in the humid, clammy air. It was getting dark and their bodies cast long shadows on the earth in the unkempt backyard. In the distance a crow cawed.

After what seemed like forever, Semantha's face took on a look of revulsion overlaid with resignation. She dropped the branch, took off her clothes and stood naked, her body stiffly erect, her arms widely outstretched.

"Come with your knife," she said. "I'm ready. Come on."

Marco did not move. He was anguished, not sure what to do.

"What's wrong?" Semantha said. "Are you too much of a coward? Come on, you miserable excuse for a man. Come on."

Then, inflamed by the affront, Marco's cheeks puffed out and his breathing became heavy. Spittle dripped from his mouth.

He'd had enough. He ran to Semantha and plunged the dagger into her chest. Blood splattered on his clothes and face. He struck her again and again, in furious hatred. A high-pitched, groan-like scream emitted from her mouth each time he struck.

After his last strike, she stopped breathing and dropped to the ground. For a moment, Marco did not move. He stared at Samantha's body. The last light from the setting sun faded away.

"Ooooh!" Marco screamed as he fell to his knees in front of Semantha's body. He began to howl with uncontrolled passion.

"God, my God, what in the name of all Hades have I done? My life is ruined! The two women I loved are dead…ooooh!"

Again, I've killed. Nooo… Too many people dead! Misery, hatred, destruction, Eternal damnation… Too much, too much, great God almighty, too much. He waved his arms and spun around again and again. He headed for the river.

Marco took off his bloody clothes and jumped into the cold water. It felt harsh and unforgiving. He swam down to the muddy bottom and clutched a reed. He took a deep breath and felt his lungs fill with water. His chest became a heavy rock pulling him down into oblivion. Spontaneously he grabbed his throat and coughed but to no effect.

Komm, Susser Tod, he thought. *What's done is done. It all returns to nothing.*

Bright purple and white lights flashed in his mind, then a warm and accepting undifferentiated glow. He sensed himself moving toward it. Finally, blackness.

Moments later, an old woman carrying a very large, old-fashioned kerosene lantern walked to the shore and jumped in.

XI

ERZULIE WIPED the cold water from Marco's shivering body and covered him with her cloak. She rolled him onto his back and gave him a hard punch on his chest. He coughed and river water spewed from his mouth. She hit him again. He coughed again, more water.

"Ohhh!" Marco howled as his arm covered his eyes. He laid there moaning for a minute. Then he stopped and struggled to sit up. In the dim lantern light, he saw a strange old woman wearing only underclothes. The lantern gave her an otherworldly aura as the deepening shadows hid part of her face in darkness.

"What are you doing? I want to die. I must…" His only thought was to return to the enveloping peace death promised. He stood up, staggered a bit, and took a step toward the river. But his knees buckled under him, and he fell back to the ground. He struggled to get up again.

"No, you don't," Erzulie said. She gave him a judo cut right to the neck. He fell back down and hit the ground hard. This time he did not try to get back up.

"Why?" he asked, looking up at the old woman.

"Death's too good for you. Look." She waved her arm as she raised the lantern so he could see the bodies. "Two women died and one, my little pet." Erzulie broke into tears as she cupped her face in her hands. "I loved her so much."

"So did I, I guess. She just…"

"Wait," Erzulie exclaimed. "Marco?"

"Who are you?"

"Why did you kill my pet? She was all I had!"

Lover… my pet… no…agg! Marco's brain began to whirl. Images of devils, snakes, giant river rats, men with whips, torture chambers, suddenly vividly appeared then vanished in an instant.

"Where am I, who am I? What is happening to me? Too much, too much." He held his head in his hands, trying to stop his mind from running away, but couldn't. He pulled hard on his hair, shook his head, and waved his arms. He felt like he had been overtaken by a perverse, diabolical force. He struggled to his feet and began to pace around Erzulie and her lantern, making growling noises like a wild beast on the hunt.

"You are the devil! Have you come to torture me?" Marco screamed.

Erzulie stood watching Marco with dread written on her face.

Marco's mind went blank.

XII

Marco's eyes opened. He moaned. He was in a small, windowless room with gray padded walls, lying on a cot with a thin yellowed blanket. He was dressed in an orange jumpsuit and confined to a straitjacket, its straps hugging him tight like a boa constrictor crushing its prey. A steel door with a small window and bars was closed, but he could hear the yelling and screaming of other men outside. The frigid space smelled musty and strongly of urine. His head throbbed and he had a sharp pain in his right upper arm. He felt nauseated and vomited into the seatless porcelain commode next to the cot. Murky water came out.

"Whaaa!" he screamed at the top of his voice.

"Hey, pretty boy's awake," he heard someone yell.

"Mine first…" someone else said. "Easy with that ol' straitjacket."

Someone laughed. "Gonna be a good time tonight."

Other male voices whistled and shrieked. Marco heard metal banging on metal.

A key turned in the lock. The door opened and an immense guard, weighing maybe 300 pounds, walked in. A patch on his sleeve read *Berrien County Jail. Sergeant.*

"You awake?" the man asked.

Marco nodded. He was too groggy to speak.

"C'mon, buster boy. You gonna see the doc an' then you gonna get booked. You put on quite a show for the boys last night. Pretty crazy when you come in, screaming and ranting. Insane shit."

Marco rubbed his eyes. "What happened? Where am I?" he asked.

The guard's face contorted. "Shuddup. I'll tell you when you can speak."

The guard pulled Marco up from the cot and pushed him through the door. Holding Marco by his straitjacket, the guard marched him down the corridor past the other cells in the block. The prisoners cackled and whistled.

"Bitch!" someone yelled, another "Sweet ass!" A third, "You's my booty." Marco hardly heard them. He felt detached, numb, like he was there, but not really.

*   *   *

Marco's mind escaped. Instead of being shoved down the prison corridor, he pictured himself processing down the aisle in Roosevelt Chapel wearing his flowing black robe with the PhD sash resting on his shoulders. His colleagues clapped as their eyes followed him, their adulation lifting Marco to the pinnacle of self-satisfaction and glowing pride. A chamber ensemble played *Pomp and Circumstance*. Dean Ricmond welcomed him to the dais and opened the ceremony.

"We are all delighted to be here to invest Dr. Marco Adamos with tenure. It is a reflection not only of his academic accomplishments, which are substantial, but also of his service to the work of Fermilab and the broader scientific community. Doctor, we salute you," he said.

Eyes closed, the dean bowed slightly in Marco's direction. Cynthia, sitting in the first row of the auditorium, wiped tears away with a hanky. Marco couldn't have been happier.

*   *   *

"Stop dragging your feet and move along," the guard said, jerking Marco back to the present. He gave Marco a rough push. Marco winced and groaned. "The doc's waiting for ya."

They arrived at the end of the cellblock and a buzzer sounded, allowing the guard to open a gate to the block. He pushed Marco down the hallway to a door with a stenciled sign that read *Medical.* The guard knocked, and when the voice inside said "Ya," he opened the door and shoved Marco in.

"Stand here," he said to Marco. "I'll be outside, Doc." He pulled the door shut as he walked out.

"Welcome, Adamos," a man said, not looking up from a file he was examining. He was wearing a soiled white coat and was seated at a gray metal desk. A plastic clip-on name tag said *Medical Director.* He looked at Marco, offered him a weak smile, and motioned with his hand. "Sit down. I'm Jim Stevens. Call me Doc. I handle the psychiatric cases here at the jail."

"Psychiatric?" Marco asked.

Stevens put down his pen. His eyes surveyed Marco up and down as if he was looking for signs of madness. He took out a hanky and blew his nose.

"You were pretty agitated when you came in last night. I had to give you a big dose of Pentobarbital. That got you calmed down. Your arm hurt?"

"Can you take this thing off me?"

"Sure," Stephens said. He walked over, loosened the straps, and let the straitjacket fall to Marco's lap. Marco sighed and began rubbing his arms. "Let's see how you do without it."

"I want to call my attorney."

"They'll handle that when you're booked. First thing after an injection of Pento, we've got to make sure you're not having a reaction, and your episode is under control. Let me see your right arm." A big lump on his bicep was black and blue.

Episode? Holy Christ...

"The guard will bring you a Xanax every four hours. It's not optional. Take it, hear me? That'll keep you under control."

Under control?

"And you'll be on the suicide watch."

*   *   *

"I'M IN BARCELONA, Marco," Frank said, sounding irritated. Frank Douglas was Marco's longtime friend and lawyer. "I'll get on the next flight I can, but I won't be back probably until tomorrow or Tuesday. I'll try to get in touch with someone else to come and bail you out, but it's Sunday. Sorry. What about Cynthia?"

"She's dead."

"God almighty. No."

"Frank, I need you so much. I don't know what's going on. Please come as soon as you can. I'm scared to death. Please. The other prisoners are—"

"What in the name of the Lord? What happened?"

"…threatening me. I'm so scared." Marco then told Frank as much as he remembered from the night before, which wasn't much. The last thing Marco remembered was standing next to that old broad along the river.

"What am I going to do?" Marco asked.

"Boy, you can really get yourself into some humdingers," Frank said. "Don't plan on getting any sleep tonight. And don't offer them any information. Don't answer any questions. Did they book you yet?"

"Yes."

"Charged with?"

"First degree murder." Marco shivered as a tingle went up his spine. "I'm—"

The door to the telephone room opened. A guard poked his head in and yelled, "Time's up," He grabbed Marco by the arm and jerked him to his feet. "Back to your cell."

"But I'm not done—"

"Yes, you are." The guard grabbed the receiver and put it back on the cradle.

It was the same march back to his cell as when he left, with the same catcalls, and the same threats. The guard opened his cell door and shoved him in.

"Chow at noon." He slammed the cell door shut and locked it. The sound of the key seemed isolating and final. Marco laid down on the cot and tried to breathe deeply to calm himself. He wished he had learned how to meditate like his orthopedic surgeon friend had recommended.

As he lay there, his head began to clear, and bits and pieces of his memory returned. The gruesome details of his wife's terrible murder and his role in it played over and over. That he delivered the deadly wound drove him to distraction. One time after another, he thought about what he could have done differently to save her. He cursed himself. *I'm a wretched godforsaken creature,* he repeatedly thought.

Marco began beating his head against the padded wall. *Four deaths, my Lord, four deaths. Will it never end?* Marco was sweating profusely, but yet he shook as if he was outside on a freezing day. *No one to call or help. Can I make it through the night?*

A guard banged on the door. "Hey, in there! No more punching your head like that or you'll get the restraints."

Marco laid back down and stared at the ceiling.

*   *   *

He recalled the lecture he had given to the quantum physics section of the National Academy of Sciences only two months ago.

"…and that nano-second power delay I utilized to get the data has been a breakthrough in accelerator technology. It is now recognized around the world. Cerne has adopted it."

The attendees clapped.

"But I owe everything to my friend and mentor Gordon Fellsteon, head of my department at Fermilab. He gave me the chance I needed." Marco looked into the crowd and waved his hand as if to say, "Stand up, Doctor!"

A tall man with a full head of white hair rose and smiled broadly. He waved as the audience clapped some more.

But now, Marco buried his head in the dirty yellow pillow and began to weep with unremitting sobs of anguish, thinking about his lie. The power delay wasn't his innovation at all. Just chance when Saul hit the coils. *Oh God, take my life, please God.*

Despite the din outside and the hostile surroundings, he cried himself to sleep.

*   *   *

MARCO DIDN'T SLEEP long.

"Get yourself up," a guard hollered as he unlocked Marco's cell door. "You's got a visitor."

Those were the best words Marco had heard for a long time. *What a relief, Frank came through.* Marco thanked his lucky stars for a friend like Frank. The tightness in his shoulders and back relaxed.

But no lawyer was sitting on the other side of the glass when he went to the visitor's room. Instead, it was the old lady who Marco saw immediately before his mind went blank, the person who claimed to have been Semantha's lover. She was still dressed in her black robe. Marco shook. *What's she doing here?*

"I've come to bond you out," she said with a thin, pretend smile. "Thank God I had enough in the mattress."

"I, I, I…" Marco was so dumbfounded he could not form words.

"But here's something for you." Erzulie shoved a daisy into the two-way tray with her gnarled right hand. "Play that game. You know, 'She loves me.'"

"Now? But I…"

"Just do it." Erzulie smirked, her face taking on a bitter and angry look. Marco saw he was in no position to offend his rescuer.

He pulled the petals off the flower, one by one. They fell to the metal shelf in front of the visitor's window as he repeated the words of the game. When only one petal was left, he pulled it off and said, "She loves me." He was silent for a minute. "What's this supposed to mean?" Marco asked.

"You'll find out."

*   *   *

"Why'd you do this?" Marco asked Erzulie as they walked out of the courthouse. The sky was overcast but it was a warm June day. Still, Marco shivered as if from the cold.

Erzulie motioned for them to sit down on a park bench in front of the Courthouse, right next to the statue of General Grant. A strong wind blew Marco's oily, disheveled hair into knots. He stroked the stubble on his face as he acclimated to the outside light.

"How much do you remember?" Erzulie asked. She stared at him as if waiting for an answer. Her face looked sad. Her lips were down-turned, and her eyes were partly closed like she had not slept for days. A couple of scraggly white hairs grew out from her chin. Years of anguish had scored her brow and cheeks with deep wrinkles.

A young couple dressed as if they were out on a date strolled by, laughing and smiling. To Marco, it seemed like they were from another planet, so distant was their happiness from his misery. He recalled the good times with Cynthia and longed to be with her. That, too, seemed like a universe away.

"A little is coming back, but nothing from after you told me who you were."

"Yeah, you got too crazy for me to handle, so I had to call the police. Against my better judgment. They usually muck things up in this town. And they don't like me, to boot."

Marco recalled when Saul was stalking him at Fermilab, and the police came. They were no help then, either. He rubbed his forehead.

"But to answer your question, at first I thought, fuck 'im; he killed my pet…let 'im rot. But then I thought about what I had done to my little pet, leaving her alone to face Clem. I began to feel guilty."

Erzulie looked away and a tear came to her eye. She wiped it away with her finger. "I decided not to let my own shit get in the way this time. And I know Semantha would have wanted me to help you."

Erzulie stopped talking. She moved close and turned so her eyes were inches from Marco's. She took his hand in hers. Marco could feel her leathery skin and hot breath on his face.

"Besides, I always try to find a way to help people fix up what needs fixing, if I can," she said meekly, almost as a plea. "So, I came."

Marco was flabbergasted by Erzulie's statement, especially coming from this weird, witch-looking character. *Admirable*, he thought. But then he recalled times when he had done exactly the opposite, tear down rather than mend. The thought made him uneasy, ashamed. But no time for internal self-flagellation right then, he decided. He searched for a way to change the subject.

"Clem? He seemed pretty crazy to me," Marco said.

"Yes, but I could control him if I needed to." Erzulie's brow wrinkled. "I abandoned her to him. I was feeling jealous and hurt."

Erzulie cleared her throat.

"I didn't want to feel that way again. I knew what would happen if you stayed in there," she said, nodding her head in the direction of the jailhouse. "From what Semantha told me about you, there probably wouldn't have been much left of you after a couple of days."

At that moment, a police car went by with its siren blaring. The sound sent a shiver up Marco's spine. Without thinking, he grabbed Erzulie's hand, seeking solace.

"Don't worry, my son, it's not for you," she said, patting his hand like he was a schoolboy. Having her sitting with him calmed Marco. He shuddered at the thought of what would have happened if she had not come. Just then, the tinny-sounding clock in the old church tower nearby struck three. Marco had lost track of time.

"And, what else do I have to do?" Erzulie chuckled. "It gets pretty lonely out there in the woods." Despite her brittle, dried-out look, there was a sweetness in her voice, like Marco's mother on those rare occasions when she spent an afternoon with him.

"Thank you so much," Marco said, not knowing what else he could say or do. Ignoring Erzulie's rank smell, he threw his arms around her and gave her a tight hug. He could feel her bony frame through her robe. "I don't know what I would have done…"

Erzulie placed her finger on Marco's lips, shook her head, and gave the hint of a smile. "There, there, my sweet boy. You are out…at least for now."

"Out of the slammer, but nothing else. I don't even have a place to stay in this godforsaken county. No family, no friends, my lawyer out of the country. Easier to die."

"A retreat to the void is no answer. There are motels…"

"I lost my wallet with my credit cards, and I can't leave the county until the arraignment, which is not until next week." He sighed. "I guess you could say I'm homeless." Marco thought of a pamphlet he had seen once which said that everyone is only a few chance occurrences away from homelessness. He remembered how, at the time, he had been sure such a thing could never happen to him.

Erzulie looked down as if in thought. After a minute, she pushed back a couple of stray hairs from her forehead and placed her hand on his knee.

"You can come and stay with me," she said in a quiet whisper, patting his knee slowly, a motherly gesture that Marco took as assurance of her intentions. A smile appeared on her face, likely happy that she might have a visitor. "My truck is right across the street." She waived at a rusty, old blue Dodge pickup truck.

"I didn't even get your name, my friend," Marco said as he stood up, took her by the arm, and began walking to the truck.

Erzulie didn't respond.

*   *   *

THE NEXT MORNING, Marco awoke in Semantha's old room, coughing and spitting up phlegm. It felt strange sleeping on the same cot as the woman he had killed. He could feel her presence, smell her smells. When he thought about what else had happened on that bed, his stomach turned. He wondered how he would get in touch with Frank when he came back from Barcelona. His cellphone had disappeared in all the commotion.

As he sat up, he gasped for air. His throat was sore and his lungs on fire. He put his hand on his forehead. It felt red hot, but he shivered as if it was freezing. When he tried to stand up, he fell back to the cot, quite dizzy. He heard Erzulie banging some pots around outside his space. She pulled aside the curtain divider and peered in.

"Some bad humors, eh Marco?" she asked.

Marco broke out into a fit of coughing. He made no effort to cover his mouth.

"That's a bad one," Erzulie said. "It sounds like pneumonia. Probably something you picked up in that hellhole."

Marco coughed some more and then tried to clear his throat. "My lungs, uh…, are…"

"You're going to need treatment. Pneumonia doesn't cure itself."

"God almighty, more pain. When will it stop?"

"You must have really pissed off someone in the spirit world." Erzulie grimaced.

"You know a doctor?" Marco asked.

"Yes, me."

"No, I mean a real doctor."

Erzulie furrowed her eyebrow. "You don't think I'm real?" A blast emitted from Erzulie's eyes, and she began to breathe more heavily. Marco could see that the old broad had a temper.

"You never did tell me your name," Marco said.

"Erzulie Perez. That's Dr. Erzulie Perez, MD, to you. I nursed Semantha back to life. Took a little time and some of my special potions, but she came back."

"But you—"

"I know… Don't look like a doctor. Well, I'm also a Santera."

"Santera?"

"Priest of Santeria."

"Santeria?" Marco asked.

Erzulie's face turned crimson. "You want my help or not?"

Marco laid back down and slept for a while. When he got up, he parted the curtain and discovered Erzulie kneeling on the bare floor in front of a little altar next to the stove and sink. It was covered with a gold cloth and a burning white candle was sitting on it. Letters on the side of the candle, looking a little like "ASF," had been crudely carved by hand.

A saucer with some slowly burning substance was situated next to the candle. White smoke rose from it, filling the hovel with an incandescent fog, smelling like a mixture of anise, basil, and marigold.

An unadorned doll was next to the saucer, as well as three gray stones, smooth like they had been at the bottom of a fast-moving brook for centuries. Marco noticed that a strand of curly, jet-black hair had been sewn into the doll's chest. It looked like his. He felt violated.

Apparently unaware that Marco was watching, Erzulie picked up the doll and held it high.

"Ghede and Loco, come," she said. "Oshun, here is Marco," she said to the doll, staring intently at it. She paused. "Marco," she said more loudly. She paused again. "Marco," she said at the top of her voice. She then sprinkled the doll with some water from a bowl sitting on the floor next to the altar.

She began to chant in a thin, high-pitched tone.

"Oriate, Orisha fifetu.

Aro gog, Orisha fifetu..." [2]

*   *   *

AFTER REPEATING the same phrase over and over, she blew into the doll's mouth and nose. She set the doll down and her head dropped to the tabletop. Her arms fell limply to her sides. Her body began to shake all over.

____

[2] "Master, bring life through Orisha; We call upon the Orisha with devotion.

Marco stood riveted, watching. He recalled the bizarre ritual he had been forced to see when he lay in front of the altar at the black mass. *Tame by comparison, but still…* By now, nothing phased him.

Suddenly Erzulie jumped to her feet, grabbed a nail that had been sitting on the table, and drove it into the doll's chest with an old spoon. Marco let out a gasp and Erzulie gave him a momentary sideways glance. She grabbed the doll, walked over to Marco, and shook it in his face.

"Wake up." She was silent for a minute. "You should feel better very soon." She placed her free hand on Marco's forehead. "Your fever has already come down."

"What kind of….?" Marco's face scrunched up.

"Don't question me, you toad," Erzulie said, her voice raised, her eyes narrowed. "I call on my orisha for you and you get upset. What gives with you?"

"I appreciate what you're trying to do, but…" He stopped and thought for a second, finally deciding he shouldn't argue with her. "I really do." He tried to smile.

Erzulie seemed to calm. Her raised eyebrows fell back to normal.

"I've got some potion for you to drink," she said. "It'll finish off the job." Erzulie took out a gold-colored plastic chalice, filled it with some dark, thick, heavy liquid from a glass bottle stored below the sink, and offered it to him. Marco could smell the musty odor of the potion. He held up his hand as if to say, "No thanks" with a slight sneer.

But he did feel better than the night before. He thought it must have been a quick-acting bug his body fended off easily after a good sleep. "Still, I do thank you for offering…I guess."

"Don't thank me, thank Oshun. She's my orisha. Oshun is the goddess of love and sweetness and the youngest of the orishas. She rules the rivers, where I found Semantha and, I guess, you. She told me she kept the river from drowning you. The river's not done with you yet."

"I still don't understand." Marco rubbed his brow. "I can't imagine you like me very much."

Erzulie looked grim. "I told you yesterday. It gets pretty lonely out here." She offered the chalice again. He held up his hand a second time.

"So, what were you doing with the foolish doll?"

Erzulie shook her head and scowled. "Not a foolish doll. It's voodoo. Powerful. You'll see." Erzulie's eyes grew wide. She again held the chalice in front of Marco. "Here. You'll feel better."

"You believe in all this crap?" he asked.

Erzulie pounded her bony finger into Marco's chest.

"Boy, you've got so much to learn and not much time." She went silent for a second. "What we believe is what's real, not all this phony science. Talk about hocus-pocus. Objects made up of mostly empty space, c'mon."

Marco decided it was not the right time to get into a debate about the nature of matter, but he didn't find the comparison persuasive.

Erzulie then started to swoon, swaying back and forth like a worshiper at the Wailing Wall. Her head went back, and the pupils of her eyes disappeared into her head.

"The world is filled…*filled*… with spirits," she said as she swayed. Her voice quivered like she was possessed. "I feel them in this room, with us, right now. Oh you cursed being, feel them or be, be, be damned for all eternity!"

Macy the cat arched his back, squealed, and ran out of the room.

The hair on the back of Marco's neck stood up and a chill ran down his spine. He dropped to his knees, astonished by Erzulie's passion and power.

"Believe, you devil!" Erzulie shrieked. "Believe and they will act. Try it for God's sake. Try it, you fool!"

Erzulie's eyes were wide with passion, her white hair stood on end and sweat beaded on her forehead.

Marco began to tremble despite himself. For a moment, he stopped thinking. Then he began to breathe heavily, like he, too, had been possessed.

"Frank, please, Frank," he uttered over and over. Then he fainted dead away.

When he awoke, Erzulie stood over him. "You feel it?"

Marco did not reply, but the spell had been broken. "It's Tuesday, right?" he asked in a monotone.

"Yes."

Frank would probably be back by now.

"Can I use your phone?" Marco asked.

"No phone. They disturb my privacy. If I need to make a call, I drive into Watervliet. It's only four miles. I'll take you."

Marco wanted no favors from this deranged old woman. He couldn't imagine what was in the chalice.

"I'll walk. But thanks for the place to stay." He was trying to act calm but inside he was seething with anxiety. What he had just witnessed ate at his soul, and his uncertain future gnawed at his being.

Erzulie squinted as she placed her hand on his shoulder.

"Good luck, and I mean that. I cast a shell oracle before you woke up. It said I'll be seeing you again."

XIII

"No cushy plea deal this time, " Frank said. He and Marco were meeting in Frank's walnut-paneled Chicago office on LaSalle Street to strategize about how to handle his indictment. The Berrien County Prosecutor, Martin Dunland, had allowed Marco to leave the county for the meeting.

Marco had known Frank since he coached Marco in junior high Little League softball. He was a well-respected criminal defense lawyer and also a passionate sailor. Marco had learned how to sail on Frank's boat, *Provocateur*, and he was behind the wheel when Marco first spied Semantha sailing on *Blind Faith*.

Marco had given no thought to his appearance before he showed up at Frank's. He toted two days of stubble and had not showered for a week. His curly hair was unkempt, and he smelled of alcohol. His shirt was wrinkled and his pants stained. At the present, he didn't care how he appeared. Particularly, he didn't care what Frank thought. But it had been hard to ignore the look of disgust on Frank's face when he had first walked in.

"But Frank," Marco said. "Before—"

"Marco, this is not like before. Dunland is adamant about it, and frankly, I get his point. It's hard for me to fathom why you did what you did. I don't see how you can excuse yourself."

Frank spoke from behind his immense walnut desk, giving him the aura of power and authority. He sat stiffly, looking like the headmaster at a reform school about to discipline an errant juvenile inmate. Even though it was Saturday, he had dressed in a suit and tie, probably steeling for a difficult conversation with Marco.

Upon hearing Frank's words, Marco slouched down in his chair, feeling like he had been hit by a sledgehammer. Until now, Frank had been a reliably sympathetic friend, more like an older brother, ready to excuse, console and justify. It was Frank who had negotiated a very favorable plea deal with Dunland after Marco had voluntarily turned himself in when he thought he had drowned Semantha. Now, the way he was speaking, Marco felt Frank's recrimination, not his love and support.

"So, what's his deal?" Marco brushed his hand through his disheveled hair and then wiped it on his pants.

"Plead guilty to first degree murder, spend ten years in prison, and five on probation after that. That's his offer. Oh, and a $100,000 fine."

Marco sucked in air and flinched. "Oh my God." He squirmed around on Frank's posh leather side chair, unsuccessfully trying to find a comfortable position.

"That's not so bad, as plea offers go in capital cases, particularly double murders. I've seen worse." Frank went to the bar, made himself a cup of coffee and returned to his desk.

"Ten years, Frank, ten years." Marco shook his head as the news sank in. He pounded his fist on the arm of the chair. "No." He shook his head. "No."

"Can't he see that Cynthia was a mistake, a horrible accident?" Marco's words sounded like a desperate plea. "I'm devastated by her loss. Doesn't Dunland understand I was trying to save her from Semantha?" Marco's knee began to shake. He was breathing heavily, like he was gasping for air.

"Yeah, I told Dunland that, but he thinks he can prove that you were having marital difficulties, and you wanted her gone. That will be a tough proof for Dunland, but he can probably get your difficulties in evidence, so the jury will know that in reaching their verdict."

Frank stopped speaking for a second and looked toward his large, leaded-glass window. "Remember, my dear friend." There was sarcasm in his voice and harshness in his words. "There are no witnesses who can confirm your version of the facts, and your fingerprints are all over the knife that killed Cynthia."

"And Semantha's, too. That's how my fingerprints got on the dagger."

Frank rubbed the side of his head and hesitated, a silence Marco found disturbing. Frank took a sip of coffee, looking like he was thinking about what to say next. He looked at Marco with a raised right eyebrow.

"You gonna testify at trial? That's the only way to get this stuff in the record. You don't have to, but I can tell you without question that Dunland will brutalize you on cross-examination if you do. And if he rattles you, you are done. You could get life."

Frank took out his pen and began to doodle on a legal pad.

"He'll take your Ivy League education and cushy job and stick it up your behind. The jury will think you are a first-class cur deserving everything you get. He may be a small-town lawyer, but he knows his juries."

"But Semantha..." Marco raised his hands looking exasperated. "Semantha... Doesn't he understand that I was out of my mind?"

"That worked before, Marco, but Dunland says he's not going to get sucked down that rabbit hole again. His words. And I don't disagree."

Marco placed his hands on the sides of his head in horror as he thought about the prospect of a public trial then jail time. "No, no, no," he said as he shook his head.

"Dunland thinks he went too light the last time," Frank continued. "And it's his fault this happened. He says the light penalty from before only made you feel above the law. He was unmoved and intent, Marco. I'm sorry to be the bearer of bad news." There was a matter-of-fact tone in Frank's voice.

"What about this guy Dunland? You know him?"

"My friends over in Michigan say he's a straight-shooter. He wants to run for mayor of Benton Harbor, a tough sell as a white man in an African American community. It's interesting, though. He keeps very quiet about his background, almost as if he is hiding something."

"Does that help us?"

"Neither here nor there." Frank shrugged. "We will have no chance to turn this into a referendum on Dunland's quest to be mayor—nor would that play well to the jury."

Marco sighed.

"But what's for sure is that he has every incentive to project the image of a tough guy on crime, and this one, as I am certain you can imagine, has attracted a great deal of attention. Dunland has good reason to play the bad guy."

"Can't we find out what he's trying to hide?" Marco asked.

Frank shook his head.

"I'm not sure he is trying to hide anything, but even if he were, how could we use that against him? The judge will not allow us to go into that before the jury, and if we threaten to expose something about him, that's a separate crime. Maybe you and I would get adjoining cells." Frank shook his head again.

Marco sat silently, head now resting on his hands. Neither said anything for a few minutes.

"No nice way to say this, my friend," Frank said, his lips pursed. "Honestly, you didn't learn your lesson from the last time." Frank shrugged.

Marco was taken back by Frank's brusqueness. He felt a lump in his throat.

"But Frank, I was kidnapped and brought back to Michigan." Marco compulsively rubbed his hand on the back of his neck. He craved Frank's understanding but had no idea how to get it.

"And you could have escaped as soon as Semantha freed you," Frank said. "There was no reason to have a fucking extravaganza with that woman, regardless of how rock-hard she got you." Frank's face pinched up. He shook his finger at Marco like he was a rabble-rousing preacher at a tent crusade. "After all my dear boy, you *were* married."

Marco looked down for several minutes, deep in thought. He was fighting panic, thanks to Frank's vitriol. He took in a couple of deep breaths and shook his head. There was a forlorn look on his face, his lips turned down and his brow furled.

"So, you're not going to help me, then?" Marco put his face in his hands and, in stormy anguish, began to cry. Frank unceremoniously pushed a box of Kleenex toward Marco from across his desk but otherwise did not move. His face was set as if in stone. Neither said anything for what seemed like hours. Eventually, feeling the urgency of the moment, Marco raised his head.

"What am I going to do, Frank?" Marco said. "Don't let me down, please."

"You've let yourself down." He spoke low and mean. "There's no easy fix."

*   *   *

FRANK THEN STOOD, walked to the office window, pulled the sheer drape aside, and stared out at the boat traffic on the Chicago River. He came to this window often to think things through, but this time the concern was much more poignant. He sighed. He stood there for a few minutes contemplating Marco's plight. He clutched his forehead and shook his head back and forth. He couldn't see how he could win the day for Marco, and he had plenty of other, more meritorious, cases where he could do some good. Why would he want to sacrifice meaningful work for a lost cause?

But then he recalled a conversation he had with Marco's father, now probably twenty years ago. He had met Ezekiel at a meeting of the Harvard Club of Chicago, and they became regular tennis opponents. They had just finished their weekly match at the East Bank Club and were having a glass of wine at the bar.

"Never tell Marco I said this, but Mariana and I haven't been very good parents," Ezekiel had said. "We've been too busy with our own lives. We sort of ignored him, and sometimes we were a little rough. Hit him too hard once in a while, you know."

"He's a very good kid," Frank had said, remembering Marco's star performance at the state softball championship.

"A little headstrong and arrogant, but he idolizes you. You're like the older brother he never had. Help him when you can. We're going to try, too," Ezekiel said, looking uncertain.

"You can count on me, regardless…" Frank said instantly, feeling honored and humbled by Ezekiel's unexpected request. Shortly after that, Mariana and Ezekiel were killed by an attack of piranha when their boat tipped over during a tour of the headwaters of the Amazon River. Their deaths turned Frank's promise into a blood oath.

As he peered out the window, Frank felt his eyes water. He took out a hanky and patted them dry, hoping Marco did not notice. He was disgusted and appalled by Marco's intemperate act; so what if it was in the heat of passion? Frank hated violence, even though that was usually his clients' standard stock-in-trade. And this act was so senseless, and committed by someone who should have known better, who Frank expected would have acted differently. He felt personally let down.

After all the things I did for this man… Marco deserved nothing from him. He shook his head again. And, looking back, he saw that Marco always did have a false bravado and arrogance that irritated him.

Frank hesitated as he mulled his reaction. He then turned and looked at Marco sitting over in front of his desk, looking like a lost sheep. Seeing Marco like that plucked on Frank's heartstrings, stirring feelings deep inside. In the end, he could not let Marco down or break the solemn promise he had made to his deceased friend. Family helps family. Like Marco, Frank had no one to call family other than Marco; his sailing buddies were only that, merely buddies. Marco had always been Frank's brother, son, and dear friend rolled into one. He felt uniquely connected to Marco. No question, he had to try to help Marco piece together his shattered life.

"Alright, let's begin," Frank said, still looking out the window. He again sighed.

He brushed his hand through his thick salt-and-pepper hair, put away his hanky, and turned to walk back toward Marco. He took off his suit jacket and threw it on a coat tree in the corner. He pulled off his tie, threw it on his desk, and sat down at the head of his conference table. He motioned for Marco to come and sit next to him.

Marco's face lit up and a toothy smile appeared on his face. He straightened up in his chair. "Thank you, Frank," he whispered. "I'll never forget this. I will love you until I die."

Frank tried to ignore Marco's comment—he thought it too ingratiating and blatantly manipulative—but inside he hoped Marco's sentiment was sincere. He wanted to love this fallen man, once having so much promise and now reduced to a creature fighting for his life. He was determined to find a way. He took his pen in hand and pulled up a legal pad.

"What did you tell that old witch?" Frank asked. "What's her name, Erzulie, something like that? Her testimony at trial could kill you."

"I have no idea. By then my mind was whirling like a funnel cloud. I was insane. But don't call her a witch, she's not a witch. She did bail me out, after all."

Marco raised his eyebrows, as if he just had an epiphany. "Insane? Can't I get off claiming temporary insanity?"

Frank walked over to his desk and pulled out a yellow legal pad filled with notes from the stack on the corner of his desk. Its binder read *Douglas and Associates, Attorneys and Counselors*. Frank stood behind his desk and read, holding the pad in his hands.

"You can always plead not guilty by way of insanity, yes. But my associate and I did some research. In Michigan, that's anything but a Get Out Of Jail Free card."

Frank studied his notes for a moment longer.

"Michigan follows the majority rule about an insanity plea. You have to prove that, at the time of the crime, you were mentally insane as defined by law, to the point that you did not understand the wrongfulness of your actions."

Frank looked up from his notes. He stopped talking for a minute; took off his glasses and laid them on the desk, right next to his half-finished copy of *War and Peace.* Frank knew he wouldn't have a chance to finish it for a while. He stared intensely at Marco.

"That does not seem to fit the Marco I know."

"Meaning?" Marco's face puckered up.

"It's got to be, at your deepest level, you appreciated that killing Semantha was wrong." Frank rubbed his eye. "Pleading insanity seems like a half-baked excuse. Too easy. So different from before when you insisted on holding yourself accountable, to hell with the cost. Ask yourself what changed from before."

Marco opened his mouth as if to answer Frank's question, but Frank held up his hand.

"You should understand something else. Even if the jury agrees, the judge will probably sentence you to indefinite confinement in a psychiatric hospital. What my friends in Michigan tell me is that, many times, confined people are locked away and forgotten. They end up spending more time in the psychiatric hospital that they would have in prison."

"But certainly, Frank, there are hospitals—"

"And these psychiatric hospitals, they are not fun places. I don't know if this still happens, but it used to be common for patients to be injected with Thorazine. Turned them into walking zombies. Have you heard of the 'Thorazine shuffle'?"

Frank noticed Marco swallow hard.

"I thought there was something called 'temporary insanity'? Sort of prove that you acted out of some sort of passion but then returned to normal."

"Right, there is that one additional possibility. It's called 'irresistible impulse temporary insanity.'" Frank looked at his notes again. "Have you heard of Lorena Bobbitt? She was tried for cutting off her husband's penis—"

"Oh," Marco said as he winced. "Bet that hurt." He tried to laugh, but the sound came out like a cough.

"Well, she was accused of a crime labeled 'marital sexual assault,' but she was found not guilty. Irresistible impulse was her defense."

"That's good." Marco's lips turned slightly upward in a half smile.

"And she didn't get confined to a psychiatric hospital."

Marco snickered with a devious tone. "Sounds just right. Let's go for—"

"Sounds right? Let's go for it?" Frank's eyes clouded over with venom. "Don't be so flip. This is not like ordering dessert at a French restaurant. Sometimes Marco, you can be so arrogant—even when your life is at stake."

"Sorry." Marco's voice lacked conviction.

"But you still have to prove that you suffered from some underlying mental defect. In your case, I am not sure what that would be, but I do know that if you go this route, your mental status and sanity will be subject to public scrutiny. Lots of court-appointed psychiatrists examining you and testifying from the witness stand about the intimate details of what goes on in your complicated head. Who knows what they could say? Ready for that?"

Without an invitation, Marco walked to Frank's bar and poured himself a double scotch. He looked into his drink for a minute, poured it down his throat in a single gulp, then turned to Frank.

"Sounds like a ticket to no more career. And what woman would ever even want to touch me again? But do I have any options?"

"Well, the plea deal."

Marco closed his eyes and shook his head.

"Then roll the dice and take your chances for a not-guilty verdict from the jury. On these facts, a virtual impossibility." Frank's words were cold and a little mean.

"And my chances with the irresistible impulse defense?"

Frank looked at his notes one more time, then deposited the legal pad back on the stack of papers.

"Slim. Our research confirms that Michigan law is not terribly clear on whether this defense can be employed, so there is always a question as to whether the judge will allow it in the first place. Nationally, the temporary insanity defense is used in only about one percent of criminal cases, and it succeeds only about one time in four when it is offered."

Marco shook his head again.

"It would be a ton of work for both of us. Very costly psychiatric testimony, maybe six figures," Frank said. "You'll have to come up with money for that, and I assume you don't have the money to pay me. An incredible investment for both of us without much likelihood of success."

Frank tapped his fingers on the desk as he thought.

"And after all of that, we'd need to fight to keep you out of some state psych hospital. Let me put it to you bluntly." He waited a moment for effect.

"If your name was anything but Marco Adamos, I'd tell you I have better things to do."

Marco looked unfazed by Frank's words. By now he seemed impervious to more bad news.

"So, I really need to thread the needle?" he asked, sounding like he did not fully appreciate the import of what Frank had said.

"Yep," Frank said. "And if they don't buy your defense, the judge will likely impose a very long sentence. Could be twenty years, maybe life."

Frank peered into Marco's bloodshot eyes. "You don't have a bunch of great options, but my advice: Try to negotiate a better plea. I can probably reduce the numbers some. That makes the most sense."

"No, Frank. I won't. I can't."

"But going forward will be very expensive. Risky, and for what? A life sentence or an indefinite stay in the nuthouse?"

Frank walked over to where Marco sat and looked down at him, his six-foot-four-inch frame towering over his old friend.

"And frankly, you don't really fit the definition of insanity in Michigan, no place that I know. Most judges will tell you that anyone who commits murder in the first degree is, in one sense, insane to begin with. So, it takes more than the act alone to make out a successful insanity plea."

They argued back and forth. It became hot. Finally, Frank went quiet. He looked exhausted, his face showed his unease. He raised his hand as if to say, "Stop." He exhaled with a long sigh.

"But you are my client. I will proceed as you wish," he said without emotion.

*　　*　　*

Marco left Frank's office and went around the corner to St. Peter's church where the Saturday afternoon Mass was underway. He sat in the back, dazed, watching the priest ramble through the ritual in the near-empty church, just a few old ladies and a couple of unshaven middle-aged men who looked homeless. The church felt like a shell, devoid of life. The priest went on about the forgiving power of God, but Marco was not consoled. *Is there balm in Gilead?* he wondered. He saw himself facing a future permeated with misery and brutality, nothing else. Like the sign over the gates to hell in Dante's *Inferno*, "Abandon all hope ye who enter here."

Marco left before the service was over, walked by the brown-robed brother standing in the vestibule without responding to his "Good day," and headed directly for a storefront bar he knew on North Milwaukee Avenue, Old Richard's Tavern. Cheap drinks. He spent the next two days drunk and buying booze for prostitutes. One of them offered him a free blowjob, but he could not imagine partaking. He was not even sure he could perform, he was so consumed by what would happen at his impending arraignment.

XIV

FRANK LED MARCO into the courtroom for the arraignment. In compliance with Frank's directions, Marco had sobered up and tried to look presentable. In the past, Marco would have needed no reminder about the importance of his appearance as he went from international conference to conference promoting his ideas. Now, his clothes, while clean, were not well pressed. His sports jacket, frayed and ratty, hung loosely from his shoulders. Marco looked skinny as a rail and his hands shook as if in alcohol withdrawal.

Brad Coulter accompanied them. He was a local attorney Frank had hired to be a part of the defense team. It still irritated Frank when he remembered what Marco had said when he had proposed hiring Coulter.

"Frank, can't you handle this by yourself? How much is this going to cost me?" *My God*, Frank had thought at the time. *What does he expect?* It was more than good enough that he was providing his services as a courtesy to Marco and his family.

"Whatever it costs, it costs," Frank had replied to Marco, scowling. "I'm not going to hop in the car and drive way over to Benton Harbor for a routine court appearance he can handle. He also knows the judge very well. I do not. Besides, he knows Berrien County like the back of his hand. We need his help in navigating this process."

"But…"

"It's done, Marco."

Frank was already grateful for Coulter's insights. Coulter had told him about the icy relationship between the judge and Martin Dunland. Apparently, they had known each other for years, way back to when Dunland was assistant county prosecutor and Judge Williamson was the one and only county public defender. The rumor was that Williamson had thought of Dunland, even then, as uninspired and colorless. After Williamson assumed the bench, Dunland had cases before him. Typically, following some initial bluster and grandstanding, Dunland would ask the judge to approve a plea deal rather than have a trial. Some people in the Berrien County criminal trial bar called Dunland "Plea Deal Martin," others "Marty the Meek."

The arraignment hearing was held in Courtroom 3, right-hand side, second floor in the Berrien County Court Building in downtown Benton Harbor. It had been built in 1932, in Greek revival style, with a faux dome in the center of the roof. The courtroom was large but shabby, the walls painted government-yellow years ago, its high ceilings making it seem even more bleak. Badly scratched walnut wainscoting extended to shoulder high, and incandescent dish-shaped lighting fixtures infused everything in the room with a dank, yellowish hew. Behind the bar, three rows of pew-like wooden benches were already filled with spectators, including a row reserved for the press. This trial was big news in this sleepy, post-industrial town.

An old walnut bench, which dominated the room, was raised so high that even when the lawyers were standing, they had to look up at the judge. A name tag prominently displayed in its center read *Senior Circuit Judge Anthony J. Williamson*. A stenciled sign on the opaque glass window of the door to the left of the bench read *Jury Room*. An identical door on the other side said *Chambers*. The doors and the letters appeared to be original. A court reporter was already sitting at his machine at the foot of the judge's bench, waiting to record the hearing.

Frank, Marco, and Coulter walked to the defense table facing the prosecution, both perpendicular to the bench and the judge. By tradition, the prosecution table was situated closer to the jury box. Frank and Brad began unloading documents from their briefcases. Dunland and his assistant, a blustery-looking female, sat at the prosecution table. They had already unpacked their papers from two banker's boxes and had organized them in neat rows on their table. They both acknowledged Frank with a formal, cold nod as if to say, "We see you are here but be ready to battle." Frank and Coulter nodded in return. Marco's cheek twitched.

Dunland stood up after Frank and Brad had unpacked their briefcases and escorted the woman with her over to Frank.

"Meet Eunice Peterson, Frank. She's the new assistant prosecutor, replacing Cynthia Sandi… er, Adamos," Dunland said. Peterson frowned as she shook Frank's hand but was careful not to look at Marco, who had also stood up for the introduction. Marco, too, looked straight ahead. He had been admonished by both Frank and Brad to keep a poker face during the hearing, say nothing, and avoid eye contact with the prosecution.

At exactly two, according to the old, tired electric wall clock above the jury box, the Chambers door opened and the court clerk, followed by the judge, entered.

The clerk stood behind a desk and announced, "People versus Adamos. Come to order."

The low din coming from the crowd ceased and the room fell silent. The judge—tall and white-haired, a little porky and wearing a non-conventional deep blue robe—lumbered slowly, deliberately, up the steps to his seat behind the bench. He walked with a slight limp, a Korean war wound, Coulter had told Frank. Wearing a bright red power tie, he acted like a man in control and confident. As he went up the stairs, his robe brushed against the flag of the United States to the right of the bench. It fluttered slightly, as if from a puff of a breeze. He sat down under what looked like a bronze casting of the great seal of the State of Michigan. The U.S. flag, along with the Michigan flag on the other side of the bench, framed him with the aura of additional gravitas.

Coulter had told Frank that Judge Williamson was from an old-line Benton Harbor family with enough clout to get their lesser stars like Anthony elected to positions in county government. His years on the bench had taught him how to appear courtly and wise. Coulter said he didn't particularly like Williamson, that sometimes his rulings were way out in left field. "Erratic," he had called them. Frank was not worried about that. Frank thought that the judge looked friendly, and Frank trusted his own instincts about people.

"We only have one case on the call this afternoon," the judge said, alternating his gaze between the two tables. "Let's go. Mr. Dunland, read the indictment."

Dunland stood up, cleared his throat, and said, "Yes, Your Honor." He cleared his throat again. Frank thought he didn't look too happy, not like the easy-going guy he had dealt with the first time Marco had been to this courthouse. He began reading.

People of the State of Michigan
v
Marco Antonius Adamos,
Case Number 1994 CR 245.

The people charge as follows:

MARCO ANTONIUS ADAMOS

Defendant herein, did commit murder in the first degree in that he intentionally, and with malice aforethought, did trespass with force of arms upon the following persons:

Count I Cynthia Adamos
Count II Semantha...

Dunland hesitated.
"Papa...Papa--drounoluis... Papadiamantopoulos."

He cleared his throat again. "Ahem.

***Thereby taking the life of said person, er, persons. In
violation of Michigan Compiled Laws Section 750.316."***

The Judge then looked at the defense table.

"The defendant will rise."

Marco stood.

The judge, squinting his eyes and furrowing his forehead like a stringent overlord, peered down at him. "Mr. Adamos, how do you plead?"

Marco grimaced.

"Not guilty, Your Honor. But…I was insane when this happened."

Frank touched Marco on the sleeve and said loudly, "Just respond, Mr. Adamos."

Marco can't keep himself in check, Frank thought. *He doesn't listen.* Frank's face showed a twinge of irritation.

"All right," the judge said in a baritone voice well-suited to his role. "Mr. Dunland, when will you be able to provide Mr. Douglas with a list of witnesses and written discovery?"

"Thirty days, Your Honor, but I already know I will be calling only the chief inspector and the coroner who did the autopsies."

Frank was quite surprised. He thought this was not that much of an open-and-shut case. He would have expected that at least he would seek to call that old lady who pulled Marco out of the water. *Was Dunland overly confident?*

The judge then looked at Frank.

"What about you, Mr. Douglas?" Frank thought he sounded deferential.

"Thirty days after that, but so Mr. Dunland does not feel sandbagged, I will be calling a forensic psychiatrist to testify about my client's state of mind at the time of the murder."

Dunland suddenly turned to Frank. He raised his eyebrows, appearing flummoxed.

"What will be the subject matter of the expert's opinions?" the judge asked with a flat affect, sounding like he was ordering at a lunch counter.

"He will testify that my client acted based on an irresistible impulse." Frank swallowed hard. Despite his search to date, he had found no expert who agreed with that conclusion, who was qualified, and who was willing to testify. He now had to make good on his promise to the judge. He had his work cut out for him.

Dunland shook his head. "Your Honor, I don't think Michigan law—"

"Well, Mr. Douglas, you have the right, but I will order you to provide the State a report from this expert within thirty days of receiving their disclosures."

Frank silently breathed a huge sigh of relief. As Frank had informed Marco at their meeting, Dunland was right, Michigan law was not that clear. Now though, the judge had just decided that Marco could evoke this defense and, importantly, without a long, drawn-out battle.

What luck, Frank thought. *Maybe Marco's good luck has returned.* Externally, Frank's face remained fixed, locked, unemotional.

"Yes, Your Honor," he said, sounding like the nun had just told him to lead the classroom in prayer. "I was already planning to provide a report to the State."

Williamson nodded his head and smiled at Frank ever so slightly. Frank was unsure as to whether the judge was bending over backwards to help Marco because he believed that a conviction was inevitable, so why not give the defendant everything he asked for, or whether he didn't like Dunland or the case. Could be that the judge was a bit star-struck by a big-time Chicago attorney or Marco's status in the scientific community. Many possibilities.

But Frank was sure about one thing. Williamson seldom got the chance to preside over such a substantial case. This very possibly was the biggest, most twisted lawsuit he had tried since being elected to the bench, and, even with his impassive countenance, he looked engaged and expectant. Perhaps he was having the time of his life.

"But," the judge continued, "We're going to need to review this again at the time of drafting the jury instructions. We may need to craft a limiting instruction."

Dunland shook his head.

"But, but, but, Judge," Dunland said. "Michigan law is not clear…"

"Mr. Dunland, I know Michigan law." He turned his head toward Dunland. His voice seeped with irritation. "Mr. Douglas will have the right to call this expert. This is, after all, a capital case, and we want all the facts before the jury, not merely what you want to present, Mr. Dunland." The judge turned to Frank. Instantly, the pique disappeared from his face. Chameleon-like, he smiled.

"Well then, Judge, I will need to call my own expert," Dunland said, sounding like he had been caught off-guard and was casting about for a way to regain a bit of control. It seemed Dunland was suddenly worried that this was not such a simple case as it had originally appeared.

Williamson lifted his hand as if speaking *ex cathedra*.

"So here's what we are going to do." He made a slight knifing motion, as if the parties should understand that this was his final word.

"The State will have thirty days to make its disclosures, another thirty to disclose its expert, and then the defendant thirty days after that to disclose. Both sides will provide full reports with supporting documents along with the disclosure." Williamson cleared his throat before he went on.

"Then we will set this matter for final preliminary hearing in 120 days, at which time we will set a trial date."

"But Judge, the state will need time to arrange for an examination of the defendant."

Williamson looked miffed, like he was disgusted by Dunland. "Forty-five, then, Mr. Dunland. Get it done by then or waive your right to present an expert." He scowled, then turned to Frank.

"And with regard to the trial date, Mr. Douglas, I know you are busy and working in Chicago. We will do our best to set a date which is convenient for you."

Frank thought he saw Williamson's eyes flutter a little, but maybe he was seeing things. What was for sure was that in all of his years, he had never seen a judge so accommodating. Usually, it was the opposite. Judges typically expected the attorneys to kowtow to the court's schedule, not vice versa.

Frank didn't know what to make of this development, but he sure didn't want to look this particular gift horse in the mouth, and he very definitely did not want to break the spell by misbehaving in court or permitting Marco to do so. Cultivating a positive relationship with the judge, even in a jury case, was part of Frank's core strategy because he had seen over and over how a friendly judge could have a significant impact on the jury. The jury tends to align with the judge's attitudes, not just because he is a power figure in the courtroom, but also because the judge is supposedly neutral, like them.

Judge Williamson stood and began to descend the steps toward the door that said *Chambers*. The clerk yelled, "All rise." Everyone stood up. The second the judge was gone, the spectators began to mutter. Some headed for Marco and Frank. Frank pulled Marco behind him and rushed to the door, pushing several people aside. He didn't need any of the hoopla; all he wanted was a not-guilty verdict.

As soon as they exited the courtroom, Marco's mouth fell agape, and he halted. He put his hand on Frank's chest as if telling him to stop, as well. There was Erzulie, standing there with a couple of people by her side, including a young Spanish-looking guy touting an ear-to-ear smile. Erzulie was dressed in a navy-blue pants suit and a pearl necklace hung around her neck. She reminded Frank of a retired old-maid schoolteacher who lived down the street when he was growing up. Marco grabbed Frank's arm and pulled him in her direction.

He looked at Erzulie and started to speak. "What….?" "How did you know… What are you…?"

Frank placed his hand on Marco's shoulder. "Best not to talk here," he said.

"Your lawyer's right. Come to my house tonight, both of you."

*   *   *

MARCO would remember the dinner for the rest of his life.

"The cops interviewed me what seems like a dozen times," Erzulie said. "Same questions over and over, ya know, how was he acting, where were the bodies lying, was there a sign of a struggle, did Semantha have a weapon, on and on. I hate cops. They piss me off. Actually, the whole government. They are all puffed up hypocrites, up to no good."

Red-faced and agitated, Erzulie sat at the head of the one and only table in her hovel-cave, droning on and on about the injustices of the system. The room smelled of freshly cooked turnips and rutabagas, matching the acrid words emitting from Erzulie's mouth. Marco and Frank listened in stony silence. When she finally stopped, she lit her pipe and took a long drag. The look on her face changed instantly from hostile to content. A flat, toothless smile came to her lips.

"But on to better things. I made you a great natural roast." She got up and stirred the pot sitting on her two-burner hotplate. "Eat up," she said as she scooped a slop of the roast of nuts, vegetables, and mushrooms onto Frank's plate.

Macy jumped up on the table as if wanting to share in the feast. Erzulie pushed her back down.

"Mind your manners, cat," she said.

After staring at the concoction for a moment, Frank took his fork and pushed the pasty goo around on his plate. He took only a couple of bites, mostly of the morel mushrooms which had somehow survived Erzulie's chopping knife. Then he carefully put his fork on the edge of his plate and deliberately wiped his mouth with the paper towel napkin. He folded it and tucked it beneath the plate.

Marco could tell Frank was uncomfortable from the way he sat, still and formal, and from the anguished look in his eyes. And with his Chicago-casual clothes and Gucci shoes, no question he was out of place.

Sensing Frank's revulsion, Marco was freshly grateful for how far Frank was willing to go to help him. He couldn't imagine anyone who could be more loyal or more dedicated, not even Melissa. His eyes met Frank's and became soft. The shadow of a smile came to his lips. Frank nodded his head slightly toward Marco and rolled his eyes. In return, Marco smiled more broadly, shutting his eyes and holding his smile in place for a second. Marco knew Frank had gotten his message.

"So, what did you tell the police?" Frank asked Erzulie.

"I told them over and over that your client went berserk as soon as I pulled him out of the water and revived him. First, he screamed at me, telling me he wanted to die. He said I was the devil for rescuing him. He wouldn't stop."

Erzulie went silent while she took a couple of spoonfuls of her vegetarian concoction. "Good stuff," she said. Neither Marco nor Frank said anything.

"I was pretty upset, too," she continued. "I screamed at him that he had killed my lover. He got this blank look on his face, but then, after a second, he started muttering to himself—meaningless gibberish, spitting and pacing from the river to the bodies then back, over and over."

Erzulie began making knifing motions with her hands held high above her.

"Then he looked at me with mean, ferocious eyes—I thought the eyes of a murderer—and began to come at me. I ran to my truck and got out of there. I stopped at the first gas station down the road and called the police."

Frank looked intently at Erzulie. She returned his gaze, their eyes locked as if each was testing the other's mettle. Marco could sense tension between them.

"What was the crime scene like when you arrived?" Frank asked.

"Well, there was this woman lying there—I later found it was Marco's wife—blood still oozing out of her throat, and about forty feet away, Semantha…" Erzulie cried a little, wiped a tear from her eye, then continued. "Naked, covered with knife wounds. I thought about Caesar at the Senate on the ides of March. To me, the treachery was the same."

Erzulie looked away and gagged as if she was about to vomit. Again, she calmed down and continued. "Her clothes were lying next to her. Her favorite pink silk jumpsuit. I loved that outfit, so sexy. A large branch was next to her. I got the impression that she had been holding it when she was attacked."

Erzulie looked at Marco and glared.

She appeared to be filled with disgust. But then her face cleared. The anguished look disappeared.

"But sweetie," she said still looking at Marco. "I do understand. You were crazy."

"How big was the branch?" Frank asked.

"Big enough to do serious damage. It was pretty long, as best I can remember."

Frank frowned and turned to Marco. "You didn't tell me about the branch. Did she threaten you?"

"No. Uh…yes. Uh …well, maybe. I'm not really sure. Everything is pretty much a blur from that day."

"What else have you forgotten?" Frank asked, his voice steeped with sarcasm. He then turned to Erzulie.

"Ms. Perez, will you tell the jury what you just told me?" Frank asked.

Erzulie closed her eyes and looked troubled. She pondered for some time.

"I…I…I guess, uh, I will help." She didn't sound too happy about the prospect.

"Thank you," Frank said. He stood to leave.

"Don't go yet," Erzulie said, beaming. She pulled out a bottle from behind the short drape covering the shelves in her galley and poured a clear liquid into three shot glasses embossed with the initials *UM* and a university seal on the side. She gave one each to Marco and Frank, raised hers, then said, "I have a toast."

Frank looked at the glass and smelled the liquid inside. "What the hell is this?" he asked.

"What the hell? Don't be such a stick. It's only a little home-brewed moonshine. It's not a brujeria, if that's what ya thinkin'. Don't be snooty, Douglas."

Frank and Marco raised their glasses.

"To the success of my plan," she said, then looked at Marco.

"Your plan?" he asked as he downed the liquor. It felt hot as it slid down his throat, but also very good. It had been a while since he had drunk anything.

"Be here tomorrow night. You'll see." Putting her finger to her mouth, Erzulie said no more. She then stood up, opened the door, and gestured for Frank and Marco to leave.

*   *   *

"Oshun will listen," Erzulie said as she and Marco drove toward the Casa in Paw Paw the next night. The truck was old and creaky and the ride rough, but the engine worked fine.

"Tonight, I'm going to summon her to intervene for you with the jury."

Marco was quite skeptical, but with the desperateness of his situation, he was prepared to entertain any possible solution, even magic. So, when Erzulie invited him to come to the Santeria ceremony, he agreed.

"I still don't understand. Why are you doing all this?" he asked as they got close to the town.

Erzulie held her thoughts and took a few breaths.

"You have suffered enough," she said solemnly, her lips turned down. "Semantha told me the whole story from the other side of the abyss. She wants me to help you believe. Her love for you is that great."

"After I killed her twice?"

"She was blind to your faults. You were her route to respectability." Erzulie shook her head. "She was so very needy. I had hoped…"

"Respectability?" Marco asked with a slight lift of his eyebrow.

Erzulie shrugged.

"Think for a minute," she said. "Semantha was very accomplished, extraordinary, but stuck in a world of low-life weirdos. Theo—well, Pappie—was her savior, but she also knew that he was on the fringe, way, way out. She wanted to escape with every sinew in her body but saw no way out. Then you happened along. Her hope of connecting with you was pretty much a fantasy, but it gave her something to live for."

Marco was overcome with sadness. Semantha's short life had truly been tragic. Remembering her, he bowed his head and closed his eyes. He reverently crossed himself as they pulled up to the Casa.

Inside, the drums beat furiously. Men dressed all in white walked in two at a time and bowed before the drummers. Erzulie followed, carrying a doll dressed in a miniature business suit. She placed it on a small altar which looked exactly like the one Marco had seen in Erzulie's hovel, only bigger.

Marco found a place to stand along the wall, trying to look inconspicuous in what seemed to him like a very strange place. After the opening ceremony, a shirtless male dancer with a long, flowing scarf came up to Marco and forcefully pulled him into the middle of the floor with the other congregants. He was the same person who had been standing next to Erzulie when Marco and Frank had exited the courtroom the previous day.

A circle of dancers formed around them, gyrating to the beat of the drums and chanting in unison. The dancer threw his scarf around Marco and pulled it tight as he pumped on Marco with his hips.

"Ah yes," he yelled loudly, throwing his head and shoulders back and spinning Marco around. "Loosen up. Let it happen…feel it!" The circle chanted "Aro gogo. Orisha fifetu."

The dancer put his mouth close to Marco's ear.

"They're saying 'the curse is being lifted by the orishas,'" he whispered. "I'm Cisco, Semantha's first lover. She's here with us tonight. Believe and feel her." He gave Marco a couple more spins.

Marco felt stiff, like a stick planted deep in a field surrounded by flowing grass swaying in the breeze. He wished he could let himself go. He wondered why he was so inhibited as he watched the people in the room freely spin and swoon.

What is real, and what is fake? Marco asked himself. He was no longer sure. He scowled. *How did I go so wrong?* He watched as the chicken's neck was cut and its blood flowed onto the altar. He needed time to contemplate, maybe change his approach to things, but for now, his priority was to try to save himself.

XV

"It's TIME to decide whether you will testify," Frank said at the beginning of their strategy meeting. The trial date was fast approaching, and he, Coulter and Marco were sitting around the breakfast table in Brad's kitchen. His place was on a bluff overlooking the lake south of Benton Harbor. Frank liked being close to the water, even though his boat was in Chicago. He was sure that the beach below Brad's house would give him a secluded place to walk and clear his mind if he needed time alone during the trial.

A belligerent look came to Marco's face, like a pouty child inflamed because he was being punished unfairly.

"Since you mentioned the question of testifying before, Frank, I've thought a lot about it," Marco said with his lower jaw stuck out. "If I don't need to, I…" He raised his voice. "Won't." He shook his head. "Why would I want to expose myself to abuse? Can't you cross-examine the shit out of Dunland's witnesses and make this case go away? Isn't that your job?"

Frank frowned, then got up and paced around the room. Arms tightly folded, he stood in front of the refrigerator and glared down at Marco, who was sipping a beer as if nothing important was afoot.

"My job?" His tone was elevated, a scowl on his face. "God Almighty couldn't make this case go away through cross-examination alone. Your expectation is mind-boggling," he growled. "And you're acting like a baby. It doesn't become you."

"But Frank—"

"No buts, Marco. It's my duty to tell you that you don't need to testify. But I think you must."

"But…but…but Frank, I have already gone through so much pain. Think about that smelly, slime-bucket psychiatrist Dunland forced me to see, his never-ending psychological tests. I've already told you how I felt after it was all over. Like a subhuman animal."

"I've heard all this before. What's new?"

"But did I tell you it took me a bottle of gin to get over that horrible experience?"

"Don't blame me. You're the one who insisted on this strategy." Frank's face turned crimson.

"How much do you expect me to take?" Marco held out his hand as if sliding down the side of a hill out of control and looking for a twig to grasp.

"What's up with you?" Frank asked. There was roughness in his voice. "That sounds like a game of guilt trip to me. Well, I'm not playing. Get over it and take some responsibility. This is your mess, not mine." Frank slammed his fist against the refrigerator.

Coulter placed his hand on Frank's arm, as if to calm him.

"If I may interject," Coulter said quietly. "In a case like this, the jury will want to hear your denials. And then there's the issue of your wife's murder. You're the only one who can testify about how that happened."

Marco started to weep. "I can't, only—"

"And remember," Coulter said, "it's to your advantage if cross-examination becomes too brutal. That will evoke sympathy with the jury."

Marco jerked as if he had just put his finger on an open power line.

"Brutal? If Dunland gets too vicious, can't you object?"

"Not a good idea. If we do too much of that," Coulter said, "the jury will think we are worried and that you have something to hide."

"Like maybe that you are guilty," Frank said with an edge to his voice. "Or maybe that you are so weak, you can't stand up for yourself. We will object only if Dunland is egregious in his misuse of the rules."

Frank opened the refrigerator door and took out his own beer.

"Brad's right, Marco," Frank said, gesturing to Brad. "You'll be somewhat on your own on the witness stand, but you have my—our—advice that you must testify. We'll prepare you. Brad's got a reputation as being quite the guy on cross-examination. He'll work you over a few times before the trial."

"And Dunland is not all that clever, anyway," Brad added. "You'll be fine."

Frank sat down, his beer in hand. "Okay, that's settled. Now we've got to talk about the expert witness. After looking everywhere, I've finally found one."

Brad made a motion with his hands as if clapping.

"Great work, Frank," Brad said. Marco sat with a blank look.

"He's qualified, willing to support our case, and most important, he's been down this road before, so he knows how to avoid the chuckholes."

"Ok, let's have at it, Frank." Marco smiled and looked relieved.

"He requires a $100,000 up-front retainer."

Marco's smile disappeared like a ghost fading into the air. He coughed and ran his hand across his forehead.

"I'm paying that?"

"You don't expect me to pay, do you?"

"Well…" Marco hesitated a moment too long.

"Christ almighty! Get over that idea, Marco. You're family, yes, but this is your freight, not mine."

"That's about all the money I have, Frank."

"Maybe you should have thought about that before you stabbed Semantha. Now's a little late." Brad again put his hand on Frank's sleeve and held it there.

"Frank and I have met with him already," Brad said. "He's solid. But, true, he's very pricey—well above the local market. And that's something for you to think about in deciding to go forward."

"Do I have a choice, guys?" Marco asked.

"Dunland will be entitled to examine him about his fees before the jury," Frank said. "And there's a chance the jury will discount his testimony because of that alone. You know, the hired gun thing."

"Actually a good chance of that," Brad said. "This is a working-class community."

Frank brusquely removed Coulter's hand from his sleeve as if to say he could handle himself. "I've looked high and low for an expert. He's the only game in town. For you that is."

Marco's head dropped. He was in anguish. Everything he knew had been turned inside out.

XVI

"ALL RISE!" the clerk called out.

Everyone in the packed courtroom stood up except Judge Williamson. "Mr. Clerk, summon the jury," he said.

Jury selection had been long and difficult. Unfortunately, it had not gone as well as Frank had hoped. The jury pool was filled with "law and order" people, all notoriously prosecution-oriented. Frank exhausted his four *no cause* objections very quickly. For any others Frank feared would be predisposed toward guilt, he had to object *for cause*, and each of his objections became a fight. Dunland even argued about whether Frank had cause when he moved to exclude one potential juror whose mother had been killed in a knifing at the high school. The judge denied Frank's objection. That person was seated.

Otherwise, Judge Williamson had been fair-minded about Frank's *for cause* objections. Yet, overall, the jurors selected were not a very friendly bunch. Frank wondered if it had been a mistake to demand a jury. Maybe it would have been better to try the case before the judge, but too late now.

Frank watched as the twelve jurors plus two alternates walked silently, stoically, to their seats in the jury box and sat down. God. Two retired high school math teachers, six construction workers, four housewives—one a retired school psychologist—the Swiss wife of a Grand Rapids businessman, and the owner of an Italian beef quick service restaurant. Not a compassionate one among them, as far as Frank could see, and a couple completely reactionary. But at least there were no Baptist ministers.

Usually calm and somewhat detached when he was at trial, Frank felt a churning in his stomach upon seeing the jury come in. The outcome of this case was too critical for a man with whom he had such a long and deep connection.

While Judge Williamson administered the oath, the members of the jury sat in stony silence looking straight ahead, a few with their arms crossed. No one looked toward Frank, a gesture Frank usually took as a sign the juror was favorably disposed to his client's case. Frank did not see even one juror he thought would reliably side with Marco and his rather avant-garde defense, but then it was early. Possibly the Swiss lady—it depended on her politics—or the housewife wearing a red dress and caked-on makeup. She looked fiercely independent, like she might have a mind of her own. But even she kept her gaze fixed resolutely straight ahead as she sat down.

Several jurors took out small cardboard fans that read *Baird and Jacobson Funeral Home* and began stirring the air. South Michigan was in the midst of a brutal October heat wave and the County Building air conditioning was broken. The windows in the stuffy courtroom were wide open, but there was no breeze. Occasionally the noise of a passing motorcycle or delivery truck disturbed the quiet of the courtroom. It would be a challenge to keep the jurors alert and listening.

Frank did not like the cards stacked so much against him, but he was used to swimming upstream against the odds. At Frank's sixty-second birthday party the week earlier, Frank's assistant gave a toast, saying that this would be his 210th jury trial, with an overall score of 147 "not guilties," twenty-three hung juries, and only forty convictions. It was an admirable track record. Frank had based his very successful practice on his reputation as a winner in the most difficult cases, a master of lost causes. And he prided himself on his demeanor in the courtroom—not cutthroat and mean like some attorneys, but rather decent, straightforward, but yet incisive like a sword when called for. One of his clients had once called him a 'kitten-skinned wolf.'

Frank nonetheless had a reason to hope. He knew he could count on Erzulie, and his high-priced expert would be adept at handling cross-examination. Frank had picked Dr. Fullerman precisely because he was a seasoned jury trial veteran who knew how to look the jury in the eyes as he testified and could project a confident, knowledgeable demeanor. Frank only wished Fullerman didn't sound like an effete eastern patrician—probably a turn-off for this lower middle-class jury. But Frank had not been able to find anyone else with sufficient gravitas. So, at the end of the day, Marco's fate rested on the shoulders of Dr. Izzie Fullerman, M.D., PhD, now $100,000 richer.

If, however, the defense had any hope of success, Marco had to behave. Frank had been annoyed when Marco had embellished his plea with his own editorial even after Frank had admonished him not to do that sort of thing, with or without a jury present. Frank was irritated with how many times he had to remind Marco to sit up, shut up, and remain poker faced. Marco was not making this case any easier to try.

And Marco would need to eat humble pie. None of his haughty arrogance. A jury could spot that a million miles away.

Though Frank had left his $2000 designer three-piece suit at home, still he was a commanding figure in the courtroom with his svelte frame and flowing hair combed back Gary Cooper-style. His presence made Dunland appear like a back bench oaf.

Unlike for the preliminary hearing, where Marco looked downright shabby, Marco had this time followed Frank's directions, showing up clean shaven, with a fresh, short-trimmed haircut and in a modest, conservative black suit, no tie. Frank had also purchased a pair of black-rimmed glasses for Marco to wear. He thought it made Marco look more boyish and innocent. Jurors paid attention to how people look. Little things matter.

Both parties made their opening statements, then Dunland called his first witness, his chief investigator. This was always the part of the state's case Frank hated the most. It would give Dunland the opportunity to paint a grizzly picture of the crime scene and inflame the jury. At least the judge had limited the number of photos the jury could see to five for each victim, a ruling which would blunt the worst of the display. In Frank's last murder trial, the prosecutor had spent a day showing pictures to the jury. That was a lot to overcome. Nonetheless, the five photos were very graphic, both Cynthia and Semantha lying in pools of their own blood with their mouths agape, their open eyes frozen with a look of dazed agony.

Dunland presented his case the first day, mostly seated behind the prosecution table, reading his questions from his notes. *Not a great way to win friends and influence people,* Frank thought. But Dunland had learned how to minimize his southern drawl so that he sounded like a distinguished old-school gentleman, not a cracker from some hick town in Louisiana.

On cross-examination of the inspector, Frank asked only a couple of questions.

"Officer Darby," Frank asked. "The handle of the knife you testified about was covered with Ms. Papadiamantopoulos' fingerprints, correct?"

"Yes," Darby responded, "along with those of Mr. Adamos. But I wouldn't say 'covered.' I would say more of his than hers."

"Just answer the question," the judge said. "You may proceed, Mr. Douglas."

"And Ms. Papadiamantopoulos' clothes, they were some distance away from where the body lay, correct?"

"Yes."

"How far?"

"I would say forty feet. It was a good distance."

"And they were covered with blood stains, correct?"

"They were."

"Well, Mr. Darby, you're a seasoned investigator. I presume you ran an analysis to determine whose blood was on those clothes?"

"We did not. We presumed the blood was that of Ms. Adamos."

Frank was surprised by that response. He had anticipated asking the court for permission to run an overnight analysis of the blood on Semantha's clothes, a request Dunland would certainly oppose. With Darby's answer, that would not be necessary.

"One last question," Frank continued. "Ms. Papadiamantopoulos' body, it was about thirty feet away from Ms. Adamos' body, correct?"

"That's right."

"That's all I have, Your Honor."

"Adjourned for the day. We'll continue tomorrow at nine a.m.," the judge said as he stepped down from the bench. As soon as the door to his chambers shut, the crowd began to mutter as the reporters rushed headlong toward the doors.

*   *   *

THE SECOND DAY, before the jury came in, Dunland asked to have a conference with the judge and Frank in chambers. Frank insisted that the court reporter record the conversation to be sure that Dunland did not try any funny business.

The judge's chamber was outfitted like the courtroom, heavy, dated and worn. The lawyers and court reporter stood in front of the judge's remarkably small beat-up wooden desk as he sat in his overstuffed leather chair wearing his robe. A credenza with family pictures and a few plexiglass awards the judge had received sat behind him.

"What's up, Counselor?" the judge asked, peering intensely at Dunland.

"It's about the dolls," he said.

"Dolls?" the judge asked.

"I'm not sure you noticed, Your Honor, but small ragdolls dressed like me have been found propped up against the Grant statue in front of the courthouse the last couple of nights."

He turned his head toward Frank.

"I believe we have a troubling case of attempted jury tampering here." Dunland scowled. "Every juror can see them as they walk in."

The judge looked over his horn-rimmed glasses at Dunland and raised his eyebrow.

"So what do you make of this, Mr. Dunland? I don't understand."

Dunland looked peeved.

"These dolls…"

"What about 'em?" Judge Williamson interrupted. "Get to the point."

"The… the… the defense is trying to spook the jury with these, er ah, v-v-v voodoo dolls, scare them." Dunland was pretty agitated, maybe thrown off by the judge's obvious hostility. It was not his habit to stutter.

"Come on, Mr. Dunland. What basis do you have for that claim?" the judge said. "Maybe it's the voters sending you a message before the next election." He snickered with a mean tinge to his laugh.

Dunland turned red.

"But, but, but Judge…."

"Do you have anything else you want to bring up, Mr. Dunland?" Judge Williamson seemed vexed.

"No, Your Honor." Dunland said looking downtrodden, like he was a schoolboy just reprimanded by the parish priest.

The voodoo dolls did not come up again before the judge, but at the first recess of the day, Dunland pulled Frank aside.

"Counselor, pleeeaase stop with the dolls." His voice shook.

"They bother you, Martin?" Frank asked.

"No, no, no, it's just that…" Frank waived his hand as if dismissing the entire incident. "It's every day, with a pin in a different part of my body. The last one right in my balls. You'd be freaked out too."

"The judge was not impressed. Neither am I." In truth, Frank found the whole thing amusing, especially the judge's reaction.

Dunland scowled. "Williamson has never liked me from the day I showed up as the new assistant DA. He keeps making cracks about moving to Benton Harbor from Baton Rouge."

"Why did you do that?"

"I'm not on trial here, Frank."

"Well, at any rate, the defense has nothing to do with this. Why are you asking me?"

Dunland turned abruptly and scurried away like a dog running with his tail between his legs. Frank watched him go, wondering why a few dolls had gotten to him.

Strange, Frank thought. *Got to be more to this.* But Frank did tell Marco to get Erzulie to cool it with the magic. That night she told Marco that she had already cast the spell, so more dolls were not needed.

Dunland next called Dr. Joseph Seaner, the county coroner and a board-certified pathologist. He described in graphic detail the gruesome condition of the bodies when he performed the autopsies. This testimony, like showing the pictures, was not a good moment for the defense. Again, Frank had only a couple of questions on cross-examination.

"Dr Seaner," Frank said. "Both decedents were killed by knife wounds, correct?"

"Yes."

"Same knife?"

"Yes."

"According to your pathology report, Ms. Papadiamantopoulos was stabbed right in the heart, correct?"

"Yes. Actually, multiple times, but certainly in the heart."

"And she was not wearing clothes when she was stabbed, correct?"

"I believe that's the case. I did look at the clothes when I did the exam and there was no evidence that the knife had gone through the pantsuit she apparently was wearing."

Frank held back for a second, then moved out into the center of the courtroom from where he was standing to the left of the jury box. He turned and looked directly at the jury as he continued his examination.

"Ms. Adamos, on the other hand, was stabbed in the neck, correct?"

"Yes."

"In the carotid artery?"

"Yes, precisely."

"Only once?"

"Yes, only once."

"And as best you can tell, the knife was inserted, then pulled out by the attacker, correct?"

"That's a fair assumption, yes."

"That's going to cause blood to spurt into the air, correct?"

"It depends on a number of factors, but it could. I don't know if it did in this case."

"Finally, according to your report the wound was in the shape of a triangle, not just a straight in and out with the knife, correct?"

"Yes, that's what I found."

"So, it would be fair to conclude that the knife was inserted, then some force pushed it to the side before it was extracted, correct?"

"Again, a fair assumption, but I cannot say for sure."

"No more questions." Frank sat down.

"Great job, Frank," Marco said in a whisper that could be heard throughout the courtroom. Frank turned to Marco and glowered. He noticed that Marco's forehead was wet with sweat.

"Outside," Frank said at the next break. He pulled Marco out of the courtroom and into the witness room across the hall. He slammed the door shut.

"I told you don't do that, ever," he said.

"But it's my life, Frank"

"Which you have given to me to save." Frank glared at Marco. "Let me do my work." He walked out of the room, leaving Marco sitting alone.

*　　*　　*

THE THIRD DAY, Dunland called Dr. Roger Millerham to the stand. He was the psychiatrist Dunland had hired to counter Dr. Fullerman.

Frank had carried out an in-depth investigation of Millerham's background and expertise. It turned out Millerham was an associate professor at Central Michigan College of Medicine, a second-tier medical school, and he had testified almost exclusively for the prosecution in cases involving the insanity defense. He'd published, but only a few second-rate articles in lesser-known journals, not a single one peer-reviewed. Frank knew the type.

Dunland spent quite a while asking Millerham questions about his background and experience even though Frank had offered to stipulate that he was an expert. Millerham was of dubious expertise and questionable impartiality, but Frank knew the judge would allow him to testify, so why make a point of his credentials? It would only make Frank look like a jerk. He also knew that Dunland would want to slog slowly through Millerham's qualifications item by item to make sure the jury heard about his background. Dunland's questioning was difficult to endure, but Frank did not see a choice.

Then Dunland asked Millerham about what he had done to examine Marco, his four-hour interview, the bank of tests, and the meeting with the clinical psychologist. Eventually, Dunland got to the point.

"Dr. Millerham, have you formed any opinions about Dr. Adamos' state of mind at the time he killed his wife and Ms. Papadiamantopoulos?"

Frank was amused that Dunland had finally learned how to pronounce Semantha's last name, but he couldn't let Dunland get by with that question.

"Object, Your Honor. It's up to the jury to decide whether my client killed his wife."

"Rephrase, Mr. Dunland. The jury will disregard that question," the judge said, boredom dripping from his voice.

"Trying again. Dr. Millerham, have you formed opinions about Dr. Adamos' state of mind at the time of the deaths?"

"I have. Based on my interview, the psychological tests, and the interview with my psychologist, Dr. Adamos was mentally sane. Furious, yes, but in control of his impulses."

"Were his actions influenced by any symptoms of a condition known as Post Traumatic Stress Disorder?"

"I found no such evidence."

"Did he have the capacity to understand the difference between right and wrong?" Dunland asked.

Millerham turned to the jury and looked directly at them. Plainly, he had provided expert testimony in a jury trial before. He paused for a second.

"Absolutely. As I noted, he was extremely livid, but he still had the mind to apprehend what was right and what would be wrong." He spoke calmly, with assurance.

Frank looked at the jury. They seemed to be listening but did not appear to be jolted by the testimony.

Dunland looked at Frank. "Your witness." There was a note of arrogance in his voice, like he was confident this case was now on ice.

Frank stood and walked directly to the witness box. He peered at Millerham for a time from no more than three feet away. Before cross-examination, Frank liked to establish his control with a stare. Millerham looked away, a plus for Frank.

"Dr. Millerham, my name is Frank Douglas. I represent Marco Adamos. I have a couple of questions."

Millerham smirked like he was in control and could handle anything.

"Is the name Bessel A. van der Kolk familiar to you?"

Dunland jumped to his feet.

"Objection, Your Honor. I request a sidebar."

The judge looked like he had just woken up. "Yes." He turned to Frank. "I would like to find out how that's relevant. Come into chambers."

As soon as the judge, the lawyers, and the court reporter had stuffed into the judge's office, Williamson looked at Frank.

"What are you up to, Mr. Douglas?"

"Your honor, van der Kolk is one of the nation's leading experts on the effects of Post Traumatic Stress Disorder. And, as Dr. Fullerman wrote in his report, that led directly to his conduct on the day in question."

"Your Honor," Dunland responded. "We know what Fullerman's report says, but this van der Kolk was not mentioned."

Frank had brought a copy of the report and attachments with him.

"Your Honor, you can look for yourself. Attachment 6, a chapter from his recently published book, *The Complexity of Adaptation to Trauma. Self-regulation, Stimulus Discrimination, and Characterological Development.* That's a mouthful for a title," Frank said with a purposeful grin. "But it's there." Frank pointed the report at Dunland then offered it to the court.

The judge waved his hand as if implying he did not need to see it. He focused on Dunland, looking like he was going to jump out of his skin.

"Mr. Dunland, you didn't do your homework. Objection *de-nied.*" He emphasized the word "denied" when he spoke.

Dunland's head dropped. Frank knew how Dunland felt. He had been there when he was a junior attorney, coming face-to-face with the calamity of a game-changing stupid mistake.

Back in the courtroom, Williamson addressed the jury. Whenever he talked, they looked at him as if they were paying attention.

"Ladies and gentlemen, this was the first sidebar of the trial. Sometimes the parties request the opportunity to discuss a legal issue outside the hearing of the jury so as not to prejudice the impartiality of the deliberations. You are instructed not to place any weight on that in reaching your conclusions. Proceed, Mr. Douglas."

"So, Dr. Millerham, my question to you is, are you familiar with the name Bessel A. van der Kolk?" Frank smiled inside. Certainly, the jury would figure out he had won that little skirmish.

"Er yes, he's an expert on the effects of trauma on personality."

"So, you consider him authoritative in that field?"

Millerham squirmed in his seat. The look of confidence drained from his face. He took out a handkerchief and wiped a bit of sweat from his forehead. Only two questions into his cross-examination and he was already looking shaken. Frank thought maybe he could wrap this faker up in knots, but there was no reason to do that. He could be seen as the aggressor and his client's case would suffer.

"I, I suppose," Millerham finally responded. "Lots of people are raving about his new book."

"Thank you, Doctor. Then just two questions about your examination of Mr. Adamos. Did you use any form of Trauma Symptom Inventory in assessing whether he was suffering from PTSD?"

"What's that?"

Frank did a mental summersault. The answer couldn't be better.

"One last question, Doctor." There was a hint of sarcasm in Frank's voice when he said the word "Doctor." "Did you employ any PK scale in evaluating the MMPI test you administered?"

Millerham took his index finger and ran it back and forth along the inside of his collar. He cleared his throat.

"I'm not sure what that is, Mr. Douglas."

Frank was delighted. Millerham had destroyed his own credibility. No need for Frank to try to squeeze anything more from him. Frank looked over at Dunland. He was furiously reading something from Fullerman's report, probably Attachment 6. But it was too late now.

"No more questions, Your Honor," Frank said.

"Mr. Dunland?"

Dunland raised his head from the report. His eyes danced on the edge of panic.

"No redirect, Your Honor."

Outside the courtroom, Marco asked Frank why he hadn't tried harder to discredit Millerham.

"Wait for Fullerman's testimony," Frank said. "Cross-examination is for impugning the testimony, not beating up the person."

*   *   *

ON THE FOURTH DAY of the trial, Dunland looked calm but not quite as confident as when the trial began. He stood up and told the judge that the state rested. He had not called Erzulie—good news for Frank. Now when he called her as part of the defense case, it would look to the jury like the prosecution was afraid of what she had to say.

Dunland sat down.

"Your case, Mr. Douglas," the judge said.

To Frank, those words were like a rousing call to arms, his chance to recast the evidence to suit the interest of his client. He loved this moment. He felt a surge of adrenaline and was riveted to the task at hand. As he stood up, he turned to Marco.

"Here goes," he whispered and offered Marco a small smile, even though at that minute he was uninterested in anything Marco was thinking or feeling. The spotlight was his and his alone.

He walked out from behind the defense table and proceeded to the middle of the courtroom where he slowly surveyed the room. For Frank, a trial is theater. As a main character, he had to be active and engaged, in motion, projecting bold confidence. He usually examined and cross-examined his witnesses standing a little to the side of the jury box to make it seem like he was one of the jurors asking the questions. As he walked and talked, he would sometimes look at the jurors, sometimes at the judge, and sometimes he would go to the prosecution table and look directly at Dunland. And no notes, ever. Frank tried his cases from memory.

"I call Dr. Erzulie Perez," he said. His voice reverberated off every corner of the high-ceilinged courtroom. The mosaic tile floor and the wood-paneled walls made for a slight echo.

Frank asked Erzulie only a couple of questions, mostly about how Marco was acting when she came to the old farmhouse on the river.

"And you called the police to the crime scene, is that correct?" Frank asked.

"Yes."

"Why?"

"I was scared to death. Mr. Adamos was acting crazy as a loon, crazier, foaming at the mouth, everything. I thought he may try to kill me. He knew where I lived."

Frank first looked at Dunland and then at the jury. Dunland was scowling. Maybe he realized that Erzulie's answer had slid past him. She shouldn't have been allowed to tell the jury that Marco was acting crazy since she was not an expert on whether Marco was legally insane, and her amateur opinion could have a prejudicial effect. But now, if Dunland asked to strike her testimony, that would only highlight the answer with the jury. One of Frank's favorite sayings came to mind. *You can't un-ring the bell.*

The eyes of every juror were fixed on Erzulie, as Frank had hoped. The juror Frank thought he might be able to win, the lady in the red dress, nodded slightly when his eyes met hers. *Progress,* Frank thought.

Frank had no more questions for Perez. He was happy with what she had said and was hopeful that her testimony would advance the ball toward acquittal. But he also knew she was very vulnerable. If he was doing the cross, he would probe into her sordid history and strange lifestyle, making sure the jury heard every bizarre detail. And he would point out that it was Erzulie who had saved Marco from drowning, trying to paint her as afflicted by a pathologic savior complex. Skillful cross-examination could easily neutralize the positive benefits of her testimony.

He waited to see what Dunland would do.

"Your witness," the judge said to Dunland.

"No questions, Your Honor," he replied.

Frank was shocked. Dunland had missed a golden opportunity. He couldn't imagine why. Maybe Dunland was following the old lawyer's rule that you don't ask a question unless you already pretty well know the answer. Maybe Dunland decided there was no reason to bother about her testimony as he had proved the murder and Marco's involvement, and didn't want to overplay his hand. Neither explanation made good sense to Frank.

The Perez testimony stands. More Adamos good luck, Frank thought.

"Mr. Douglas, call your next witness," the judge said.

"I call Marco Adamos."

Someone in the packed courtroom gasped. It was an audacious move. But Frank and Brad had spent days preparing Marco. It was essential the jury understand that he was trying to save Cynthia when the knife plunged into her neck. His testimony was also critical because part of Fullerman's testimony would be based on Marco's distraught state of mind due to Cynthia's death.

Frank had to call him, but he also knew Marco. Despite all the preparation, he was worried about how Marco would react to push back from Dunland. Frank could easily see Marco blowing up and saying almost anything, throwing everything away in a hot outburst.

*   *   *

"No more questions," Frank said looking at Dunland when he was finished with direct examination. It was Dunland's turn. On the outside, Frank seemed calm, almost serene. Inside, he was close to panicked. This was the ball game.

Dunland got up and walked over to Marco. He looked Marco directly in the eye and stared at him for a while.

Frank blanched. Marco was not good at staring an opponent down, but, for once, he looked back politely as a slight smile came to his lips. He appeared humble, not intimidated.

"Let's see, Doctor. You are a scientist, correct?" Dunland asked, without even introducing himself. He moved closer and stared at Marco more intently.

"Yes."

Got your PhD from MIT, correct?"

"That's right."

Some time ago now?"

"1985."

"And now you are an associate professor at the University of Chicago practicing at the Fermilab National Accelerator Laboratory, correct?"

"Yes. Well, I was...."

"And you've published extensively in good-quality scientific journals, correct?"

"I've published some. I wouldn't say extensively."

"But you've published."

"Yes."

So far so good, Frank thought. *Keep your cool, boy.*

"Doctor, to get where you are in your career took a great deal of work, I would assume, correct?"

Now it begins.

"Yes." Marco's voice was soft, but more importantly, not timid.

"Hours spent pouring over articles and textbooks. Days, weeks, even months performing experiments, writing reports, all that, correct?"

"Yes," Marco said, sounding meek.

"And a great deal of good old-fashioned discipline, right?"

"I would say focus, but sure."

"Call it what you want. Focus, discipline, whatever, you had to concentrate, correct? Had to stay focused?"

Dunland was upping the ante, getting a little argumentative.

"Yes."

Frank felt the tension building. He hoped the jury did not see his hand quiver slightly. Dunland looked at Marco in silence for what seemed like an hour.

"I'll bet there were times, probably many times," Dunland finally continued, "when you wanted to go out and have a beer with friends, but you continued to work, right?"

Marco fidgeted in his chair and looked down.

Oh, my God, Frank thought. He had told Marco over and over to keep looking at the jury, not looking down. Averting his eyes could be interpreted as a guilty reaction.

"I loved my work, Mr. Dunland," Marco responded, looking slightly sheepish.

Good, Frank thought.

"You loved your work, so you kept yourself under control, correct?"

"I was submerged in my work," Marco said without hesitation, sounding irritated and with an almost imperceptible frown.

Is he beginning to crack? Frank wondered.

"And I'll bet that, to get where you are, you had to bite your tongue every so often, right?"

"Part of life, Mr. Dunland." The soft expression had returned to Marco's face. Frank calmed some.

"Yes, part of life, Dr. Adamos. Life your victims no longer enjoy, right?"

Frank jumped to his feet. "Objection," he said.

"Sustained," the judge said. "The jury will disregard that question. Proceed Mr. Dunland."

Good, Frank thought. The objection broke Dunland's rhythm slightly and gave Marco a touch of support.

"But you didn't haul off and slug your professor if you didn't like a grade or punch your boss if you didn't get the raise you wanted, right?"

"I respected them too much," Marco responded, again sounding confident.

"You didn't lose control and try to hurt them, correct?"

Dunland was zeroing in. Frank held his breath waiting to see what Marco would say.

"I did not try to hurt them, no."

He's doing pretty well, Frank thought. *No anger, no arrogance, no frustrated scowls. But we're not done yet.*

"Dr. Adamos, isn't it fair to say that you have gotten to where you are because you kept yourself under control when you needed to?" Dunland asked with a scowl.

The judge, the jury and the spectators were all looking at Marco, unquestionably waiting for his answer. Frank saw a bit of panic in Marco's eyes. Marco looked toward him as if begging for an answer. Frank stared back blankly. Marco paused for a second.

"Mr. Dunland, I've often wondered how I've gotten to where I am, but I would say it was because of many things, including a lot of luck," he eventually said.

Not bad, Frank thought, *but far from over.*

Dunland shook his head and looked at the jury.

"But you do agree with me that controlling yourself when you needed to was an important part of your success, correct?"

A look of fear swept over Marco's face.

A big test, Frank thought. *Can he get through this one?*

Again, Marco paused. Again, Marco looked at Frank. Again, Frank looked back expressionless. Marco was on his own.

"Self-control is always important. I'm not sure how much that played in my success., Mr. Dunland, but…" Marco hesitated again.

"But what, Mr. Adamos?" Dunland asked.

"No buts, Mr. Dunland. I don't want to argue."

Frank had told Marco not to argue with Dunland. Merely answer the questions, he had said. Frank could clear up problems on redirect if needed.

"Finish your sentence, Mr. Adamos," Dunland said.

Marco looked at the judge.

"You have to answer, Mr. Adamos," Williamson said.

"I'm only human."

Out of that one, Frank thought. *Not wonderful, but not fatal either.* Marco was holding up.

As cross-examination continued, Dunland tried, over and over, to get Macro to admit that he had mastered the art of self-control, regardless of the situation and in a host of different circumstances. Marco squirmed on the hard oak chair in the witness box but never went further than conceding that, in one case or the other, he had kept his cool. Frank hoped the jury would not think him cagey.

Frank was relieved when, after two hours of interrogation, Dunland said, "No more questions." It had not been perfect, but it was not a disaster. No outbursts and no nasty arguments.

"Redirect, Mr. Douglas," the judge said.

"No questions, Your Honor." Dunland had not impeached Marco's testimony showing that he was not Cynthia's killer, didn't really try. No reason to rehash or rehabilitate what Marco had already said. It was good enough as it was.

*   *   *

ON THE FIFTH DAY, the lady in red, as Marco now thought of her, had changed from the red dress she had worn each day before to one almost identical in style and vintage except it was bright green. Frank was superstitious enough to be heartened by the change.

Red to green—like a streetlight. Maybe a real crack in the wall, he thought.

"I call Dr. Izzie Fullerman," Frank said in a quiet, small voice. Frank liked to change his cadence and tone from time to time to keep the jury interested and listening, and now, by speaking quietly, he emphasized the import of the testimony he was about to elicit.

A short, rotund man navigated through the crowd of spectators and ambled toward the witness stand. He walked with a pronounced limp, a feature Frank liked. Made him seem more human, more sympathetic. But his fancy Italian suit, accented with a starched white shirt and gold bow tie, would be a turn-off for the plain folks in the jury—maybe not to the Swiss lady or the clinical psychologist, but most of them.

After a torrent of objections from Dunland, all of which the judge overruled, Frank proceeded with his examination. He asked about Fullerman's credentials—MD from Harvard, PhD from Cambridge—anticipating that the jury would see he was far more qualified than Millerham. He also asked what he had done to examine Marco and the research he had performed to prepare to testify.

"I'm pretty familiar with the current understanding of the effects of trauma on human behavior," Fullerman said. "I know one of the leading experts on the subject, Bessel A. van der Kolk. A couple of months ago, he asked me to read an advanced draft of the chapter in his new book on that subject. Chapter Nine, I believe."

"I'm going to show you now an exhibit, I've marked it Adamos Exhibit One for identification," Frank said. "Is this the chapter in the book to which you referred?"

"That's it," he said after feigning to examine the document.

"Your Honor, I move the admission of Adamos Exhibit One into the record."

The court looked at Dunland. "Any objections, Mr. Dunland?"

"No, Your Honor," Dunland said meekly, looking down as if he knew he had already lost the battle over the chapter in van der Kolk's book.

"Admitted," the judge said. "Proceed, Mr. Douglas. We will publish all of the exhibits to the jury when they are charged."

"Is there anything in particular in this article upon which you relied in forming your opinions?"

Fullerman threw his head back a little; the corners of his lips went up making the barest shadow of a smirk.

"Not forming them, but in confirming them." Frank wished Fullerman would not be quite so haughty, but he did like the answer.

"Several times in this chapter," Fullerman continued, "he underscores what my own experience demonstrates, which is that someone suffering from PTSD has difficulty controlling his or her impulses. These impulses can get so strong that they compromise reason. Let me say that more clearly: the impulse obliterates reason."

"Do you consider yourself to be an expert on diagnosing and treating PTSD?"

"Yes."

"Did you determine whether Mr. Adamos suffered from PTSD as part of your examination?"

"Yes. I employed two standard, very well-recognized diagnostic tools for PTSD, the Trauma Symptom Inventory and the PK Scale of the Minnesota Multiphasic Personality Inventory, commonly referred to as the MMPI. They both showed strong evidence that Mr. Adamos suffered from a severe case of PTSD, I presume from everything he went through here in Michigan. But the test does not diagnose a cause, only the manifestation of symptoms."

Frank looked at the jury. They were listening, the most he could wish for in this sweltering courtroom. He hoped that they got the point. Fullerman had just destroyed Millerham.

Frank looked around the room. Dunland looked like he had just choked on a mouse, and the judge appeared comfortable and satisfied, as if he had eaten a piece of cherry pie à la mode. He noticed in the corner that a court illustrator was working away. He reminded himself to have his assistant order some copies.

Frank then asked Fullerman the marquee questions, the ones he hoped would sway the day for his client.

"Doctor, as a result of your examinations, have you reached any conclusions about Mr. Adamos' state of mind at that old farmhouse?"

"I have," Fullerman said, sounding in charge.

"Please tell the jury what you have concluded."

Fullerman pulled on his right earlobe for a few seconds, looked at each juror individually, and then in a quiet voice—almost a whisper—he began. *This man is good,* Frank thought. *Worth every penny.*

"Dr. Adamos suffers from some narcissistic tendencies, not uncommon in persons like him who are extremely talented and unusually handsome. But in his case, those tendencies are overlaid by great insecurities, in my view resulting from his abusive and unloving parents. When he was a child and then a teenager, he felt isolated and alone because he had no family life to speak of. For that reason, too much is never quite enough, especially as far as his relationships with women are concerned."

"How has that played out in Dr. Adamos' conduct in this case?" Frank asked from his usual position next to the jury box.

The jury seemed engaged, all looking at Fullerman. The lady in red, now green, sat on the edge of her seat.

"Typically, in a man with Dr. Adamos' psychosocial makeup," Fullerman said, "it is very difficult to form lasting supportive bonds with women. They tend to translate their legitimate desire for closeness into a sexual agenda, as I believe he has. This has also led to a great deal of ambivalence about what Mr. Adamos wants and how to get it. To his credit, he seeks genuine intimacy, but he is still driven by carnal desire."

Fullerman stopped speaking and again surveyed the jury.

"And there is one extremely unique aspect to Dr. Adamos' psychosocial makeup which was very evident during my examination."

"What's that?" Frank asked, hoping that the jurors were asking themselves the same question.

Fullerman brushed back the few gray hairs on his mostly bald head, cleared his throat, and leaned forward in his seat.

"In my opinion, the murder of his wife, especially in the unique way it happened, aggravated the Post Traumatic Stress Disorder from which he suffered as a result of his capture and abuse at the hands of the satanic cult, in which Ms. Papadiamantopoulos was a key player. His PTSD was in remission until he saw his wife murdered, sadly playing an unwitting part in her death. This caused... Well, in the vernacular, his brain blew a fuse. I do believe he loved his wife, to the extent he could actually love any woman."

"You mean Cynthia Adamos?" Frank asked.

"I believe that's her name."

"Have you formed any opinions as to Dr. Adamos' state of mind when he stabbed Semantha Papadiamantopoulos?"

At that moment, Erzulie, who had been sitting quietly in the back of the courtroom, stood up, climbed over the other spectators sitting in her row, and ran for the door holding her left hand on the side of her head. As she opened the door, her face tightened into a pout. "Michalik," she said in a loud whisper. The door made a noisy thud as it slammed shut behind her and a murmur arose among the spectators.

The judge banged down his gavel.

"Order," he shouted. But then he looked at Dr. Fullerman and smiled. "Sorry, Doctor. Please continue."

"I have formed some opinions, Your Honor." Fullerman looked at Williamson, then at the jury.

"What are they?" Frank asked.

"Based upon the testing my staff performed, my interview with him, and the extensive psychosocial history I collected, Dr. Adamos was insane when he killed Ms. Papadiamantopoulos, in the sense that his capacity to think clearly and rationally had been overridden, perhaps you could say overwhelmed, by the series of events to which he had been subjected." Fullerman spoke with pompous arrogance.

Way too full of himself, Way too many big words. But still great, Frank thought. He was ready to ask the lynchpin question.

"Doctor, in your considered opinion, within a reasonable degree of medical certainty, did Dr. Adamos have the capacity to control his actions at the time of the death of Ms. Papadiamantopoulos?"

"He did not. His act was as a result of an uncontrollable impulse precipitated by all that had happened to him—way back to his initial capture, now years ago. And I might add, at that moment in his insanity, all the pain, suffering, and humiliation he had experienced for well more than a year was personified by Ms. Papadiamantopolos as she stood there before him," Fullerman said and then went silent for a second.

"And I might add, nothing in Mr. Adamos' life had prepared him for this moment. It was qualitatively and quantitatively different from anything he had ever experienced before."

Frank looked over at Marco, who sat at the table with his head buried in his hands crying quietly, even though Frank had told him not to. Frank also saw out of the corner of his eye that a couple more of the jurors seemed to have perked up, particularly the retired sixty-five-year-old psychologist and the Swiss lady, although she was hard to read. Other jurors stared blankly at Marco, revealing no hint of emotion. Frank wondered what they were thinking.

"No more questions," Frank said. He felt like a gardener who had planted some seeds, and had to wait to see whether they would grow.

*   *   *

"...And in conclusion, ladies and gentlemen of the jury..." Frank stood right in front of the jury box with his hands resting on the railing that separated the box from the rest of the courtroom. He had been talking to them for more than an hour in a calm, relaxed voice, as if he was an old friend.

He paused mid-sentence, looked at each of them one by one, then lifted his arms and motioned with his hands outstretched as if making an invitation. He raised his voice. "The evidence presented to you shows that Mr. Adamos did not kill or intend to kill his wife, Cynthia. Rather it was Ms. Papadiamantopoulos who thrust the knife into his wife's neck just as he was trying to deflect it away. Ms. Papadiamantopoulos' clothes were soaked in Ms. Adamos' blood. That would not have occurred if Ms. Papadiamantopoulos did not cause Ms. Adamos' death."

"Further, the murder weapon carried her fingerprints, and the wound had a triangular shape, as if the knife had been pushed to the side after it entered the body. It is reasonable to infer that happened when Mr. Adamos hit Ms. Papadiamantopoulos' hand, trying to stop her."

Frank looked down for an instant and shook his head. "...regrettably a moment too late."

"The State has therefore not proved that Marco Adamos killed or intended to kill his wife, let alone proved he was culpable beyond a reasonable doubt."

Frank pulled a handkerchief from his pocket and wiped his brow.

Before he continued, he looked up at the judge, then again at each member of the jury, finally letting his gaze fall on the woman in green.

"Further, in testimony that the State has not refuted, you have heard from one of the nation's leading forensic psychiatrists, Izzie Fullerman, M.D."

Frank emphasized the letters "MD."

"He testified that Mr. Adamos suffered from Post Traumatic Stress

Disorder caused by the very person standing in front of him on that horrid night, that is Ms. Papadiamantopoulos. As a result of that condition, he was not in control of his emotions and acted by reason of his uncontrollable impulse when he stabbed her."

"Therefore, again, the State has not proved that, under the laws of the State of Michigan, Mr. Adamos is legally culpable for the murder of Semantha Papadiamantopoulos."

By this point, the eyes of every member of the jury were fixed on Frank. He took a moment and, in his mind, reviewed what he had said to be sure he had made his points. He felt comfortable that they had listened. *Enough,* he thought.

"Therefore, ladies and gentlemen, we implore you, I implore you, to find the Defendant, Marco Antonius Adamos, not guilty of the murder of Cynthia Adamos. We implore you to find the Defendant Marco Adamos not culpable for the murder of Semantha Papadiamantopoulos, due to temporary insanity."

Frank turned and surveyed the rest of the courtroom, the judge, the spectators, even Dunland and Peterson. They were all looking at Frank, not moving. Frank walked over and stood in front of Dunland and Peterson, looking down at them almost with disdain.

"Marco Adamos rests," he said.

*   *   *

"You were incredible," Marco said as he and Frank walked toward the doorway to the courtroom. He had never seen Frank in action before. Marco marveled at how smooth and commanding he had been before the jury.

"We will see if they are persuaded," Frank said, taking off his suit coat. Judge Williamson had refused Dunland's request that everyone be allowed to take off their coat jackets.

"Mr. Dunland, this is a murder trial, not a picnic in the park," the Judge had said with a scowl.

Marco took Frank's damp coat and threw it over his own sleeve. Frank had enough to carry, lugging the oversized trial briefcase.

"They must have been persuaded. Who wouldn't be?" Marco said. Frank stopped walking and stared at Marco.

"It's only the opinions of twelve people that matter and you're not one of them," he said.

"How do you think it went?" Marco asked.

Frank said nothing. He opened the courtroom door and propelled Marco through the squeezing crowd milling around outside the courtroom. Frank looked straight ahead, ignoring the torrent of questions, and pushed Marco into the witness room across the hall from the courtroom. He shut and locked the door.

"There, that's better, away from those crazies." Frank threw himself down on the single chair in the room as if he bore the weight of the world.

"To answer your question, it's hard to say. I've learned through experience that I'm way too close to the case to accurately assess the outcome. So, after a trial, I try to blank it out of my mind, think about something silly, try to relax."

He sighed.

"But I've also learned that it's way too easy for someone like you to become dazzled by the foot work. You don't appreciate that what matters is the number of times the ball goes through the basket. Dunland made some good points."

"I didn't see them…like what?"

"He painted you like this entitled man used to getting your own way." Frank shook his head. "And he was effective in pointing out that you spent a lifetime controlling your impulses. His message to the jury?" Frank shrugged. "You don't get to what you have accomplished without a whole lot of self-control. So, your defense is way too convenient. At least, that's what he argues."

Marco's anxiety rose when Frank said that. Awash with overconfidence, he had missed that point while the trial was underway. But now what Frank said made sense. Marco decided to focus on positives as an antidote for his apprehensions.

"But Fullerman did great, I must admit, worth the price," he said. "I got scared when Dunland asked him if I might act on a violent impulse again. His response was classic. 'Only if he's captured by another satanist cult.' Perfect."

"Yeah, I heard someone in the courtroom snicker when he said that," Frank said. "That shut down one of Dunland's main arguments. Without that response, I'm sure he would have argued that you remain a threat and should not be let free." Frank smiled weakly. "I take some credit for Fullerman's response."

"How so?"

"In my meetings with him, I emphasized over and over how strangely unique this case was. He got the point."

"But Frank, what do you…?"

Frank stood and motioned toward the door.

"C'mon, let's wade through the vipers outside and get out of here. Kibitzing is for old men sitting in the park playing Checkers. Besides, I'm starving."

Frank opened the door and found the hallway surprisingly empty, except for Erzulie, who stood there in her old-maid aunt pantsuit, wearing her pearl necklace, undoubtedly her only piece of jewelry.

"Congratulations, Mr. Douglas," Erzulie said. "Great closing argument. You made Dunland look like so much chopped liver."

Frank stopped and smiled at her.

"I thought you were vegetarian?" he said, throwing a quixotic look her way. Erzulie smiled back.

"Can I walk out with you?"

"Free country," Frank said as he continued to walk toward the steps down to the front door. Marco could see that Frank wanted to get away. His slow walk and slightly bent-over shoulders told Marco that Frank was drained.

"What's next?" she asked as they walked down the steps. Frank did not answer but he stopped at the landing and pointed out the open window. Thunder clouds were rolling in.

"Look guys, we're not done yet," Frank said. A Channel 16 mobile unit sat out front with a reporter and cameraman standing next to it.

"Shit," he said. "Ms. Perez, we can't be seen with you. Can you leave first, and try to avoid talking with them?"

"Okay. I'll go see my friend in the clerk's office. Ya know, Semantha's old boyfriend."

That statement rankled Marco. He wondered how he could have ever let himself get so taken by such a slut. But he was also a little jealous.

"One big happy family, eh?" Frank said as he looked at Erzulie.

Erzulie did not respond to Frank's dig but continued down the hallway.

Outside, the scorching heat and the hot sun peeking out between the clouds hit them hard. It had been stuffy inside the building but was much worse in the bright sunshine. The reporter walked up to them as soon as they cleared the door. His armpits were visibly moist with sweat.

"How about an interview, Counselor? That was an impressive performance," he said.

"No comment," Frank said as he brushed by.

"How long before the jury decides?" he yelled at Frank as he continued to walk toward his car. "The longer, the better," Frank said without looking back.

*   *   *

FRANK PUSHED the "Max" button on the car's air conditioning. The cold air felt refreshing, like a sip of ice water after a long uphill run.

What to do now? Frank thought.

It could be days before the jury reached a verdict, depending on whether they took the *irresistible impulse* defense seriously. The longer they stayed out, the more likely they were doing so. Return in a day or two, Marco is done. Frank did not want to say that to Marco, however. What was going on in that jury room—whether the woman in green, maybe the Swiss woman, maybe the psychologist was with us or against us, what others thought about the defense—was all useless speculation. No reason to get Marco's hopes up too high without basis, nor dash them on the rocks unnecessarily.

But he was cautiously optimistic. He had clearly outlawyered Dunland and his intuition told him that the jury had paid close attention to his arguments. Frank felt he had connected with them, person to person, a critical step to a verdict in his favor. Marco had survived cross-examination reasonably well and Fullerman was…. Well, Fullerman was Fullerman.

Still, Frank was tense. He always hated the time spent waiting for the jury to return a verdict. Not only was there a natural letdown after the adrenaline-soaked trial, but he also couldn't concentrate on anything until the jury came in—no other case, no brief, no newspaper, no magazine, no TV, not even taking out the garbage, nothing could hold him. Mostly he sat around and, depending on the time of day, drank coffee or bourbon.

He decided to drive Marco to South Haven for dinner, get away from the locals and all their questions. As he drove, Frank thought back to the first time he and Marco had come to the Berrien County Courthouse. Then, Marco had decided to voluntarily turn himself in, regardless of the consequences. Now Marco seemed to be doing everything possible to shirk responsibility, even depleting his life savings for Dr. Fullerman's testimony, and maybe evoking a crazy voodoo curse to try to tip the scales of justice his way; Frank didn't know.

What had changed? Up till now, Marco had not answered that question and Frank still wondered. The Marco sitting next to him now was not the same man he had counseled after the first incident. He absolutely wasn't the same person he had coached in the high school youth league.

Frank chose a tiny Ma and Pop restaurant in downtown South Haven for dinner and, as soon as they sat down, ordered two glasses of Merlot.

"What changed from the last time?" he asked.

"What do you mean?"

"You wanted to fight this time. Last time you wanted to take responsibility."

"I don't think anything's different." Marco fiddled with his wine glass, then took a sip.

Frank was surprised by Marco's flip reaction to such an important question. But Frank was too emotionally depleted for a deep conversation. He let the comment ride. Maybe the subject would come up again in the future.

They ate in silence. Frank's mind wandered to what he would do after the trial. Maybe it was time for one of his Miami Beach getaways. Hang out with the beauties on the Twelfth Street Beach. He missed the Cardozo Hotel and loved the whole Art Deco strip.

"So what do we do now?" Marco asked as they walked toward the door after Frank had paid the bill.

"Wait."

"How long?"

"Hard to say." Frank was not in a mood to explain more. They got in the car and drove to Benton Harbor. Neither spoke until they got back to the rental house.

"When you were preparing your closing argument, Erzulie walked up to me," Marco said as he and Frank sipped a beer in the kitchen.

"You should stay away from that old buzzard," Frank said, unbuttoning his now sweat-stained white shirt.

"She said that the jury would deliberate for three days. That would mean we will know on Thursday, or so she says."

Frank took off his shirt and threw it on the extra chair. He looked at Marco with a slight smirk.

"How would she know?" Frank asked, shaking his head.

"In Santeria, she told me, they have this thing they do with seashells."

Frank shrugged his shoulders. "Quaint," he said.

"Three days… That's a long time if your life's on the line, Frank. I won't sleep a minute."

So? Frank thought. Frank was tiring of Marco's relentless narcissism. He went straight to bed.

*   *   *

MARCO SPENT his time pacing around the house wearing an old pair of workout pants and a yellowing T-shirt. Sometimes he stared out the window at nothing. Sometimes he tried to watch TV. Sometimes he sat with his head in his hands. Frank had seen many clients go through the same thing. Marco's reaction was one of the worst.

Late Thursday morning, Frank got a call from the Court Clerk.

"Put on some decent clothes and get cleaned up," Frank said to Marco. "Like now. The jury's coming back."

Frank drove Marco to the courthouse and they went up the old, worn marble stairs to the courtroom. Dunland was already sitting there.

"Good afternoon, Counselor," Frank said and feigned a smile.

"What took you so long?" Dunland responded. He then looked at the clerk sitting at his desk beside the bench. "Tell the judge we are all here."

A moment later, Judge Williamson emerged from chambers, took the bench, and directed his attention to the clerk. He stumbled a little walking up the stairs, as if he had gone back to the days of the three-martini lunch.

"Summon the jury," he said.

The clerk went to the jury room, knocked on the door, then opened it. "Ladies and gentlemen, attend to the court."

Frank looked at Marco. He was shaking like a leaf. His face was puffy and his eyes bloodshot. Marco looked like a fallen spirit in

Dante's *Inferno*, dreading imminent final judgment and powerless to do anything besides take it.

The jury shuffled in looking serious. No one smiled. But Frank was heartened when first the Swiss lady, then the lady in green—today wearing a large necklace with a cross—nodded slightly in his direction.

Good instinct, he thought, patting himself on the back.

Nonetheless, Frank was anything but calm as the jurors solemnly and slowly, one by one, went into the jury box. They stood until all were in front of their seats, then they all sat down at the same time. He felt like the bottom had dropped out of his stomach as it twisted and turned. The man sitting next to him, in whom he had invested so much, was about to receive the decision that would overshadow the remainder of his life. Frank swallowed hard but he tried to keep a poker face, something he always found very difficult.

The judge looked at the jury. "Madam Foreman, have you reached a verdict?"

Frank was shocked when the lady in green stood. No one in the packed courtroom moved. All eyes were on her. She pulled out a piece of paper.

The lady stood there for a moment, looked around the courtroom, then brushed her hair back. "As to Count I, we the jury find the Defendant Marco Antonio Adamos..." She ceased speaking for a moment as if she wanted to add to the drama. "Not guilty."

A murmur went through the audience. A reporter jumped up and ran for the door. Marco grabbed Frank's knee under the table and squeezed hard. Frank motioned with his hand to stay calm.

"As to Count II, we have not reached a verdict," she said in a quiet, apologetic voice. Frank glanced at Dunland, who scowled and shook his head.

"We are deadlocked," the woman continued. "And after trying very hard for three days, we cannot break the deadlock."

Frank fought the grin pulling at his lips. He had convinced at least one juror that Marco's defense was good. Maybe more. He looked at

Marco. He was smiling, the first smile he had seen on Marco's lips for quite some time.

Judge Williamson looked miffed, but he had obviously been through this before. "I want you to return to the jury room and try once again to reach a verdict. It is in the best interest of justice that you do so. And I caution you in the strongest possible terms. Assure yourselves that your vote for guilt or innocence is based upon the evidence you have heard and the jury instructions I have given you. Nothing else." The Judge stopped talking, peered at the jury from above his glasses and squinted. "No petty bickering or trivial excuses for your vote. And you are sequestered until you reach a verdict or again conclude you cannot."

"All rise," the clerk intoned, and everyone stood up as the jury shuffled out.

"Don't go very far," the judge said to the lawyers after the door to the jury room closed. Frank and Marco went outside the courtroom to one of the wooden benches and sat down.

"The judge, Dunland, all of us, we know this jury is hopelessly deadlocked," Frank said. "The judge sent them back to be sure."

"Frank, I'm—"

"Say nothing, Marco. This plane will land shortly. Hopefully it will be a smooth landing."

Frank was right. About two hours later, the clerk called them back into the courtroom and the lady in green again told the court that the jury was deadlocked and could not reconcile their differences. The judge thanked them for their service and discharged them. Frank and Dunland both asked for the opportunity to interview the jurors and the judge agreed. Frank made a beeline for the lady in green. He grabbed her in the hallway as she headed for the stairs.

"Miss Freedman, the judge has given us the right to ask you what you thought of the case. What can you tell me?" Frank asked.

"You mean other than I had to get a babysitter for ten days and waste my time hearing about how your client treats women? Everyone wanted to throw him in jail and throw away the key."

"Except you, I'll bet."

"No one thought he had acted to intentionally kill his wife. That witch Semantha, that was another matter. My new friend Pascale—she's from Switzerland—and I were the only ones who thought Dr. Fullerman's testimony made sense. We sort of put ourselves in your client's shoes and asked what we would do in those circumstances. There's Pascale over there."

Freedman motioned for a tall, elegantly dressed middle-aged woman to come over. She was across the hall talking to Dunland.

"We had to fend off a lot of pressure," Freedman continued. "We sort of reinforced each other fighting against the reactionaries. I wouldn't have been able to stand the pressure without her."

Pascale nodded back at Freeman, shaking her head "no," and put her finger on her watch. She started walking toward the stairs.

"Nobody asked the question while we were being examined to be on the jury," Freedman continued. "But she told me during a lunch break that she's the wife of the drummer at that crazy voodoo church. Strange coincidence, don't you think?"

More than merely a strange coincidence, Frank thought. Had that come out, she would have been disqualified for cause, and by now Marco would probably be in the prisoner van on the way to the Iona Correctional Facility. And to think he would have used a no-cause challenge to keep her off the jury if he had any left. Funny the way things happen.

*   *   *

"DUNLAND'S DEAD," Frank said to Marco as he put down his phone. They were getting ready to leave to return to Chicago. Marco looked up from packing his suitcase. His jaw dropped and a shocked look came to his face.

"That was Eunice Peterson. Remember? The assistant DA in Berrien County, I guess taking over for Dunland. She wanted me to know right away because she said she would need some extra time before the retrial."

"Retrial?" Marco said with a sour frown. "But I thought you said…" Marco's eyebrows drooped.

"Yeah, I suspect Dunland's talk about a plea deal is off the table now. Peterson sounded pretty gun-ho about a retrial."

Marco's stomach sank like a bag of rocks on its way to the bottom of a lake.

"How'd he die?"

"They say natural causes. Sudden, massive heart attack. That's what Peterson said, anyway. Nobody expected this, not his wife— who's shattered—nor his three teenage kids, not the county administrator, who loved Martin. Dunland appeared to be in great health but apparently, he had a bad heart. He tried to keep that to himself."

Marco looked miffed. "More bad luck for me," he said. He snapped his fingers like someone who had just missed his bet in a game of penny roulette.

Frank's eyes fixed on Marco.

"Don't you ever think about anything but yourself?" Frank growled, his face red and his eyes narrow slats.

"Really. You've already exhausted your bank of good luck for your lifetime, a couple of lifetimes, maybe. What's wrong with you? You murdered a woman in cold blood and all you can think about is trying to squeeze out a good plea deal for yourself. Give some thought to this human tragedy, would you…for two seconds…"

Panic spread through Marco's body. Something told him he had just drained the last drop from Frank's reservoir of goodwill.

"I'm…I'm…I'm sorry," Marco said, almost in a whisper. "I didn't mean it that way."

Frank held up his hand, like he wanted Marco to be still. He stared at Marco for a while, saying nothing. The silence between them grew thick and oppressive, charged.

"Marco, this is the last stop on the train to nowhere," Frank finally said. He jumped to his feet, grabbed his bag, and walked toward the door. On the way out, he turned around and looked at Marco, now sitting on the bed but holding his gaze on Frank, his mouth open, his face drained.

"I need some time to myself. Get back to Chicago on your own. I need to decide what to do. I'm not sure I want to continue with you. I'm exhausted—not only with the case, but with your attitude. Everything about you disgusts me right now."

"No, no, please…" Marco said as he ran to Frank, fell to his feet and hugged his legs. "Don't go. I need you so much." He began to cry, dizzy with emotion. His long, curly hair brushed Frank's shoes as he shook his head from side to side.

Frank looked down at him and glowered. "Another tearjerker, Marco? Well, I'm not buying it this time. Your tears are so much salt water, as far as I'm concerned." He pushed Marco away, went out to his car and drove away.

Marco stood in the doorway watching the car disappear. He sat down on the front porch, stunned by the intensity of his mentor's unanticipated reaction, too numb to even cry. Over and over, he ran one hand, then the other, through his hair.

What have I done? Marco thought.

He picked up a rock and threw it down the lane, then another and another, each time pitching the stone harder and farther than the last. He felt as if he was alone on a desert island thousands of miles from anywhere, with no food, no water, not even anyone to talk with. Was this what genuine loneliness felt like? He couldn't imagine his life without Frank. He had always been like his rock.

Now he had nobody.

Nobody. Nobody, nobody, except… Marco found himself walking down the road to see Erzulie.

XVII

"You're back," Erzulie said, standing in her open front door. Marco was thankful she was home though embarrassed by his own disheveled appearance. His shirt, unbuttoned and pulled out from his pants, hung wet with sweat. His tie was loose around his neck. And he smelled. Marco offered Erzulie a weak smile.

"What you want? You here to thank me for your great victory yesterday?" Erzulie asked.

"Can I stay with you for a couple of days?" Marco dropped his bag on the ground next to the welcome mat.

"What happened? Where's Frank?"

"He went back to Chicago. Had an emergency." Marco did not want to tell Erzulie that he had left in a huff. It was too painful for him to acknowledge to himself, let alone say aloud to someone else.

"And I can't leave the county right now anyway. If I do, that would be a violation of the terms of release."

"What about that place you were staying?"

"Frank was paying for that. I'm out of money. Fullerman was extremely expensive."

Erzulie motioned for Marco to come in. The hovel's strange smells and decrepit appearance seemed familiar to him, almost like he was home.

"No thanks for your victory?" Erzulie asked as she pulled up a chair for Marco and sat down herself. Marco knitted his brow.

"What you mean? It was all Frank and Fullerman. And it wasn't a victory anyway, only a stay."

Erzulie was silent for a few seconds.

"Oshun and I cast a spell on Dunland."

"Spell? Lord almighty, he died. Which turns out to be very bad for me."

"Oshun has a mind of her own." She paused. "Sorry." Erzulie put her pipe in her mouth, then lit it. She reached down and petted Macy, who was rubbing himself against her leg.

"Did your spell have something to do with the dolls outside the courtroom?" Marco asked.

"The dolls?" Erzulie shook her head back and forth. "I didn't have anything to do with them."

"Who did?" A knowing smile appeared on Erzulie's lips.

"Have you met Cisco?"

"The dancer?"

"Yep. I'm not really sure, but he knew Martin's story. I told him."

"The story?"

*   *   *

MARTIN looked up from his algebra notebook and saw his father's looming figure standing in the door to his room. Frederick had that evil look that spelled trouble. Martin wanted to run, but he knew there was nowhere to go.

It was a blistering hot Sunday in the delta and Frederick was shirtless, wearing only work pants held up with a big, wide belt. He had a working man's chest covered in hair. He yanked Martin out of his study chair in his tiny bedroom, dragged him to the living room, and stood him at attention. Martin's mother, Mildred, was also there. Even though it was three in the afternoon, she was wearing only her yellowed terrycloth house robe, her hair wound up in a towel. Her left eye was a puffy black and blue. Bags accented the other. Their tiny two-bedroom bungalow was stuffy and smelled of beer.

"Well, did ya do it?" Frederick asked, spitting out his words. Martin stood quiet, stiff with fear. He began to shake.

"W,w,what, sir? Please…"

Frederick pulled off his belt. Even though he was almost seventeen, Frederick did not hesitate to whip Martin, like he always had. As a 300-pound Baton Rouge dock worker, Frederick could easily over-power Martin when he wanted to—and he wanted to a lot.

"Don't ya play dumb, you fuckin' piece of shit." Frederick raised his belt high and gave Martin a light slap across the face.

"Fess up. Ya knocked up one of them Haitian girls from the camp, didn't ya?"

Frederick doubled his belt and started tapping his calloused hand with it. It made a smacking sound every time it hit his palm.

"I, I, I…" Martin was too petrified to respond.

"So this mean ol' nigger comes by, I guess her pa, an' tells me that if ya don't marry this little floozy, they's gonna put a curse on me an' yer ma."

"We don't need that, baby," Martin's mother said tentatively, shak-ing her head. "Haint ya heard what them voodoo folks can do with them dolls? We've already had enough bad luck for a—"

"Hush up, woman," Frederick said as he gave her a slap across the face. "Git outta man's work."

Frederick grabbed Martin by the seat of his pants and spun him around, giving his behind a stroke with the belt as he turned. "Well, what's ya say, Marty my boy? Don't ya lie to me, hear?"

"She's a slut, Pa. She's got a rep."

"You haint answerin' my question, boy. She says she can prove it." He gave Martin another wack. His body jerked.

"How?" Martin said between sobs.

"Says she saw yer scar down there, ya know what I'm talkin' about. An' wit' a nigger girl, disgrace. Drop em."

"Please, please, please, Pa."

Mildred grabbed Frederick and pushed him away. She stood in front of Martin holding her arms wide open, for sure trying to protect him from her husband's venom. She had a look of terror on her face.

"Please, no more, Fred."

Frederick slapped Mildred to the floor. Then he wacked Martin until he was numb and stopped crying. After a couple more strokes, he dropped the belt and pulled his son's face close to his.

"But we haint gonna have ya marrying no Haitian whore, so you gonna say it weren't you, got it?"

"What am I gonna' say about the scar?"

"I don't care. Say ya told her about it at lunch, say she was being gang-banged and you had your pants off waiting yer turn, I don't care. Make sumpum up, say sumpum. Got it?"

"Yes, Pa."

Martin pulled up his pants and ran to his bedroom where he took shelter with his books.

*   *   *

THE NEXT DAY was senior honors day and Martin had the morning off from school. He didn't need to go until the assembly in the afternoon, which was where he was to learn whether he was going to receive a scholarship for LSU. He wasn't about to miss that.

Frederick had already gone to work when he heard Mildred shriek "No!"

Martin came running out from his room still clutching his open algebra notebook, pencil lodged above his ear.

"What's wrong, Ma?" Martin asked. But then he saw them: dolls propped against the tree and positioned all over the front porch.

"They's comin' after us, son. See there." Mildred pointed at the two misshapen red and black stick-doll figures with crude faces and plumes of brightly colored feathers.

"Don't let them upset you. They're only dolls."

"Dolls? Ask Fannie over in Shenandoah. Her cat died straight away after seein' one. Betsy o'r in Zackery, same. Her pigs up and ran away. Liz in Broussard, dead. Dead, mind ya. Just withered away. Even the Klan's scared. Talk is they're afraid to even go close to the bayou so long as they're there." Mildred shook and ran her hand through her gray, crinkled hair.

"Calm down, Ma. That's only superstition."

"Superstition? Talk to Mattie. She's gone to Congo Square o'r in New Orleans. She told me what she seen there. Hexes, curses, God almighty. They're gonna get us all. They're gonna get ya." Mildred threw her arms around her son and hugged him tight.

"I don't want nothing' to happen to you, my boy. I jus' want ya to get outta this hell hole, go to school like ya want, make something of yourself."

"Maybe I should marry her. I mean…I like her and all that."

Mildred grabbed Martin by the shoulders, shaking her head.

"Your pop will kill ya. He'll kill her to boot. No joke."

Frederick did not show up that night. He was on one of his binges.

The next morning, more dolls showed up, but this time accompanied by a decapitated chicken.

"No, not again!" Mildred screamed, even louder than the day before. She began pacing around the living room, then back and forth to the kitchen. She took a swig of the moonshine from the refrigerator each time she went by.

"Please, Ma. They're only dolls."

There was a wild look in Mildred's eyes. "We are cursed, we are cursed, we are cursed," she shouted. But then the moonshine took effect and she dropped to the floor.

"I'm feeling a little dizzy," she said as she gasped for air.

Martin ran to her, lifted her up to a sitting position and held her close.

"Please, Ma, get a hold of yourself."

"You gotta get to school, boy. Big day for you."

"I'm not leaving you, Ma, until you get over this." Mildred passed out and Martin pulled her up onto the couch, where she slept.

That night, well after dark, Frederick showed up and found Mildred still sleeping on the couch. He gave her a couple of slaps.

"You's a floozy drunk," he shouted as she woke. She offered no resistance. He slapped her a couple of times more, then raped her, groaning loudly with his final thrust.

Martin lay on his bed listening, horror stricken. Once when he was younger, he had tried to protect his mother but paid dearly with a daily thrashing for a week. He cried silently, hoping Frederick would pass out and forget about him.

Instead, he heard Frederick pull the cord of the overhead light in the kitchen.

"Fuckin' shit," he yelled. "I'm gonna get those devils." Martin assumed he had found the dolls and the chicken Mildred had thrown in the wastebasket.

Frederick pulled out his gun, got in his pickup, and drove away. He never showed up again.

Mildred rose from the couch. "No more," she screamed and ran out the door into the bayou.

Now Martin was all alone in the house. He shivered uncontrollably even though it was almost a hundred degrees and more humid than the jungle. He wasn't sure how or why, but he had seen what the dolls could do. He went to the kitchen, then outside, searching for them. He was going to burn them, but they had all disappeared.

*   *   *

"So, CISCO KNEW the dolls would spook Dunland?" Marco asked Erzulie.

"'I think all he wanted was to throw Dunland off track, get him to make some kind of mistake. I'm sure he had no idea he would end up dying. That wouldn't be like Cisco. He's as good natured as you'll find." Erzulie's face softened and her lips broke out in a twinkling smile. Suddenly she looked years younger.

Marco stood and walked to the window, hoping against hope that he would see Frank's car pulling up. No such luck.

"Who knows what was going on in Dunland's mind?" Erzulie continued. "Maybe he believed it was the return of the dolls from Louisiana. Could be anything."

"So he's yanked back to a horrific childhood memory, he goes off the deep end, and then suffers a massive heart attack. Is that what you're saying?"

"Er…" Erzulie ceased for a second "A reasonable conclusion, wouldn't you agree? I learned in medical school that stress alone can kill, so why not some dolls?"

"Evil," Marco said, furrowing his eyebrows.

Erzulie massaged her forehead.

"Look, Marco, voodoo is not an evil practice. It's like Santeria. It's got some quirky twists, but it's really about human fulfillment and success. Not dark magic, not evil. No strange malevolent powers floating around ready to do mischief." She looked Marco squarely in the eye. Then she squeezed up her face and knifed with her hand.

"My curse, the dolls, the rosary, a crucifix, Santeria, all of it. If people believe, these things have power. That's it." Erzulie lit her pipe and took a long drag.

"Look, it's all in the mind. Spooking out Martin's mother, reviving Semantha, curing Clem's mom, all of it. Science calls it the placebo effect, but it's real."

"That makes you out to be some kind of charlatan."

Erzulie shook her head 'no.' and squinted.

"Because I make people feel better, help them get in touch with their own power, bring energy? What's wrong with that? Religion's been doing that for five thousand years, and with no better basis." She stopped speaking and let silence add to the impact. "Remember what that famous author said—What was his name?— 'There's nothing in the sky above or earth below that thinking doesn't make it so.'"

"Where's Cisco in this?" Marco asked. "He's got to be pissed with me. I murdered his old girlfriend after all."

"Cisco didn't care about Semantha. She had dumped him one too many times, and he's happily married now. But he really didn't like Dunland. Dunland tried to get him fired once. Said he spent too much time in the courthouse socializing. I think he was jealous because everybody loves Cisco and people didn't like Martin."

Erzulie went to her hot plate and put on some water for tea.

"He was at the Casa when I put the hex on Dunland, so apparently he decided to give it an extra push, help make my magic work. That would be my guess."

"What's Cisco to you?"

"We like to talk and laugh at the Casa. He's very charming."

Marco helped himself to some tea. After Frank had left, he had no interest in eating or drinking, but he knew he had to have something.

"Cisco tries to be helpful, and he practically worships me," Erzulie continued. "He tells me over and over that I have mystical powers, and I think he really believes that."

Marco's lips turned down and his cheeks turned slightly red.

"Lady, keep your mystical powers to yourself," he said. "Now, thanks to you, I feel responsible for the death of yet another person, and for what? A temporary delay in the inevitable."

"One step at a time, Marco." Erzulie shrugged. "So far my plan is working."

Her plan? Marco thought. *That's the second time she talked about her 'plan.'* He hadn't asked her for help, and her way of helping was too weird. Too destructive. Scaring people with voodoo dolls, playing on their fears and superstitions, dredging up old trauma to haunt anew.

Marco's head reeled like he was caught inside a tornado cloud. His wife dead, his career in shambles, on trial for murder, abandoned by his one and only friend, and now caught in a bizarre cesspool of magic and psychological sorcery.

He thought back to that day he insisted on going sailing with Frank and they encountered *Blind Faith*. What a monumental catastrophe. It had been a miserable day on the water and things had only gone from catastrophe to catastrophe since then. Such a small act but with such horrendous consequences. He felt shipwrecked, floating on a tiny piece of debris in a vast dark ocean.

Marco went to the window and looked down the road again. No Frank yet.

*   *   *

"Dunland's death, was that part of your plan?" Marco asked Erzulie.

"I'm sorry about that." Erzulie rubbed her chin. "I had a warm spot in my heart for Martin."

"Yeah, how so?" Marco slanted his head, looking incredulous.

"Another weird story. I did a post-residency fellowship in neurology at Baton Rouge General Hospital. He was a freshman at LSU and he came to my unit because he suffered recurring nightmares. He was my first patient, told me everything." Erzulie ran her hand through her hair and took a sip of her tea. "I befriended him."

"Merely friends?"

"Yes, but pretty good friends. I felt sorry for him. He was so lonely and afraid. And I was all alone, too, so far away from Michigan. I felt out of place."

"No sex?"

"Not even a kiss." Erzulie dropped her head. She appeared sad, like she had recalled a bad memory.

"Well, he tried once, but I never was into skinny, bookish white boys. And way too needy. Damaged goods. And to boot, he was twelve years younger and very emotionally immature. Not for me."

Marco sensed there was more to this story. Erzulie returned her gaze to Marco and her face brightened.

"When I finished my fellowship and came back to Michigan, he transferred to Michigan State. I suppose to stay close."

"I saw him at the trial," Marco said. "He didn't even nod his head in your direction."

Erzulie pulled on her earlobe while she thought. "Yeah, he didn't want to have anything more to do with me when I lost my license. My guess, he worried that being my friend would be bad for his career."

Erzulie stopped talking and took Macy into her lap. The cat purred as she stroked him.

"Maybe that's why he didn't ask me any questions at the trial. My bet, he was afraid of what I might say. I could have laid him out in lavender, and he knew it."

Erzulie shook her head.

"I got sort of pissed when Martin shut me off. One day, when Cisco told me Martin was trying to get him fired, I blurted out the story. Not too ethical on my part, but..." Her voice trailed off and she again looked to the floor.

Marco studied Erzulie, creaky and gaunt. Not his cup of tea, but he knew that this was no time to walk out on her, to confront her, to condemn her, although he wanted to scream, "Get away!" He had to think about his own survival. At the moment, she was his lifeline. Where would he even go? No family, no friends. The world had become an alien planet. *Maybe it always has been, but I was too self-absorbed to notice,* he thought.

"Please, Erzulie, no more voodoo." He tried to sound polite considering how much he needed her right then."Anyway, dolls, spells, the power of suggestion, none of that is going to get me out of this. One of these days I will need to go before a jury again. I can't count on another Swiss lady or lady in red or green to save me."

Erzulie put her pipe down and peered at Marco. She stretched out her hand over the table as if she wanted to touch him. He moved to avoid her finger. She then tilted her head and studied Marco. Her face took on a steely, stern look.

"Look, Marco, you've got lots of problems, but they all start with you. Probably end there, too. You've never really had to struggle, really struggle. Think about poor Dunland, may God rest his soul, his story. He made it out of a cesspool all by himself.

"What have you done?"

Marco looked down as if shamed by what Erzulie had said. *Is she right?*

*   *   *

THE DOOR OPENED. Cisco walked into the hovel without knocking. He nodded at Marco as if he had expected to find him there and then went to the hotplate to pour himself a cup of tea. He sat down on the remaining chair.

"I heard Dunland died," he said with a gleam in his eye. "No big loss. He was sort of a bore anyway. Around the courthouse he had a reputation as a loser." He took a sip from his cup.

"I'm sure his wife and kids don't feel that way, sir," Marco said with a look of reproof.

"Yeah, they told everybody it was a heart attack. But the rumor is that his wife found him hanging in the attic," Cisco said.

Marco closed his eyes. He gagged but put his fist on his face to make it appear like a cough.

"What brings you barging in like you own the place, Cisco?" Erzulie asked furrowing her eyebrows. "You're interrupting my conversation with Mr. Adamos. I mean, Dr. Adamos" she said, nodding in Marco's direction.

"A bit of bad news, I'm afraid," Cisco said, looking at Erzulie. "People around the courthouse are saying you're responsible for what happened to Dunland, with the doll scare and all that."

"You know that's not true," Erzulie said.

"Probably you should lay low for a while," Cisco said. "Take a trip, whatever. It'll blow over in a couple of months." He was worried about his old friend. Most people Cisco knew thought her peculiar and would welcome an excuse to force her out of town.

"What about you? Aren't you worried?" Marco asked.

Cisco winked. "Eunice and I are on pretty good terms," he said with a half-smile, as if he didn't want to let out some state secret. "Besides every cop in town and I are good friends. Ten years as a deputy, you get some connections."

Erzulie stroked her chin and thought for a few seconds. She exhaled, sighing slightly.

"Perhaps it's time for my fall retreat to the UP, be alone with Oshun. I've not done that for a few years. Maybe I can have a seance and contact Isabella."

"Wait. What about me?" Marco asked, looking panicked. "If you go, where will I stay?"

Erzulie glowered as if saying, 'Is it always about you?'

"If I get in touch with Oshun, I can ask her to send some power your way. And you can stay here as long as you want."

Macy jumped down from Erzulie's lap, ambled over to Marco and rubbed himself against his leg.

"Don't worry, Macy. You're coming with me," Erzulie said as she leaned down to pick up her cat.

"Or you can come and stay with me," Cisco said, looking at Marco with an inviting smile. "At least I have indoor plumbing." He laughed out loud.

Erzulie packed her bag, tossing it into the back of her pickup and throwing Macy into the cab. He let out a cat-like scream as Erzulie started the motor. Cisco and Marco watched as she drove down the lane. The dust kicked up from the gravel roadway made it appear she was being taken into the clouds.

It was the last time Marco saw her.

*   *   *

A TEAR ran down Cisco's cheek as Erzulie's truck disappeared, leaving only the fading remnants of the dust cloud.

"A great lady," he said as he turned to Marco.

Marco said nothing but looked away as if retreating into the solemn crevices of his mind. Cisco motioned for them to go sit on a log across the yard from the hovel.

"Met her at a ceremony in the Casa," Cisco continued. "As soon as I walked in, she came to meet me. When she found out I was single and living alone, she was all over me." He grinned.

"Sexually?" Marco asked as he raised his left eyebrow.

"If that's what she was after, I would have tried to stay as far away from her as I could." He laughed as if amused by the thought.

"She sort of mothered me. Always bringing me food, offering to do errands for me, introducing me to everyone in the Casa. I got to know her well." He rubbed his forehead for a minute.

"She showed me a lot." His eyes took on a penetrating look.

"About voodoo and Santeria?" Marco asked.

"About how to live, what's important." He took out his penknife, picked up a stick, and began to whittle.

"I don't get that," Marco said. "She seems like nothing more than a lonely old recluse." He stood up and looked down the road again, still hoping.

"Didn't she tell you her story? It explains a lot. Listen, you may learn something."

*   *   *

"DR PEREZ, code blue in the ER," a voice said over the intercom system. "Dr Perez to the ER, STAT."

It was the third code blue that night, Erzulie noted. That's what she got for agreeing to work on the Fourth of July in this town. All these rednecks and their macho fantasies. They shoot off enough fireworks to start World War III. Lots of puncture wounds, burns, and ripped appendages to fix up.

But she didn't mind too much. She took holiday work so that the rest of the staff could have time off with their families. And working was a way to distract her from thinking about her impending disciplinary hearing. She knew her time practicing medicine may soon be coming to a precipitous close.

Even more, she yearned for Isabella on family holidays, so it was good to have a distraction. Better to sew up a couple of bumpkins than to sit at home staring at her Isabella keepsakes and getting depressed.

Her living room was a memorial to her daughter, lovingly preserved exactly like it had been the day she passed, the bronzed first shoes now turned into book ends, her first drawing—it said "Mama." The marks on the door frame recording her height every three months—she had gotten up to 58 inches—so many things, along with the legion of photographs as Isabella grew. Erzulie's favorite had been taken by a passerby at the dunes on a hot summer day.

Erzulie wished she could have frozen time somehow, hold in place all the good times they had experienced together. There were so many: taking her to school on the first day, her birthday parties, the laughs they shared, snuggling as Erzulie read her a story. Erzulie's life had revolved around Isabella. She loved being a mother.

Erzulie was the opposite of Fannie, her own mother. She had been a boozer and a floozy with no interest in her six children, and Erzulie's father had died when she was fourteen. As the oldest, Erzulie took responsibility for the children, and she reveled in it.

Her youngest brother, Jason, had a learning disability and a mild case of Tourette's Syndrome. He could not stop shaking his hands. Erzulie tutored him for hours and found a round ball he used as a fidget toy. She got him to learn to play softball with the local disabled team and went to every game. She was always by his side, encouraging him, helping him learn, pushing him gently along.

With a few accommodations—which Erzulie engineered— Jason excelled at school, eventually becoming his high school class valedictorian. In his graduation speech, delivered in a halting, slightly affected tone, he told his class that he owed his whole life to his "loving sister." Erzulie beamed with love and pride. After the speech, Erzulie vowed to do everything she could to be a mother in her own right. She also decided to go to medical school to become a pediatrician.

While Erzulie tried, she never had found another lover after being set aside by that guy Theo, Semantha's stepfather. It still made her mad and depressed to think about him choosing Satanism over her. She wondered maybe, if she had been more of a woman, could she have snagged him and set him on a less destructive path?

What would her life be like now? He was from a leading Benton Harbor family with plenty of money. And he was very intelligent—so what if he was a bit of a dreamer heavily into fantasies of one sort or another? By now they would have five handsome children. She and Theo would be growing old together.

She still remembered seeing Isabella for the first time, abandoned at the hospital ER door late one night when she was on call.

What a beautiful baby, she thought. *Would that it was mine.*

After finding out that the baby's mother had disappeared, Erzulie petitioned for temporary guardianship, then permanent adoption. Everyone thought that would be a perfect placement considering Erzulie's profession and her status in the community.

One of the steps in the adoption process had been to pick the baby's name. After considering many possibilities, she hit on the name "Isabella," meaning "God's promise." Erzulie wasn't sure about the God part, but Isabella certainly filled a hole in Erzulie's life, a promise made reality.

After the guardianship was approved, Erzulie took her nest egg and invested it in a nice home. She had one of the bedrooms converted into a nursery, decorating it in various shades of pink, with a mural of a half moon and stars covering the ceiling. She redid the kitchen and filled it with high-end appliances.

When they moved in, Erzulie looked at her darling baby in her cradle and beamed. "Isabella, my dear," she said. "This is the first day of a great future for both of us. Your mamma loves you so much."

Isabella smiled as if she understood.

*   *   *

MARCO STOOD UP and peered down the lane again, interrupting Cisco's story. He still ached for Frank and could not let go of his vague expectation that he would soon return. After a little anxious longing, he sat back down next to Cisco. Listening to Cisco's story distracted him from his many problems.

"What a fairy tale," Marco said. "It's hard to believe of that old eccentric. There's got to be more."

"That's only the beginning." Cisco looked uncharacteristically sad as his thick, black eyebrows dropped. He stopped whittling and continued.

*   *   *

WEEKS AFTER Isabella turned seven, her healthy glow faded. She ran a persistent fever, and she complained about being tired all the time. Her condition deteriorated very rapidly. Suspecting something serious, Erzulie had first taken Isabella to a childhood infectious diseases specialist and then, after routine tests showed nothing, to a pediatric oncologist in Grand Rapids. She was concerned that Isabella may have cancer.

"Isabella suffers from acute myeloid leukemia, Dr. Perez," said Jordan Smithfield, head of childhood oncology at Corewell Health. Erzulie and he were reviewing the lab results in Smithfield's clinic office, Isabella sitting next to them.

"Isabella has way too many white cells and too few red cells. And from the looks of things, aggressive treatment must begin urgently. Otherwise, she has only a month or two to live. So, I'll get her in for chemotherapy tomorrow. There is no time to waste."

Erzulie visibly shivered. She felt like she had been hit in the head with a brick. She had little faith in chemotherapy for a child with Isabella's condition. Too often she had witnessed children with similar diagnoses endure agonizing treatments, only to succumb in the end. She could not imagine watching this almost inevitable process work its way to its typical conclusion in Isabella. She saw these oncologists as little better than drug dealers on the street, pushing dubious treatments and raking in the bucks.

While Smithfield described the treatment process—as if Erzulie didn't already know—she mulled over what to do next. Maybe Santeria might work. She had seen it help others in the past. She decided to at least try it. A couple of weeks' delay in treatment wouldn't make any difference.

"This is serious," Erzulie said as she stood up, cutting off Smithfield before he had finished. "Come on Isabella, my dear. We've got some work to do." She took Isabella's arm and began guiding her to the door.

"I'll go ahead and set up the appointment, Dr. Perez," Smithfield said.

Erzulie turned back and looked at him. She felt hot frustration. *How dare he try to take over. This is my daughter, not his.*

Saying nothing in response, she shot Smithfield a mean glance, then continued for the door.

"Where are you going, Dr. Perez?"

Erzulie stopped.

"It's time to consult Oshun," she said without looking back. As soon as she said them, she regretted her words. But it was too late.

"Oshun, who's that?" Smithfield asked. "Never heard of him. Where does he practice? What's his specialty?"

Erzulie turned her head back toward Smithfield.

"Oshun is my Orisha."

"Your what?"

"My Orisha. I'm a Santera. I get in touch with Oshun regularly. She's made all the difference in my life."

"This is no time for hocus-pocus crap, Dr. Perez. Frankly, I'm shocked to hear a physician talk like this. You know the stakes are too high for playing around with magic." He knotted his forehead, took off his glasses and threw them on his desk. "Isn't Santeria a cult?"

Erzulie's face turned red. She wheeled around and walked back to Smithfield's desk. Still standing, she stared down at him. Their faces were only a few feet apart.

"Magic? I beg your pardon, Doctor," Erzulie said. "The stakes are too high to simply trust injecting poison into my dear Isabella in the name of treating her problem," she said. "Isabella is my daughter. I love her intently. I will take care of her." Her eyes were burning fire.

"I can't, uh can't, let you do this to a child. She, she, she must be treated," Smithfield said, apparently cowed by the ferocity of Erzulie's response.

Erzulie shook her finger at him.

"Make no mistake, Smithfield. I want her to get better, quickly, too. But I will not, hear me, *will not*, stand by and watch her suffer for no reason. I've seen what chemotherapy does to children. I will not have it given to my baby unless there's no choice. And I have a choice."

Smithfield stood up, his mouth agape. "Doctor, I'm astounded. Chemotherapy is the best, only option. Isabella can live. You are putting the child you love at terrible risk."

These words made Erzulie even more furious. Now, she didn't care what she said or whom she offended. All the anger she'd built up from years of harassment and exploitation at the hands of the white, male medical establishment, both in school and during her residency, boiled over in a wellspring of frustration and bitterness.

"Smithfield," Erzulie hissed. "It's you who should be ashamed, what with your prejudice against anything but the western medicine they teach at those doctor assembly lines called medical schools. They turn out carbon copies of people like you, perversely holding tight to the indoctrination you got regardless of the bigger picture."

Erzulie began shaking. "Yours is no less a cult than Santeria. All you do is make people believe in drugs to get better. It's just that your particular brand of deception has gained the upper hand."

She stormed out, slamming the glass top office door so hard it almost broke.

Two days later, a case worker came to take Isabella. The poor girl screamed and hollered but Erzulie told her that she had no choice. Erzulie was forbidden by the state child protective agency to visit her in the hospital. Six weeks later, after intense chemotherapy, Isabella died. In a month, Erzulie got a letter telling her that the State of Michigan would hold a hearing to suspend her license to practice medicine. It said for "willful endangerment of a child."

*   *   *

THE WIND STOPPED and the woods where Marco and Cisco were sitting became quiet. A red fox appeared from the brush, halted, looked toward them, then vanished.

Cisco ran his hands through his thick, black curly hair and pulled it back revealing his high, regal forehead. He wanted this man to understand why Erzulie was such a remarkable person.

"After she lost her license, which of course was inevitable, she sort of flipped out." Cisco shook his head. "Lots of wailing and cursing, pounding the kitchen table, yelling for her lost Isabella, you know. One day she threw all the nursery furniture into the street and smashed her car into it. Her weird behavior drove her family away. I thought she was done for."

Cisco finished whittling, put his knife away, and drank in the quiet for a few minutes while Marco sat looking down at the leaf-covered ground, unmoving like a marble statue. Overhead, some starlings cackled.

"Finally," Cisco continued, "she got it into her head that she should try to commune with this Santeria spirit, *Oshun*, she called her. She spent days in a trance. When she came out of her stupor, she said she had found peace."

Cisco rubbed his forehead.

"To me it seemed more like resolve. Peace? Okay. But peace arising from bitter anguish, not joy."

Cisco had been at the Casa when Erzulie came out of her trance. He remembered how her face looked, like Venus di Milo in the famous painting.

Marco raised his head and looked at Cisco. He opened his mouth as if he was about to speak. Cisco touched Marco's leg and, with a narrow smile, continued. No need for conversation at that moment.

"After that, she didn't lash out at anyone or talk about revenge. All she did was to try to help everyone she could. It was like she was searching for that happy feeling she had had with her brother and Isabella."

Cisco picked up a pebble and threw it toward the hovel. *It is a cozy looking place*, he thought.

"She had no job, no money." Cisco pointed with his hand. "This place was abandoned, and she moved in. Nobody minded. But it wasn't good for her, stuck way out in the woods. I'd come out and see her every so often, but she kept getting more and more reclusive."

An unhappy smile appeared on Cisco's face.

"My guess, when Semantha showed up, something long buried stirred inside her. Maybe her compulsion to be a mother, maybe a last gasp for finding a lover, who knows."

Cisco sighed. He never had completely gotten over the wonderful encounters he had with Semantha, although now those days seemed so far gone.

Cisco's eyes watered up. He took out a hanky and wiped away a tear.

"I still get choked up when I think about what happened to Erzulie, the tragedy she has endured."

Marco shook his head then put his face in his hands. He began to sob.

"Tragedy? What about *my* tragedy?" Marco asked, his words cascading between gasps of anguish. Cisco understood his desperation. Erzulie had told him the details during breaks at the trial. Cisco put his hand on Marco's shoulder and winked.

"You're going to come home with me and try to forget about your problems for a few days."

Marco looked up and calmed. He was silent for a minute.

"You said Erzulie taught you about life?" Marco eventually asked, his countenance still bruised with fear and grief.

"Yeah, how to deal with heartbreak and loss, turning disasters into something positive."

Marco went silent again.

"Maybe that's what I need to learn to do," he said with a forlorn, far-away gaze.

Neither spoke for a time. Then Cisco stood up and waved his hand. "Enough serious stuff, Marco. Come on and meet my wife. But you gotta stop looking down the road every ten minutes. No one's coming." A full-bodied, mahogany laugh dissolved his serious look.

XVIII

Cisco's house, a white aluminum-clapboard bungalow, sat on an over-sized lot on the outskirts of town. The big lawn surrounding it, while clean and tidy, was not carefully manicured, with scattered patches of grass interspersed with raw dirt. Much of the space was devoted to swing sets, trampolines and sandboxes. A tricycle was parked next to the front door.

"You have kids?" Marco asked as they drove up, merely to make conversation. The answer was obvious.

"My life, Marco. Tad's eight and in second grade. Mae is four. She starts kindergarten next year."

Cisco pulled his Honda Civic into the dirt and grass driveway, not so much a driveway as ruts in the grass which fit the tires of the car. He tapped the horn, and two well-fed children came running out of the house. They both were olive skinned with dark hair, and wore matching jumpsuits.

"Daddy, daddy Tad yelled as he and Mae ran to Cisco and squeezed him around the legs. Cisco picked both of them up and gave them a hug. A woman soon appeared at the front door. She was dressed in a shoulder-to-ankle housedress in muted orange cotton. It hid her rotund frame.

Marco was taken aback by her appearance. Cisco was quite striking with his curly hair, clear olive complexion and broad, eager smile. This woman, Marco assumed she was Cisco's wife, was plain and rough-hewn. Her round face was pockmarked, looked like from a severe case of teenage acne.

Cisco blushed when she ran up to him and planted a big kiss on his cheek.

"Marco, this is Patrice, my loving wife." He put his arm around her waist and squeezed her. "Patrice, meet Dr. Marco Adamos."

"Hello, Doctor, I've heard a lot about you." She offered her hand to shake. Marco wiped his on his pants and extended it to her. His palms were sweaty from the heat.

"About me?" Marco asked. "How? From Cisco?"

"You're the talk of the town, sir. But what brings you to our humble home?"

"He's going to be staying with us for a few days," Cisco said, "until his lawyer friend comes back for the retrial. Don't say anything to anyone…" Now he was looking at both Patrice and the children. "If the newspapers find out he's here, they'll be all over us."

"Welcome," Patrice said to Marco, smiling as if she was truly happy to have him. She gave him a light peck on the cheek.

Marco tried to appear nonchalant in front of these new people but inside he burned with anxiety. Frank's unexpected departure had left him with a nagging disquietude simmering in his every sinew each waking moment. Would Frank ever return?

The fear that he might not weighed Marco down, sometimes making his legs drag like heavy boards and his shoulders stoop. He felt unmoored. He had no idea how to get a new lawyer or to get ready for a retrial, where to start. He didn't even know how to contact the public defender. But losing Frank was so much worse than just not having legal representation. Frank had been at the apex of his life since he was a boy.

"Come, come, come," Cisco said, pointing to the house. "You'll love my family. I sure do."

"Daddy, push me in the swing!" Tad yelled as he grabbed Cisco's sleeve and pulled on it.

"Not now, my boy. We have to make our guest feel comfortable. Come on in Marco, it's not much, but it's home and it's paid for. He opened the screen on the front door and waved Marco in. It felt good to get into the shade. The living room's overhead fan was going full blast.

"Forgive the toys," Cisco said. "Pat tries to keep up with the mess, but it's hard. She also works from the computer in the kitchen. Does phone surveys for Nielson. It's only part time but try living on what I earn as a deputy in Berrien County." He smiled again as Pat came over and put her arm around his waist. She gazed at him with sweet eyes and a wide smile.

"I like my job. It keeps me engaged," she said. "But don't worry about the mess. We'll have it all cleaned up before you go to bed."

"Sorry, all we can offer you is the couch," Cisco said, motioning with his hand to the immense brown leather sofa that almost filled the living room. "But it's soft enough. My mother-in-law loves it." He gave one of the cushions a couple of pushes. "I hope you don't mind."

"It'll be fine." *Anyway, I'm not in much of a position to complain,* he thought. Marco recalled the suite that the National Academy of Physical Sciences had recently reserved for him at the Hotel Sofitel when he spoke to their plenary session in New York. *How far gone, how far….*

Marco dropped his bag next to the couch.

"I'm sure you want to get cleaned up," Cisco said. "The bathroom's down the hall. There's a stack of clean towels there. Throw the wet one in the hamper. Dinner in an hour."

Marco took a shower and shaved. It refreshed him after his long, disastrous day. For the first time in several days, he felt hungry. But he also wondered what Frank was doing at that moment. He imagined Frank out for a solo sail on *Provocateur*. And he dreaded tomorrow, when he would need to figure out how to deal with his problems alone.

As soon as he finished cleaning up, he returned to the living room where Cisco was watching a soccer game on their old Zenith television, which was located on the other side of the room from the couch. The moment Marco entered the room, Cisco jumped to his feet in exultation, throwing both arms high in the air, arching his back, and yelling "Gooooal!" as if he was at the game.

"My favorite team, El Tricolor," Cisco said. "They're playing La Albiceleste, in case you don't know. Argentina's national team. And they just scored. It's a grudge match. Want a beer? You look like you could use one."

"Well, er ah, I don't want to be a bother, and I don't have money to pay for your hospitality," Marco said, standing erect almost like he was at attention. He was trying hard to hide his humiliation. He wasn't used to being the one in need. He preferred playing the gracious host.

"C'mon Marco, you're my guest," Cisco said.

"Guest?" Marco said. "Aren't you taking a risk even having me here? You an officer of the court and all that?" Marco asked.

"You heard what I said to Erzulie. With Dunland gone, I'm in. Everybody loves me. Besides, you're not a fugitive or something, only a guy down on his luck."

"But. I should pay…"

Cisco interrupted, placing his finger on his lips.

"Not everything is about money. Relax. Come sit." Cisco patted the cushion next to him. "Watch the game with me." He went to the refrigerator and pulled out a Hamm's, popped the lid, and handed it to Marco.

"Take a break from your troubles," he said. Cisco's eyes danced like magic, agreeable, bright and clear, framed by his two strong, black eyebrows. Marco was taken back by this man's untroubled generosity.

After a couple of beers, they all sat down for dinner, ample quantities of spaghetti and meat sauce—a little light on the meat though—and an enormous salad. Marco complimented Pat on how tasty it was, better than most restaurants, he said. His stomach began to settle for the first time since the jury had come back.

When dinner was done, Cisco belched loudly, and Pat mocked his manners. The children covered their mouths and guffawed. Cisco smiled sheepishly and stood up.

"C'mon Marco, let's watch the second game. It's a double header. This one's gonna tell us a lot about which team's got an in for the World Cup, so it's really important."

With a grand sweep of his arm and a nod of his head, Cisco motioned for Marco to come and sit next to him on the couch. But before long, he was asleep and snoring like a pig. Tad, not showing even the slightest interest in the game, came and sat down close to Marco.

"You don't like soccer either, I can tell," Tad said. His lips turned up in a bashful smile. "Daddy's out like a light. Let's watch cartoons." Without waiting for a response from Marco, he went to the TV and changed channels, turning to *Big Guy and Rusty the Boy Robot*.

"My favorite," Tad said.

Watching this children's show pegged Marco back to his own childhood. He had loved the Mickey Mouse Club and had been convinced that he would marry Anette Funicello, one of the show's teenage stars and a heartthrob of most boys Marco knew. *Funny how things evolve,* Marco thought.

Tad yelled and screamed, pointed and gestured, as the episode played itself out, sometimes giving Marco a good-natured slap on his knee with a giggle, sometimes bouncing up and down on the couch, shaking Marco. For a moment, Marco lost himself in Tad's innocent exuberance as he watched Rusty jump hurdle after hurdle on the screen. Marco laughed too, despite himself. He almost forgot that he had lost his prestigious teaching job and was on trial for murder. For right now, the dark cloud of his despair had receded to the horizon. But the persistent unsettled feeling in his stomach reminded him of what he faced. Tomorrow he would need to make plans.

Once the show was over, Tad stood on his knees next to Marco.

"Your turn," he said, his face only inches from Marco's.

"My turn?"

"Everybody gets to pick one show before bedtime, so now you choose."

Marco was unsure what to do. He barely even watched TV, let alone any television series or children's programs. He found the idea of watching TV uninteresting, not a good use of time—which he had, up to now, filled with doing research, writing papers, or—for comic relief—chasing women.

"Tad, I'm not real familiar...."

"Okey dokey, then it's *Ed, Edd n Eddie.*"

Tad walked over to the TV and changed the channel—the remote control had died years ago. Then he came back to the couch, snuggled up against Marco, and began giggling as he watched the ridiculous slapstick cartoon. Tad's body felt warm and comforting next to Marco. Soon, the boy too fell asleep, with his head resting on Marco's knee. Marco watched him in marvel and delight. He couldn't remember a time in his life when he had felt so accepted. He didn't even get up to turn the TV off. In a few minutes more, he too dozed off.

*   *   *

AT FIRST, while they intrigued him, Marco was unsure what to make out of this Ozzie and Harriet-esque family. It seemed too good to be true. Cisco and Pat were almost too loving, too accepting, too gracious, the children too sweet and innocent. He distrusted most people's warmth, and this apparently idyllic oasis from the clamor of the world was no exception. He thought there must be some hidden secret, some profound defect, some scratchy discontent. But as the days went on, Marco discovered none. They were as happy and satisfied as they seemed, devoid of guile or peevish lust.

Marco couldn't help but envy Cisco's happy little home. He thought back to his growing up years, spending his time with a series of nannies in a big empty house. By contrast with Cisco's home, it had been sterile and indifferent.

But he couldn't stop looking at his recently acquired flip phone. It had caller ID to help him fend off calls from the press. Reporters called over and over anyway. No call from Frank. That's the call he prayed for, one time after another he prayed. The call which didn't comee.

Should he call Frank? Frank had seemed very definite that he wanted time away. And he had departed only two days ago. Marco feared that, if he initiated the call, the wedge between them would only fester. So, he waited. And each day he put off until the next tackling what he needed to do. Was there a way to get back in Frank's good graces? Marco didn't have an answer.

Maybe with some time and distance…

*   *   *

ON THE FIFTH DAY of his stay, after an early dinner, Cisco and Marco sat on the tiny front porch in folding lawn chairs watching as the sun began its descent. They had spent each of the last few nights together, laughing, getting a slight beer buzz, talking about their early years growing up, high school sports they had played, professional teams, and world affairs. It was easy to talk with Cisco even though Marco was not too good at making conversation, at least outside the subject of how subatomic particles behave.

Marco intentionally avoided bringing up their mutual sexual encounters with Semantha. He was afraid to fester old wounds. It turned out his concerns were unnecessary.

"I already know about your love life," Cisco said with a touch of sarcasm but also a slight smile and a twist of his head. "But what about your friends? I'm sure they would give you a hand if you called."

Marco had always hated it when the subject of his friends came up. He had teammates when he was in high school, associates at Fermilab, and acquaintances all over the country, fellow scientists he had met at conferences. He even had some fairly close collaborators. And there was Frank, more than a friend, although Frank's ongoing interest had always been somewhat of a mystery to him.

Real friends were another matter.

"I've been too busy…" Marco said in a doleful tone as his voice trailed off. He looked down at the grass in front of the porch. He swallowed a lump in his throat.

*   *   *

Cisco threw up his arms and leapt to his feet. "Enough about your friends," he said. "C'mon, let me show you my favorite spot. I've never taken anyone, not even Pat." He grabbed Marco's hand and pulled him to the car.

They went to an uninhabited section of the river. From the road, especially in the low early evening light, it appeared to be nothing more than a concentration of foliage. But after pushing through the bushes, the two entered a small clearing. A couple of tall, old oak trees and a few vines hanging down formed something like a cathedral nave opening to the water. A rope hung from a tree branch which extended out over the river, and an old, slightly inflated inner tube was tied to it.

They walked to the river's edge. Marco looked off in the distance and saw the low fixed bridge he had first seen a couple of years before when he came looking for Semantha. The Circle's house was on the other side of the river a bit downstream from the bridge, comfortably away from Cisco's secret hideaway.

"Nice," Marco said. "How'd you find this?"

"I loved to swim in the river when I was a child. It was my way of getting out of the house and away from the teasing I got in high school from the Anglos. I was the skinny Latino kid out and the river was my second ma. I swam in the cold, the heat, the sun and the rain. I swam when it was so windy that it was all I could do not to be washed out into the lake. One day on a late fall swim, I saw this place."

The two sat down on a patch of moss covering the bank, took off their shoes, and dangled their feet in the water, letting the current massage them. Marco's toe was by now almost completely healed but he felt a bit of a sting when it touched the water.

"I love the river," Cisco said. He was silent for a moment as they gazed out on the water. "And it loves me. We're a team." He stopped again.

"The only other thing that comes close is my time at the Casa. Besides my family, of course."

"Tell me," Marco said, looking Cisco in the eye. "You're a pretty level-headed guy, if I can say it, *normal*, and I mean that as a positive. So, what do you see in this Santeria/voodoo business?"

"The Casa? To me, it's like a sort of club. I like the music and the dancing. I'm not the only one. Remember the bald guy? He's lead drummer. Well, he's a big-time businessman from Grand Rapids. Name is Tom. He comes because he likes to make music."

"What about all this with the spirits and the unseen forces?"

"I don't think about that much. It's not a big part of my life."

Marco's face turned serious. His head inclined slightly as he placed his hand on Cisco's shoulder. He waited a bit before he spoke.

"What do you want out of life, Cisco?" Marco asked quietly, partly out of curiosity, but partly because he constantly asked himself the same question.

Cisco slapped Marco's knee while emitting a rich laugh.

"I was wondering when you were going to get around to that. It seems that everything for you has to be momentous. It's like you demand a lot out of life. I'm not sure why. It's caused you a lot of pain. And for what?"

Marco offered no answer. He just looked out at the water.

"You know my friend, there are many ways to lead a happy, good life. Not only money and success," Cisco said.

"You ever hear of Lame Deer, that Sioux medicine man and philosopher?" Cisco asked after pausing for a second. "Maybe you didn't have time for reading his books, studying physics so much."

"Well...."

"He said that the meaning of life is to look at everything with a song. Why don't you try that?"

Marco went silent. He wanted to scream with delight and cry with despair all at the same instant, delight from the beauty of the insight, despair because he was beginning to see how terribly mistaken he had been all of his life.

Marco and Cisco sat quietly together as the sun began to set. The reflected light on the river danced over the light waves in orange, red, and dark blue. Cisco began to sing.

> *"Besame, besame mucho*
> *Como su fuera esta noche*
> *La ultima vez…"*

*   *   *

HE HAD A DECENT tenor singing voice and Marco was enchanted. Enchanted with the place, the water, his companion, the beautiful song. For the moment, the nagging omnipresence of his troubles again seemed to have evaporated. Marco had never felt like he did then—no past, no future, no desires. His brain was clear of all those corrosive thoughts.

"How about a swim?" Cisco eventually asked. He rose to his feet as if he had had enough serious talk for one evening.

"I don't have a suit."

"Don't need one here. We're all alone."

"But…"

"C'mon Marco…no buts. Take off your clothes, get into the tire and swing."

"But, but…."

"You want to pay me back for my hospitality? Now is your chance. Jump in."

Soon Marco and Cisco were in the water, horsing around in the warm, pleasant river, splashing each other and tackling each other from underwater. Cisco helped him crawl into the inner tube and began it swinging. Marco built up momentum, going higher and higher.

Not since I was a child, he thought. Being naked added to the sensation, total freedom.

When the swing reached its highest point, Marco let go. As he fell, he imagined himself on a journey to everlasting bliss. He hit the water, and the river enveloped him in its peaceful warmth. Closing his eyes, he floated just a little below the surface, lost in space, and separated from time. He felt cleansed, bathed in sacred water and purged of corruption. He sensed that the river had forgiven him and had invited him to a new life under its watch.

He floated to the surface, raised his arms, and jumped, emitting a scream, not a scream of fear but of exaltation. He had never felt like he felt at that minute, free of earthly desires and ambitions. He looked over and saw Cisco sitting on the shore gazing at him, smiling like a Cheshire cat. Marco returned the look. He dove back under water and swam toward the shore.

Maybe my first real friends—Cisco…and this river.

*　　*　　*

THE NEXT DAY, early Saturday morning, Marco awoke from a deep sleep when his phone rang. He had left it charging in the kitchen the night before. He looked at his watch. So early… it must be another reporter. Marco ignored the ring as he drifted toward wakefulness, recalling warmly his intimate interlude with Cisco at his secret hiding place the night before. After a minute floating in reverie, he sat up on the couch and looked around the house, a place he wished he could call home.

I never want to leave, he thought.

The phone rang again, disturbing his happy ruminations. He got up to see who was calling. A nervous tingle ran through his body when he read the screen. It said *Frank Douglas.*

Marco's mind went racing. What would he say? Was this his chance to smooth things over? Was Frank calling because he had cooled down? Did Frank miss Marco too?

He remembered a time years ago when he had recklessly crashed *Provocateur* into the dock. Frank had been furious but had quelled his anger when Marco had fallen on his knees and begged. For lesser misdeeds, all it had taken were a couple of smiles and a few tears. He was about to find out where he stood now. The first words out of Frank's mouth would tell the tale.

"Marco, I have some news for you," Frank said after he and Marco exchanged indifferent hellos. Frank spoke slowly and seriously, neither harsh like when he had walked away nor warm and friendly like it had been in the past. The difference was obvious.

"It's about the retrial," Frank said.

Marco's spirit sank.

"What about you and me? That's what I really want to hear about," Marco said.

"Yesterday as I was about to go home, Peterson called," Frank said.

"Peterson?" Marco asked, feeling a sudden twinge of unease. Why, he was not sure.

"Eunice Peterson. She's the one who took over when Dunland died."

"Oh yeah, the bitch who wants to send me the torture chamber for fifteen years." Marco immediately regretted his words. He worried that Frank may be put off all over again by his puffy arrogance.

"She wants to set a new trial date."

These words jerked Marco away from his happy little Cisco-shaped Shangri-La and back to the specter of that godforsaken old courthouse. His stomach lurched sideways and turned over.

"How about never? After all of this, can't she simply drop the charges?"

"Forget that," Frank said, not changing his indifferent tone. "But we did talk about the case. She told me Dunland had been too sure of himself and made a serious mistake not to hire a more capable psychiatrist."

Another $100,000, Marco thought. *Where's that money coming from?*

"My guess, reading between the lines," Frank continued, "is she's worried about a repeat with one or two jurors buying into your insanity defense and again refusing to budge. I suspect she knows that if the state can't convince a jury to convict the second time around, the case is over, and maybe her career as well."

Marco's face puckered up.

"Well, I guess that's something anyway," he said. "If the jury is hung the second time, all the better."

"There's more," Frank said, sounding a little more friendly. "The Adamos luck holds. She made a new offer to resolve the case. Two years in the slammer and five years on probation, no fine, nothing else. And you can go to the state prison farm, not Iona."

Hearing these words, Marco fumbled the phone and dropped it just as Cisco emerged from his bedroom. He waved with a healthy grin as he watched Marco scramble to return the phone to his ear.

"Sorry, Frank," Marco said. "I lost you for a minute. My question is, what changed?"

"I talked to some of my friends in the Berrien County trial bar because I wondered the same thing. She's pregnant with triplets and does not have the bandwidth to go through a trial right now. See why I say lucky you?"

"Lucky? To spend two years in prison and five years on probation, that doesn't feel like luck to me."

"C'mon Marco, you keep forgetting that you killed a woman in cold blood," Frank said, his voice raised. "You expect that …" Frank stopped talking. Marco knew from experience that Frank's hesitation meant he was about to say something caustic and blunt but decided against it.

"You can say it, Frank," Marco said.

"I've said enough. You know how I feel about your defense."

"Frank, I need to talk with you. I need to see you, please."

"Well, I don't know Marco, a lot of water under the bridge."

With a quirky smile on his face, Marco thought about the bridge that separated Cisco's happy river hideout from the evil that pervaded the Circle's house a bit downstream. *A lot of water under that bridge, too*, Marco thought.

"Please Frank, for all we've been through together." Frank said nothing for a time too long for Marco's comfort.

"Okay, come to Chicago," he finally said. "I will see you. I'll call Peterson on Monday. Especially under these circumstances, I'm sure she won't object to you leaving the county."

*   *   *

MARCO ARRIVED EARLY at Frank's office, before eight am, even though he knew Frank didn't usually get in until about nine. It had been great to sleep in his own bed, such as he slept at all, and drive downtown in his own car, a cheap rental car replacement for his Beemer, but still his car. It was a bitter-sweet sensation, a pleasant recollection of his past affluence but a piercing reminder of what he was about to lose. He already missed Cisco, Pat and their two charming children. He dreaded more losses to come.

Frank's assistant ushered Marco into Frank's office and motioned for him to sit down on the tan leather side chair in front of Frank's ornately carved, walnut desk. Frank's tastes ran to the classical.

As Marco waited in nervous anticipation of this critical meeting, his heart began to pound hard and sweat broke on his forehead. He tried to distract himself by looking at the artifacts scattered around Frank's office. It contained many reminders of Frank's distinguished legal career as a criminal defense attorney, showing why Frank was someone a defendant would want on his side: photos on the walls of Frank with the luminaries of the Chicago legal community and a few national political figures, the various awards sitting on the credenza behind his desk, and the gavel embossed with the seal of the American Bar Association. All the more, Marco hoped he could persuade Frank to take back his defense.

Then Marco's eyes landed on the exact reproduction of *Provocateur* sitting on a small cradle with a brass plaque reading, *The best and the sweetest.* Seeing that reminder of Frank's avocation evoked many memories, good and bad. Marco wondered if he would ever be invited for a sail again.

But it was the fancy overstuffed brown leather couch along the wall that stirred him the most. He recalled the shock he had felt sitting there when Frank told him that drowning Semantha was a felony, not only a simple innocent act in the heat of the moment. That was the beginning of his struggle back then, whether to fess up and face the consequences or hope that what he had done would never be discovered. Ultimately, he had gone to Michigan to confess after he had an epiphany caused by seeing Saul fried on the accelerator coil at the lab. *What a bizarre incident,* he thought. To this day, he had no idea how Saul got into his office and managed to tie him up, certainly planning to torture him to death— but then how he managed to break free… the ensuing struggle, throwing Saul on the coil, and watching him transformed, perhaps only in his own imagination, into the devil incarnate.

This time, there was no inner debate about what to do. All he wanted was to escape from his pain in any way possible, return to the good life at all costs, rise in his profession through whatever means. Become a famous physicist. Marco could not pinpoint what had changed from the first time, nor why.

Most of all he remembered how, the first time, Frank had come to that couch to comfort him and wipe the tears away like a loving father consoling his son. A box of tissues sat on the coffee table in front of the couch. *Maybe the same box,* Marco thought.

"Here already?" Frank asked as he walked in a little later. Upon seeing Marco, his forehead furrowed and he frowned slightly. He walked directly to his desk and sat down in his plush, overstuffed chair, then peered judgmentally toward Marco from above a pair of new horn-rimmed glasses, not taking off his suit coat. He assumed a position behind his desk holding his hands together, a posture which yelled out stern rebuke.

This is not promising, Marco thought.

Frank drummed his fingers on his desk and peered at Marco. "You wanted to talk, right?" he said. "Well, talk." Frank's tone chilled Marco.

"Frank, I'm sorry, so sorry." Marco fought back tears as his eyes watered. "I can't…You are my rock. I…" At that moment, getting Frank to help him with his legal problem was secondary. For the first time, he didn't see Frank as a means to an end but as a dear friend he cherished, loved, but lost.

"A little late for all that now," Frank said, interrupting. He took off his glasses, wiped the lenses clean, then sat them carefully on the one and only pile of papers neatly squared in the corner of the otherwise uncluttered desk.

"Please Frank, what changed?" Marco felt a pinch in his neck. He rubbed it with his hand.

"You." Frank spoke harshly. The word hit Marco like a cudgel.

"What do you mean?" he asked. But as soon as he said these words, Marco regretted them. They must have sounded confrontational when what he really felt was penitent.

"You want to hear what I think, Marco? Can you take it?"

Marco braced himself. Frank sounded like a demanding taskmaster, not a friend. Marco jerked and almost slid out of the chair. He could pretty well guess what Frank would say, truly afraid he could not take it. He sensed an end too terrible to contemplate.

"Excuse me, Frank," Marco said as he stood and headed toward the bar in the corner of the office. Frank motioned with his hand, picked up a draft brief from the stack of papers, and began reading.

Even though it was still early morning, Marco poured himself two shots of Maker's Mark bourbon from a bottle on the bar and gulped them down in rapid succession. He then scurried to the small bathroom adjacent to the bar, running as much from his own terror as from the sting of Frank's judgment.

He closed the door tight, deliberately locked it, and flushed his face with cold water. He looked intensely at his image reflected in the gold-trimmed mirror hung squarely above the marble countertop.

Yes, he was still handsome, even though he noticed some gray hairs, a few wrinkles. Yet, he did not like what he saw. No longer did his physical beauty matter. What was he really beneath the facade? Had he learned anything from all that had happened to him since Clem had abducted him? Seeing Erzulie's life, the noble way she had lived, her probing questions to him, the tragedy of Dunland's life and death, the refreshing contentment of Cisco's family, the healing encounter with the river... Frank's question and its blunt underlying message tipped the scales in his mind. Marco could no longer deny the cur he really was. Where had he gone wrong?

He thought back to when all of this had started, standing on the dock on that stormy day, insisting on taking that sailing trip. Why did he brashly put others at risk and make them endure what surely was a terrible afternoon merely to satisfy his own need for a few cheap thrills? Why had he been so selfish?

Selfish, my God, what about how he used women? His absolutely insane quest for passion that led him to Michigan in the first place? His abysmal treatment of Cynthia, a good woman, having needs he did not bother to meet or even acknowledge. Even Semantha, throwing himself at her in wanton disregard for the consequences of his passion.

He could now see why this time was different than the last. The first time he experienced a burst of gratitude after he had seen Saul incinerated and, in response, sought to put himself right with the world. Now, he was driven only by roguish selfishness.

But the very worst was taking the data which resulted when Saul hit the accelerator and pretending it was his own idea, a false pretense which lifted his career from dead end to on the road. *Appalling*, he thought. What an act of dishonesty, and by him, who hypocritically claimed to be so ethical?

He beat on his chest, groaning with every strike. He had failed at what mattered the most, sacrificing his humanity for vainglorious success, a pursuit that had left him arrogant and indifferent. His life passed before him, the steady progression from small things like winning the softball championship at all costs to the ultimate delusion, having a vague hope that someday he would win the Nobel prize in physics. He threw more cold water on his face and rubbed it in, feeling his unkempt stubble.

A deep unspeakable remorse welled up. *I am getting what I deserve. It's past time for atonement.* He stood there for a time looking at himself in the mirror, shaking his head.

*　　*　　*

MARCO RETURNED to Frank's office, finding him talking on the phone. He still had not taken off his suit jacket. He motioned to Marco to sit and covered his handset. "Just a minute," he whispered.

Frank seemed to take his time and what had begun as a business call turned friendly. Frank asked about the other person's family, their plans for the upcoming winter. He laughed and smiled. When he finally finished and put down the phone, his expression instantly changed from jovial to bellicose. He again looked at Marco with the same strident countenance as when he had first walked in.

"Proceed," he said as he again drummed his fingers on his desk.

You still want to know what I think changed?"

Marco stared at Frank and Frank held his gaze in return. Nothing was said for what seemed to Marco forever.

"I have wronged you," Marco finally said in a still, small voice. "It's pretty simple. Up until now, I have taken your friendship and caring for granted, like it was my birthright." Marco blanched as if he had been knifed. It was a self-inflicted wound, but it still hurt.

"How can I make it up to you?" Marco asked. Marco's face appeared as if a shadow.

Frank took a tissue out of his desk drawer and wiped the side of his eye. Marco was not sure, but he thought maybe Frank was crying a little, something he had never seen before, ever.

"In that bathroom I looked in the mirror and saw myself for who I really am. Not a pretty picture, Frank. It's past time for me to change."

"My God, Marco. I don't know what to say," Frank said, shaking his head. "I'm at a loss for words. That never happens."

"I'm going to start by getting a public defender in Michigan to finalize the terms of my incarceration and then pay the price for what I did to Semantha. She was a troubled woman. What she really needed from me was a little caring, not a fuck buddy anxious to get off on her good looks. And no one, no matter how misguided…nobody deserves to be knifed down in cold blood. "I…." Marco paused. "I must pay the price."

Another silence ensued. Frank's office phone rang. He pushed the Do Not Disturb" button. After some moments, Frank spoke, now looking sad and somewhat regretful.

"I will come back and represent you, Marco." Frank's voice was quiet, almost inaudible.

"No Frank, you've done enough. But will you come and visit me when I'm inside?"

"Every week," Frank replied.

They both stood up and embraced. Marco took both of Frank's hands in his and looked into his eyes. He saw only love.

"I'll be back for another sail before you know it," Marco said prior to turning to go.

As he took the elevator down to the street, he felt at peace, a peace he had never felt before, a release from all of his cares and anxieties. He was finally on the road to healing.

*   *   *

Two DAYS LATER, Marco drove to Cisco's house. As soon as he parked, Pat came running out, the children not far behind. They yelled, "Marco! Marco!" as he walked up. She gave him a big hug. Marco felt her lumpy body through her dark blue dress.

"I thought I would never see you again."

"You're not done with me so easily. I have business to attend to here." His eyes were focused and serious.

"Cisco thought you would go on the lam," she said.

"What?" Marco knotted his brow.

"Just disappear. He's seen it before, especially with folks who are not hardened criminals and have a few bucks saved up. What they would need to go through here is too much for them to bear... Sometimes they go to Argentina."

"Where's Cisco? I hope he can refer me to the public defender."

"At work. He'll be home at six. Why don't you stay with us again? We'd love to have you." She giggled as though the idea delighted her.

"No, I'll be staying at the Motel Six a bit outside of town, thanks to a loan from Frank. Enough…" Marco made a knifing motion with his hand. "…of me imposing your hospitality."

"That's too bad. But tonight, the Casa is having a big party. I'm sure you would be welcome. Why don't you stay here until Cisco gets back and we can go together?"

"You into Voodoo and Santeria too?" Marco asked with an upturned eyebrow.

"No, I love Cisco and he's into this. I don't know why. He's not really religious. I don't mind it, it seems innocent enough, and Cisco is hooked. I come along mostly to be with him. I like to watch him dance." She rolled her eyes. "Very sexy."

*　　*　　*

LATER THAT EVENING, Marco, Cisco, and Pat arrived at the Casa, as Tom began beating the kettle drums. This evening, he was dressed like a businessman on his way to a golf outing, quite a contrast to the mostly brown Latin American crowd wearing clothes like they were at a fiesta in old Mexico. But he sported a big smile and a happy look, like he was enjoying the chance to entertain. Marco and Pat joined the onlookers standing around the sides of the large living room while Cisco went to prepare for the dance.

The celebration began when four elders dressed in white walked in procession up to the drums and, one by one, bowed in front of them. They assumed positions on Tom's either side.

More people joined the congregation, then a three-person mariachi band appeared and began to play along with Tom. All four of the musicians swayed back and forth, swooning, as if possessed by the rhythm.

Cisco emerged from a side room, kicking his legs out in front of him with his head thrown back, his hair flowing down, his arms waving. He wore white pants, but no shoes, and was shirtless, showing his well-defined brown chest and stomach muscles. A long, red scarf was tied around his neck. It glided down his back. His furious gyrations were fluid and smooth, exotic like a belly dancer but also Caribbean and calypso. Marco marveled at his new friend's grace and style. He had seen Cisco dancing before but knowing him like he now did gave Marco a new appreciation for his friend's talents.

Cisco danced in a big circle around the room, the air hot and full of feeling. Marco smiled as Cisco approached him. Cisco ran his hand lightly across Marco's chest above his belly as he moved by. Glancing back, Cisco winked and grabbed for Marco's hand like he was going to pull him onto the floor to dance. Marco resisted—the last thing he wanted to do just then was dance—so he pulled his hand back and jerked to the side. He accidentally bumped hard into the woman standing next to him.

"Excuse me," he said in a monotone, giving her an oblique glance. Until that moment, Marco had not noticed her, but her neck-to-floor green muumuu-like dress made her stand out from everyone else.

"Anytime, handsome." She batted her eyes and grinned, accenting her slightly protruding top jaw and bucked teeth.

"Do I know you?" she said, offering her hand. Marco turned to look, then reflexively extended his hand back. She grabbed it and held it tightly in both of her's. They felt warm but her grasp was a little overbearing. The music and the drums got louder. She had to shout.

"Is this your first time at the Casa?" she asked.

"Second," Marco responded. The music got louder still. Marco could see this girl's lips moving but the music drowned out what she was saying. Marco was relieved. Preoccupied by his imminent departure for prison, he really didn't want to talk to anyone, and the loudness of the music gave him an excuse. And anyway, he towered over her. She appeared to be only about five-and-a-half feet tall, making hearing each other in all the noise that much more difficult.

But the girl seemed determined. With her right hand she grabbed his wrist like in a vise and pulled him toward the door, clearing a pathway through the crowd with her left. Her short, stocky body helped free the way. As Marco was being dragged outside, he looked back and noticed Cisco smiling from ear to ear.

"There, that's better," the girl said once they had gotten to the yard. "I love these celebrations, but they can get out of hand. And I really wanted to talk to you. My name's Cecilia." She gave Marco a short hug, which he did not reciprocate.

Marco thought, *Cecilia? Wasn't that the name of Semantha's aunt? No, that was Calissa.*

"What's yours?" Cecilia asked.

"Marco," he said in a neutral voice, although he was happy to be outside the hot, stuffy room and away from the noise. It was a perfect night, warm and no wind.

"I know who you are. In this town, you're famous."

"Famous? Then you know why I am here."

"Not everything, but you killed that pervert witch." Her brow arched up.

"Pervert?" Marco felt a touch of anger, a little protective of his old lover. He turned to walk away but Cecelia continued to talk, raising the pitch of her voice.

"My younger brother was one of her victims." She shook her head, looking disgusted. She touched Marco on the arm as if she wanted him to listen carefully. "Before she disappeared, she called him all the time. Sick, I would say."

By now Marco, who a second before only wished to get away, wanted to know more. He stopped to listen.

"He became quite disturbed, had to go for long-term counseling. He's a good-looking guy, but he wasn't ready for an older woman throwing herself at him like she did. I'm pretty sure he was a virgin before that happened."

How did I fail to see… Marco thought.

"Actually, about half the town thinks you did everyone a favor by killing that woman."

"A favor?" Marco repeated with probing eyes.

"Yeah, you saved two really nice young boys from the ordeal of testifying at a public trial."

"And what does the other half think?" he asked. He wasn't sure he wanted to hear the answer.

"You're just a rich snob getting what you deserve."

For the first time, Marco gave this girl a good look. Apparently in her late twenties, she had a rounded sort of Oriental-looking face with straight black hair that fell evenly over her ears and neck on the sides. Bangs in front. Her complexion was ruddy and rough. She was not beautiful, but she was not ugly, either. Marco was intrigued by her straightforwardness.

"Which side are you on?" he asked.

"It's karma, you know. I love my darling little brother. She hurt him a lot. You know about karma?" There was a devilish gleam in her eye.

"Well, I'm a scientist…"

"Sorry to hear that." She placed her hand on her mouth and pretended to snicker. "Well, she overflowed with bad karma, spread it wherever she went." Marco didn't need to be told.

"I was her lover for a while," he said.

"I know. Everyone in town knows the story, even the parts they wouldn't print in the *Herald-Palladium*. What do you think we have to do in this town but gossip?"

"Well…"

"Besides, Cisco's connected to everyone, so if you want to hear the real news, you get to know him." A wistful look appeared in her eyes.

"A while ago, I tried to get closer to him myself, you know what I mean. But I found out he was already going out with my dear friend Patrice. I didn't want to hurt her. Not that I could ever get a looker like Cisco, anyway, but I could always hope."

"So, you said you really wanted to talk with me. Why?"

"Other than you are the hottest man in fifty miles and I believe in putting myself out there." She smiled and winked. "When you're not a beauty, you've got to be aggressive. You never know."

Just then the music stopped. Marco welcomed the silence.

"The party's breaking up," Cecilia said. "Everybody's going to be coming out. How about coffee sometime soon?"

"How about a Boiler Maker?" He knew where he was going there would be no drinking and he wanted to find out what other gossip was going around about him.

*   *   *

"ARE YOU SCARED?" Cecilia asked as she poured them a glass of wine. For their first meeting, she had picked her favorite, a Chianti in an old-fashioned wicker basket. She was looking forward to getting to know more about Marco, other than what she had learned through the rumor mill, and she thought that some wine might loosen his lips.

They were sitting in the living room of her small one-bedroom apartment in a second-floor walkup in downtown Benton Harbor, no more than three blocks from the courthouse. The furnishings were all simple IKEA hand-me-downs from her older brother, an attorney on the rise in Kalamazoo. It was a week after she and Marco had met at the Casa.

"Scared? Wouldn't you be?" Marco responded, taking an outsized gulp of the ruby-red liquid. His hand shook slightly as he lifted the glass to his lips. "But I'm trying to make peace with the world and go quietly." He closed his eyes as if in thought.

"I don't understand. Why are you so interested in me?" he asked after a second. "Yesterday I signed the plea deal, and I report to Harrison in thirty days. I'm not going to be around."

Not waiting for an answer, Marco turned his head and inhaled loudly.

"Smells really good," he said smiling. "I'm very hungry. This could be my last home-cooked meal for a while."

"Come over any time before you leave," Cecilia said as she stood up and poured more wine. Then she gestured to Marco to go to the table, which was scarcely big enough for two people. She'd prepared a pot roast with boiled potatoes and watched Marco eat like he was storing up for the winter. She liked when people enjoyed her cooking, especially on those rare occasions when she had a single man for dinner.

After they had eaten, she wadded up her paper napkin, threw it on the table and took a sip of water. She knew exactly why she was so interested in him, and it was more than merely putting a hook in the water to see if any fish would bite. She was fascinated by his story and wanted to figure out what drove this almost-famous, now-fallen physicist who had suddenly landed in her life.

Was he really as egotistical as people said?

"I hadn't been planning to go to the Casa last week," she said. But it was so strange. You may think me a kook, but I had a dream where this old lady—Erzulie's her name—appeared and told me to go." Cecilia had been hesitant to tell Marco that, worrying that it would sound bizarre. But she also wanted to be sure he understood she had not come with the express hope of meeting him.

Marco pushed his chair away from the table and tilted his head to the side.

"You know her, too?" he asked, raising his eyebrow.

"In high school, I babysat Isabella when Erzulie was on call. I was a pretty depressed kid, the homely girl in a household with four good-looking football player brothers. She took me under her wing, got me involved at the Casa. She's the one who made me go out and meet people, said not to worry about rejection." A quixotic smile came to her face. "So, I guess that's why you're here," she said.

Marco shook his head as if in disbelief, letting his now way-too-long, curly hair bounce back and forth. Cecilia found him very attractive but was wary at the same time. She knew his track record with women wasn't good. That didn't matter because she couldn't imagine anything romantic happening.

"You know my whole story?" Marco asked, playing with one of his curls.

"Tell me," Cecilia said, resting her head on her up-stretched hands and staring at Marco as if a love-sick schoolgirl. She was prepared for a long narrative. He talked for the next two hours. At the end he coaxed a smile.

"Thanks Cecilia. Nobody has ever wanted to listen before," he said.

Cecilia went to bed happy that evening. She saw that this cardboard figure had a soul.

The next thirty days were some of the best she could recall. He was so different from anyone she had known before. But she also remembered what Erzulie had taught her. Disappointments come when a person expects too much.

XIX

On a cold, drizzly February day befitting the occasion, Marco and Cecilia stood outside an olive-drab van about to take Marco to the prison farm. A guard had ordered him to climb on board seconds before. Marco's apprehensions had reached a fever pitch, and he was glad Cecilia was there.

"It's been great getting to know you," she said, her eyes taking on a grave, cloudy look. "I dreaded this day as it got closer."

She batted her eyes as if she was fighting back tears.

"I've never met anyone as kind, gentle, and unassuming as you. That's something I can't say about the other rats who have populated my existence up to now, especially my shit-head dad. You've become the best friend I ever had."

Cecilia's face went from serious to whimsical. "But I never will understand particle physics, sorry."

Marco winked impishly.

"You do pretty well with the standard model, especially for some-one who never took a science course." He had been thrilled to talk with her about his life work and delighted with how much she had understood and how quickly. He too was pretty happy about getting to know Cecilia. *Talk about unassuming,* he thought.

"I have a gift for you," Cecilia said as she pulled a small bottle out of her purse. A freshly picked daisy was inside, which she took out and handed to Marco. He stared at it blankly.

"C'mon Marco, play the game," she said, waving her hand at him. A little irritated, Marco grimaced. He's getting ready to go to prison for two years and she wants him to play this silly game. He looked apprehensively at the scowling guard standing at the door to the van.

"Must I?"

"You want any visitors?' The look on her face told Marco she was serious.

He took the flower in his hand. He pulled off the first petal and said, "She loves me." He frowned. Then the second and said, "She loves me not." Frowned again. He went around to each of the petals and pulled them off one by one, making a face each time. Finally, there was only one petal left. He pulled it off and said, "She loves me."

"Don't you ever forget it, Marco." She put her hand on Marco's arm. "I don't expect you to love me the way I would like. That's okay with me. I want to be with you whenever and however I can."

"Even though I'm a convict?" Marco rubbed his forehead.

Cecilia took Marco's hand and began massaging it.

"That doesn't matter to me. I'll be waiting for you when you get out. I hope you stay here in Michigan. But I don't really expect it."

Cecilia's words comforted Marco more than any he had heard for months. A warm tingle traveled up his spine. With these words, he felt fortified for the lonely ride ahead.

He was so very happy he had been forced to play the game.

The guard grabbed Marco's arm and shoved him onto the bus.

*   *   *

THE DAY ROOM at the Harrison Work Farm was typical prison—barren with dank, gray cement block walls and old, threadbare furniture. From the moment he arrived, Marco detested spending time there. The guards were everywhere, and inmates usually had visitors, so no privacy.

There was one guard, in particular, Marco came to loathe. Overweight and bald, he watched Marco incessantly, as if he hoped Marco would break some rule.

One of Marco's friends had told him that this same guard had gotten another prisoner thrown into solitary for a week for arguing about whether inmates could play penny poker. Marco began calling him "Sadistic Sam."

His friend also told Marco that, because of Marco's status as an academic, he was a marked man with guards like Sam, so he had to be careful all the time. Marco stayed in his four-by-eight cell as much as he could.

But Marco knew that he was far better off than at Ionia, infamous for its brutality. Since the first day, he had heard stories: prison rapes, beatings, even one prisoner who had been in effect guillotined on the weight bench by an overloaded weight bar. Certainly, better than Riverside, the state prison hospital where he could have ended his life spaced out on mind-numbing pharmaceuticals. Marco shuddered when he thought about how awful that would have been, how close he got. He wasn't sure God existed, but if He did, he thanked God for what Frank had done for him.

And Cecilia, too. She was true to her word. She made the two-hour drive every other Saturday. She brought him news about what was happening with Cisco and his family, the goings on in town and the most recent activity at the Casa.

One particular Saturday, while he awaited her visit—he had been in the "house" for about a year— he thought about how important she had become to him. He was quite sure he would never have a sexual relationship with any woman ever again. The thought nauseated him. But Cecilia gave him so much else. Unlike either Cynthia or Semantha, she offered caring without expectation and loyalty without condition.

Right there in the day room, right in front of all the other prisoners, he got down on his hands and knees, bowed and prayed out loud. "Thank you, God. I'm indeed a remarkably blessed human being."

*   *   *

"PARTICLES FOR PRISONERS" was the name Marco gave to the physics course the warden approved him to teach after Marco had been in the house for about three months. Marco was grateful for this opportunity. With so much time on his hands, he was suffocating from boredom, and he ached for intellectual stimulation. Teaching the course helped him pass the time. It also soon became one of the most popular events at Harrison, attended by prisoners and guards alike. That's how he met Elisha Burnett, a fellow prisoner from Detroit serving ten years for aggravated rape.

"I flunked out of freshman science in college and lost my f—ing football scholarship," Elisha told Marco after the first class. He had waited until everyone else had cleared out to walk up to Marco, who was seated at the teacher's desk. Behind Marco was an old-fashioned chalkboard filled with equations Marco had written as he had lectured. Elisha's three-hundred-pound, six-foot-five frame towered over Marco.

"I kinda fucked up after that. Did every kinda bad shit a kid from the projects can do. Blew my NFL dream. Ya know, back then I said no more book learning, an' that's what I thought until today."

Marco stood up so he was eye-to-eye with Elisha. Despite Elisha's extra hundred pounds, Marco was not intimidated. He found Elisha's soft-spoken voice engaging.

"But I learned somethum today. It's kinda amazing when ya think about it. All them particles goin' right through us as we's standin' here. An' we don't feel shit."

Marco smiled.

After that, Marco befriended Elisha, tutoring him and teaching him the basics, starting with the three laws of motion and going on from there. Elisha proved to be a very good learner and quite inquisitive. He also spent a lot of time reading on his own.

After they had been working together for several months, out of the blue, Elisha asked Marco to explain how the Higgs boson gives particles mass. Marco's eyes widened and his jaw dropped. He lacked the words to tell Elisha how impressed he was by that question, obviously from a man with a great scientific aptitude. *What wasted potential,* he thought.

Marco began his long answer immediately, drawing diagrams in his notebook to help Elisha understand. But about midway through, Elisha put his hand on Marco's arm.

"Wait Doc, my ma just walked in." He pointed to a large, plainly dressed African American woman.

"Here ya go, Marco, come and meet my ma, LaTonya."

"Elisha loves ya, so he tells me," LaTonya said after introductions. "But he says you're gonna leave him one of these days. What ya goin' to do when you get out?"

"I'm not sure, ma'am," Marco said with an anxious grin. "I've gotta figure that out."

"My advice, get into gardenin'. It'll keep ya sane."

*   *   *

"Adamos, your visitor is here," the guard shouted as he ushered Cecilia in. *Why are they never pleasant about anything?* Marco thought.

Cecilia pulled a package out of her monstrous fake Gucci purse. "Something for you, Marco my dear." She handed him a bunch of drawings with stick figures done in bright colors, obviously painted by small children. Each said, *Hi Marco, I hope you are ok,* or words like that.

"Sweet," Marco said. "Who did these?" The drawings reminded Marco of Cisco's children, who he missed a great deal. When he thought about them, he regretted not having children himself.

"I told my class that I knew you and we talked about what it was like to be in prison. The oldest, she's seven, suggested that they send you a greeting. So here they are."

Marco started leafing through the drawings, smiling when he saw one he liked.

"I have some bad news," Cecilia said. Marco looked up.

"No more bad news, my dear," Marco said. He surprised himself by calling Cecilia "dear." He hoped she didn't read too much into that. The word had rolled off his tongue by accident.

"Erzulie's hovel flooded yesterday. Cisco went over to see. It's in shambles."

"Did she ever return?" Marco hoped he could see her again. He would apologize for the way he had acted.

"We have not heard from her. We don't expect to. I suspect she has gone home to her Orisha."

"I learned a lot from her, Cecilia."

"We all did. She was quirky but powerful."

Marco's face took on a far-away look. He mourned her passing.

*   *   *

"Today is somewhat of an anniversary," Cecilia said during her last visit, feeling hopeful and expectant. She was sitting with Marco on the worn leather couch in the day room. Sadistic Sam had stepped out to go to the bathroom, so they were in the room alone for the first time since Marco arrived.

"You'll be out in exactly one month. Are you excited?" she asked.

"I wish I could say that the time has passed quickly," Marco responded.

Marco had aged in the last two years, a few more lines under the eyes, additional gray hairs. But to Cecilia, he was beautiful, even in his dark-orange jumpsuit.

"I just bought a two-bedroom bungalow on a hill close to the Lake, way out in the country. I've got room if you need a place to stay, at least for a while."

"I've thought of asking you if I could. Not as your lover, though. I doubt I'll ever get there again with anybody."

"I know," Cecilia said with the slightest hint of a frown, but shaking her head as if in agreement. Her attachment to Marco had grown during these two years but she appreciated that Marco did not want, probably did not have the capacity for romance.

"I have no money," Marco said. "I'll look for a job, but I'm not sure how long it will take to find one."

"That's okay, Marco. I can pay the mortgage."

"I don't like being a freeloader."

"Stop." Cecilia slapped Marco teasingly on the cheek. "You should know by now we don't think that way, not in our community."

"Well, then I would like to try."

Cecilia sprouted a big smile and gushed. "Best day of my life."

She then took a breath, letting the silence seal their agreement.

"And now…" She pulled a daisy from her purse and handed it to Marco. "It's time for our regular ritual. The last one in this place."

"It always comes up the same. She loves me…" Marco grinned. "Do you search for a flower with the right number of petals each time?"

Cecilia winked.

XX

"GORDON, it's so nice for you to come by." Marco put down the pruning clippers and extended his hand to greet his old boss. "And a great surprise. I was shocked when I got your email. How did you ever find me all the way over here? But first things first." Marco turned his head toward the screen door.

"Cecilia, come out to the porch. Meet our distinguished visitor." Marco turned back to Gordon. "Cecilia is my… Well, I don't know what you call it, but we are living together. We get along nicely."

Cecilia arrived carrying a tray with a tea pot and some cups.

"Cecilia, meet Dr. Gordon Fellsteon, head of neutrino research at Fermilab where I used to work."

Cecilia put the tray down on the rusted metal garden table on the bungalow's front porch and extended her chubby hand as if offering to shake.

An acrid frown appeared on Gordon's face.

"Not anymore, Marco," he said, ignoring Cecilia's outstretched hand. "I got dismissed as department head. Nasty. Lots of internal politics." He shook his head.

"They claimed I wasn't bringing in enough grant money. And I must confess, it slowed down since you left. Your new approach brought a lot of notoriety to the department."

Marco scowled and motioned for Gordon to sit down.

"You're well off being out of the politics of particle research, Gordon," Marco said with a quick jerk of his head. "I saw how vicious it could be. Everybody wants the same research money, the same promotion and the same prizes. What a pit of vipers. Knowledge for knowledge's sake, what bull. No way to live." Marco's face squeezed up. He looked almost like he was about to spit.

Cecilia feigned an artificial smile as if trying to lighten the mood.

"Here Professor, have some yerba mate," she said, pouring the dark, muddy substance into three unmatched coffee cups on the plain wicker tray. One of them said *Harrison Correctional Facility* in dark green letters. A single daisy from Marco's garden was in a small glass vase.

"It's all we drink over here," Cecilia said. "It lifts you up and cleans you out all at once. I hope you like it strong." She giggled and offered him a cup.

Gordon smiled and lifted the cup to his mouth. As he drank, his lips puckered up. Stone-faced, he put the cup down and didn't touch it again. He waved a fly away.

"So Marco, what you been up to over here way out in the middle of nowhere? I wouldn't have expected to find you in a place like this," Gordon said with a haughty tone of voice. Cecilia's face tightened.

"Gordon, I've spent the last year and a half trying to get my life back on track. It's been a hard journey but, mainly thanks to Cecilia" — he nodded his head in her direction— "and my other terrific friends here, I'm on the road."

Marco placed his hands on the table and stayed quiet for a long time, his head bowed. He searched for the right words.

"I feel compelled to tell you something, Gordon." He hesitated. "I should have told you this years ago." He went quiet once again. "It's been heavy on my mind ever since I worked for you. I've got to get it out."

Gordon's eyes fixed on Marco's. Marco ran his hand through his hair and paused again, calling up courage. He quivered slightly.

"Remember when we had that conversation about my future at Fermilab and you told me you admired my ethics? Remember?"

"I really don't." Gordon coughed a little. "I've had so many heart-to-hearts with junior faculty over time. But I do remember that I believed you were very ethical. Why?" Marco went silent again and for a moment looked away.

"Would you have believed that I was all that ethical if you had known that the data which I relied on for my tenure application was generated by chance when Saul was electrocuted on the accelerator cables? It wasn't my idea at all. I merely took advantage of what I saw and ran with it. I pretended it was mine."

Marco sighed. His face became soft like he had thrown off a great weight. He had confessed his most serious failure to the one person whose opinion about it mattered most. Gordon furrowed his eyebrows and pushed the cup with the yerba mate toward Marco.

"Marco," he said, sounding irritated. "I knew that back then. It was obvious to me."

"Then why…" Marco scratched his head.

"Haven't you read *The Sleepwalkers?* You should. According to the book, Kepler came up with the idea that the earth revolves around the sun based on luck. No insight."

Gordon's voice took on a professorial tone as he rubbed the side of his face.

"You were no different. You recognized the pattern from the results when they became apparent. That's the mark of a very good scientist. So you're not Einstein? Few of us are. Surely not me." Gordon shook his head.

"Gordon, I'm so relieved, you have no idea," Marco said with a full, toothy smile. "I spent a lot of time in the slammer dwelling on what I did. I felt like a miserable, low-life scientific fraud." At that second, Marco resolved to go to Cisco's hiding place and thank the river for this final redemption.

"Thanks for telling Marco that, Doctor," Cecilia chimed in as she began rubbing Marco's arm. She had been sitting there quietly listening to Marco and Gordon speak while she consumed her cup of yerba mate and began working on Marco's.

"Unfortunately, Marco has been spending too much time engaged in mental self-flagellation. It's good to bring him back from the extreme."

For a minute all three were silent.

"C'mon, Gordon. Let me show you my vegetable garden." Marco rose to his feet and motioned for Gordon to start walking down the pathway. As they walked, he studied Gordon's expression, looking for any cracks in his austere, unforgiving patina. He didn't see any.

"I got the idea to garden from the mother of one of my students at Harrison, and now I love it," Marco said.

"Wait till you see my tomato plants. They produce the biggest, juiciest tomatoes you can imagine." When they got to the garden, Marco took Gordon on a tour showing him the beans, the squash, the watermelon, carrots, strawberries, all he was growing. Finally, they arrived at the tomatoes.

"Everything does so well in this rich, slightly sandy soil, but especially the tomatoes." He got down on his hands and knees, picked one off the vine and took out his pocketknife. He sliced off a piece and handed it up to Gordon. "Try this. I hope you like it better than Cecilia's tea," he said. Gordon's face remained stone-like.

"This is good. You're right," Gordon said tasting the tomato. "But, Marco, I didn't come all the way out here to talk about your vegetable garden. I have a proposal for you." Fellsteon was a person of few words, and fewer emotions, all business through and through.

"Proposal?" Marco asked.

"I got a $100,000 grant from Carnegie to write a layperson's book on the Higgs boson and how it plays out in the Higgs field. I'm sure you remember that is one of my interests."

Marco nodded.

"I'm going to need a fair amount of research, and I thought you could help me with that. I can't pay much, but this could be a steppingstone for you back into the field."

Marco rubbed his chin.

"With all that has happened," he said after a little time thinking, "I don't suspect anyone would want me involved in anything except maybe sweeping the floors at Fermilab."

"I think you're wrong. Show you still got your groove, and people will look at your past as nothing more than a curiosity. The world of science is filled with people who have, well let's say, quirky histories. This could be your chance to get back into research."

"But why me? There must be a thousand newly minted PhDs who would give their left...well, body part...to do this with you. Why not them?"

"I don't know anyone who has the sophistication, dedication, and enthusiasm you do, not to mention vast knowledge in the field. And my interest is to get all that expertise for what I can pay a beginner. So I win, you win, everybody wins if the book sells. What do you say?"

Marco thought for another minute, then again motioned for Gordon to follow him. "C'mon, Gordon. I want to show you something else."

He led Gordon down a narrow path in the knee-high sand grass to a tall dune. After they had climbed up, Marco said, "Look," and waved his hand, inviting Gordon to take in the magnificence before them. In the distance, they saw the lake and could hear the soft lapping of the waves against the sandy shore. Somewhere behind them, a seagull crooned. It was very still, a silence unknown in the city. The sky was blue, and the sun was shining, giving a gentle warmth to the land.

After they had taken in the bucolic scene for several minutes saying nothing, Marco turned to Gordon. His face radiated contentment and peace.

"Gordon," he said as he placed his hand on Gordon's shoulder, "I am deeply honored that you would drive all the way out from the lab to see me here in sleepy old Western Michigan, but I'm happy here. Cecilia is a good woman who does not pile up expectations for money, power, fame...even for sex. I love tending to my garden and watching the plants grow. I learn so much from nature that way. And in the winter, we put on snowshoes and walk over to the lake. Sometimes, we get lucky and see a sunset you can't imagine. Other times waves of ten or fifteen feet come crashing to shore. I marvel at the power in the universe, but I no longer want to play physicist and dissect it into its smallest component parts."

Marco thought about how the river had saved him. He was glad he lived close to it.

"Particularly, I no longer want to jump back on the academic merry-go-round as it spins faster and faster. It was hard to hold on before and with what I understand about life right now, it makes no sense to even try."

Fellsteon said nothing. His face took on an appearance Marco had never seen before, apparent amazement, maybe a little shock, perhaps envy, even remorse. His stoic, unchanging expression was gone. Marco thought he saw Fellsteon's head shake ever so slightly to the left and right.

"Remember what the Budda says," Marco continued. "The cause of suffering is desire, so all you need to do to be free from suffering is to eliminate your desire. I'm not there yet, but I'm sure a lot closer than when I was at Fermilab."

Another period without words followed. Fellsteon looked like he was lost in thought.

Marco embraced the silence with wonderment, savoring the unspoken communion between him and his old mentor. After a while, Fellsteon turned to Marco and took both of Marco's hands in his.

"Godspeed, my son," he said, moving their hands up and down together. "And I am proud to call you that." A single tear flowed down his tightly drawn cheek. He turned, walked back to his car, and left, saying nothing more.

Cecilia walked up and stood next to Marco as the car drove away.

"Why did he leave? Was it my tea?"

Marco snickered. "No. I'll tell you what we talked about someday. For right now, I want to keep our conversation in a little temple in my mind and savor it for myself."

"Okay. When you wish, my dear. But Frank called while you were in the garden."

"Great. He said he might drive over to see us."

"He's coming, but he's sailing on *Provocateur.* He wants to take us both out for a sail."

FIN

Thank You

Dear Reader:

I hoped you enjoyed your time with *the Mystical Spirit of the Ol' St. Joe,* the sequel to my first novel, *A Boat Named Blind Faith.* As I have told some of you, I believe writing is the process of discovery, not creation. It was a thrill writing this sequel and discovering how Marco evolved as he learned about what matters most to the end of living a fulfilled life. He grew a lot as a result of the difficulties he has experienced, and there have been some humdingers! But stay tuned, because the saga is still not quite over. Now it's Frank's turn to tell his story. Since, as I said, writing is the process of discovering, not creating, I suspect we are all in for a couple of surprises as Frank's background and deep secrets come to light.

Since I published *A Boat Named Blind Faith* and now *The Mystical Spirit of the Ol' St. Joe,* I've gotten so many emails from readers expressing their views about Marco's life and whether he really did redeem himself in the end. I would appreciate you telling me what you think. As an author, I love feedback. You can write to me at <u>blindfaith1256@ gmail.com</u> and visit me on the web at Belmont HarborBooks.com.

Finally, I need to ask you a favor. If you are so inclined, I'd love your review of *The Mystical Spirit of the Ol' St. Joe* on the sales platform of your choice. What you think is so important to me, whether good or bad. Reviews are hard to come by these days. You, the reader, have the power to make or break a book through your review.

Thank you so much for reading *The Mystical Spirit of the Ol' St. Joe* and thereby spending a little time with me.

Yours in reading,

Norm Jeddeloh

Chicago Illinois

About the Author

Norm spent many years as a civil litigator in federal courts in Illinois until he decided to focus on learning how to write creatively. For the last few years, he's been a student in the Writer's Loft of the Graham School of the University of Chicago, learning the craft and how to translate his love of words from stiff formal legal writing to evocative fiction. He also consults with up-and-coming not-for-profits and emerging entrepreneurs, helping them launch their businesses. He and his husband of 25 years live in downtown Chicago and are currently hosting their eighth foreign exchange student.